W9-BVF-831

"Virginia Kantra's stories . . . can make a believer
out of the most hardened soul."
—*New York Times* bestselling author Patricia Rice

PRAISE FOR
Sea Witch

"*Sea Witch* will definitely make your temperature rise!
Virginia Kantra delivers thrills and chills in this sizzling
new paranormal series."
—*New York Times* bestselling author Teresa Medeiros

"A breathtaking new world I intend to visit again. The
adventure, romance, and emotion held me captive. A
definite must read, and I'm so glad I didn't miss it!"
—*New York Times* bestselling author Lora Leigh

"A haunting new world of passion and danger, with a
truly wonderful hero. I'm already impatient for the next
book in what promises to be a fascinating series!"
—*USA Today* bestselling author Nalini Singh

Home Before Midnight

"Sexy and suspenseful . . . a really good read."
—*New York Times* bestselling author Karen Robards

"Virginia Kantra is a sensitive writer with a warm sense
of humor, a fine sense of sexual tension, and an unerring
sense of place."
—*BookPage*

continued . . .

Close Up

Sea Fever

VIRGINIA KANTRA

BERKLEY SENSATION, NEW YORK

THE BERKLEY PUBLISHING GROUP
Published by the Penguin Group
Penguin Group (USA) Inc.
375 Hudson Street, New York, New York 10014, USA
Penguin Group (Canada), 90 Eglinton Avenue East, Suite 700, Toronto, Ontario M4P 2Y3, Canada
(a division of Pearson Penguin Canada Inc.)
Penguin Books Ltd., 80 Strand, London WC2R 0RL, England
Penguin Group Ireland, 25 St. Stephen's Green, Dublin 2, Ireland (a division of Penguin Books Ltd.)
Penguin Group (Australia), 250 Camberwell Road, Camberwell, Victoria 3124, Australia
(a division of Pearson Australia Group Pty. Ltd.)
Penguin Books India Pvt. Ltd., 11 Community Centre, Panchsheel Park, New Delhi—110 017, India
Penguin Group (NZ), 67 Apollo Drive, Rosedale, North Shore 0632, New Zealand
(a division of Pearson New Zealand Ltd.)
Penguin Books (South Africa) (Pty.) Ltd., 24 Sturdee Avenue, Rosebank, Johannesburg 2196,
South Africa

Penguin Books Ltd., Registered Offices: 80 Strand, London WC2R 0RL, England

This is a work of fiction. Names, characters, places, and incidents either are the product of the author's imagination or are used fictitiously, and any resemblance to actual persons, living or dead, business establishments, events, or locales is entirely coincidental. The publisher does not have any control over and does not assume any responsibility for author or third-party websites or their content.

SEA FEVER

A Berkley Sensation Book / published by arrangement with the author

PRINTING HISTORY
Berkley Sensation mass-market edition / August 2008

Copyright © 2008 by Virginia Kantra.
Excerpt from *Sea Lord* copyright © 2008 by Virginia Kantra.
Cover art by Tony Mauro.
Cover design by Rita Frangie.
Cover logo by axb group.
Interior text design by Laura K. Corless.

ISBN: 978-0-425-22297-3

BERKLEY® SENSATION
Berkley Sensation Books are published by The Berkley Publishing Group,
a division of Penguin Group (USA) Inc.,
375 Hudson Street, New York, New York 10014.
BERKLEY SENSATION and the "B" design are trademarks of Penguin Group (USA) Inc.

PRINTED IN THE UNITED STATES OF AMERICA

10 9 8 7 6 5 4 3 2 1

To Phyllis S. Kantra
and Robert A. Kantra

Thanks, Mom and Dad

ACKNOWLEDGMENTS

Deepest thanks to my wonderful editor, Cindy Hwang, and the team at Berkley who do such incredible work.

To my agent, Damaris Rowland, who made this book possible.

To Melissa McClone and Kristen Dill, for listening, reading, critiquing, and supporting.

To Lieutenant A.J. Carter (ret.), Martin Urda, M.D., and all the experts who patiently gave well-thought-out responses to the most unlikely scenarios.

To my niece Marie for letting me "borrow" her tattoo.

To Jean and Will, Andrew, and Mark, who as deadline approached probably thought that their mother had been kidnapped by demons—or possibly possessed.

And to Michael. I'd be lost without you.

But his soul stood with his mother's folk,
That were of the rain-wrapped isle,
Where Patrick and Brandan westerly
Looked out at last on a landless sea
And the sun's last smile.

—G. K. Chesterton,
"The Ballad of the White Horse"

They say the sea is cold, but the sea contains
the hottest blood of all,
and the wildest, the most urgent.

—D. H. Lawrence

1

THE NIGHT THE ONLY ELIGIBLE MAN ON THE island got married, Regina Barone got drunk.

Getting laid would have been even better.

Regina looked from Bobby Kincaid, whose eyes had taken on the wet glaze of his beer bottle, to fifty-three-year-old Henry Tibbetts, who smelled like herring, and thought, *Fat chance.* Anyway, on an island with a year-round population of eleven hundred, a drunken hookup at a wedding reception could have serious consequences.

Regina knew all about consequences. She had Nick, didn't she?

The wedding tent's tiebacks fluttered in the breeze. Through the open sides, Regina could see the beach where the happy couple had exchanged their vows—a strip of shale, a tumble of rocks, a crescent of sand bordering the restless ocean.

Not your typical destination wedding. Maine, even Maine in August, was hardly Saint Croix.

Regina hefted a tray of dirty glassware and then spotted her son, standing beside her mother at the edge of the dance floor, jigging from foot to foot.

She felt her mouth and shoulders relax. The glasses could wait.

Setting down her tray, she crossed the big white tent. "Hey, good-looking."

Eight-year-old Nick turned, and she saw herself in miniature: dark, Italian eyes; thin, expressive face; big mouth.

Regina held out both her hands. "Want to show me what you've got?"

Nick's initial wariness dissolved in a grin.

Antonia Barone took his hand. Her mother was in full Mayor Mode—a hard red slash of lipstick and her two-piece navy dress. "We were just about to leave," Antonia said.

Their eyes clashed.

"Ma. One dance."

"I thought you had work to do," Antonia said.

Ever since Regina had offered to cater this wedding, her mother had been bitching about her priorities. "It's under control."

"Do you still want me to watch him tonight?"

Regina suppressed a sigh. "Yeah. Thanks. But I'd like to have a moment first."

"Please, Nonna," Nick added.

"It's not my decision," Antonia said, her voice suggesting it damn well should be. "Do what you want. You always do."

"Not recently," Regina muttered as they moved away.

But for the next ten minutes, she enjoyed the sight of

Nick hopping and sliding, clapping and turning, laughing and carrying on like any other eight-year-old.

The music shifted and slowed.

Couples took their turn on the floor.

And Regina, her sandal straps biting into her toes, delivered Nick back to her mother.

"Midnight for us, kiddo. You go home in the pumpkin coach with Grandma."

He tipped his head up to look at her. "What about you?"

Regina brushed his dark hair back from his face, letting her hand rest a moment on his smooth cheek. "I've got to work."

He nodded. "Love you."

She felt a burst of maternal love under her breastbone like heartburn. "Love *you*."

She watched them leave the white rental tent and climb the hill toward the parking lot, her square mother and skinny son casting long shadows on the park grass. The setting sun lingered on the crest, firing the bushes to fuchsia and gold like the enchanted roses in a fairy tale.

It was one of those summer evenings, one of those days, that almost made Regina believe in happy endings.

Not for her, though. Never for her.

She sighed and turned back to the tent. Her feet hurt.

Mechanic Bobby Kincaid was tending bar for the free beer and as a favor to Cal. Bobby earned good money in his father's garage. These days every sixteen-year-old on the island with lobster money burning a hole in his pocket had to have a car. Or a pickup.

Regina sidestepped as Bobby attempted to grab her ass. Too bad he was such a jerk.

"Hi, Bobby." She snagged a bottle of sparkling wine from the ice-filled cooler and wrestled the wire cage around the cork. "Let's do a quick refill of all the glasses, and then I want those cake plates off the tables."

"Hey, now," rumbled a deep male voice behind her. "You're off duty."

Regina's heart beat faster. She turned. *Strong, tanned hands, steady green eyes, and a limp he'd picked up in Iraq.* Police Chief Caleb Hunter.

The groom.

Plucking the bottle of Prosecco from her grasp, Caleb filled a rented champagne flute and offered it to her. "You're a guest. We want you to enjoy yourself tonight."

"I am enjoying myself. Any chance to serve something besides red sauce and lobster rolls . . ."

"The menu's great," Cal said. "Everything's great. Those crab patties—"

"Mini blue crab cakes with chipotle aioli and roasted red pepper sauce," Regina said.

"—are really something. You did good." His eyes were warm.

Regina flushed all over at the compliment. She *had* done well. With less than a month to plan and prepare, with only a clueless bride and the groom's awkward sister for support, Regina had pulled off the wedding she'd never had. The rented tent was warm with lantern light, bright with delphinium, daisies, and sunflowers. Crisp white linens covered the picnic tables, and she'd dressed up the folding chairs from the community center with flowing bows.

The food—*her* food, mussels steamed in garlic and white wine, bruschetta topped with basil and tomatoes, smoked wild salmon with dilled crème fraîche—was a huge success.

"Thanks," she said. "I was thinking I might talk Ma into adding some of these appetizers to our regular menu. The mussels, maybe, or—"

"Great," Cal repeated, but he wasn't listening any longer. His gaze slid beyond her to his bride, Maggie, dancing with his father.

Margred's dark hair had slipped free of its pins to wave on her neck. She'd kicked off her shoes so that the hem of her flowing white dress dragged. She was looking up at Caleb's father, laughing as he executed a clumsy turn on the floor.

The naked intensity in Cal's eyes as he watched his wife closed Regina's throat.

In her entire life, no man had ever looked at her like that, as if she were the sun and the moon and his entire world wrapped up in one. If anyone ever did, she would jump him.

If Cal ever had—

But he hadn't. Wouldn't. Ever.

"Go dance," Regina said. "It's your wedding."

"Right," Caleb said, already moving.

He turned back a moment to smile at her and order, "No more work tonight. We hired the youth group to give you a break."

"You know you have to watch those church kids like a hawk," Regina called after him.

But that was just an excuse.

The truth was she would rather schlep glasses and scrape plates than have the same conversations she'd had before with the same people she'd known all her life.

How's the weather? How's your mother? When are you getting married?

Oh, God.

She watched Cal circling the dance floor with his new bride—slowly, because of his limp—and emptiness caught her under the ribs, sharp as a cramp.

Grabbing her glass and the open bottle of Prosecco, she walked away from it all, the music, the lights, and the dancing. Away from Bobby behind the bar and Caleb with his arms around Margred.

Regina's heels punched holes in the ragged strip of grass. Drawn by the rush and retreat of water on the rocks, she wobbled across the shale. A burst of foam ran toward her feet. She plopped onto an outcrop of granite to remove her sandals. Her bare toes flexed in the cool, coarse sand.

Ah. That was better.

Really.

She poured herself another glass of wine.

The level in the bottle fell as the moon rose, flat and bright. The sky deepened until it resembled the inside of a shell, purple and gray. Regina rolled her head to look at the stars, feeling the earth whirl around her.

"Careful." The deep male voice sounded amused.

She jerked upright. The contents of her glass sloshed. "Cal?"

"No. Disappointed?"

She'd spilled on her dress. Damn it.

Regina's gaze swung to the tent and then swept the shore, searching out the owner of that voice.

There, standing barefoot at the edge of the surf as if he'd just come out of the sea instead of simply wandering away from the wedding reception.

Her heart pounded. Her head buzzed from the wine.

Not Caleb. She squinted. He was too tall, too lean, too young, too . . .

His tie was loosened, his slacks rolled up. The gray light chased across his face, illuminating the long, narrow nose; the sculpted mouth; the eyes, dark and secret as sin.

Regina felt a pulse, a flutter, of pure feminine attraction and scowled. "I don't know what you're talking about."

He laughed softly, coming closer. "They look good together—Caleb and Margred."

She recognized him then. From the ceremony. "You're his brother. Dylan. The one who—"

Went away.

She'd heard stories. She was drunk, but she recalled the basics. How, twenty-five years ago, his mother had left the island, left her husband and Caleb and her infant daughter, Lucy, taking with her the other son. This one.

"I thought you were older," Regina said.

He went very still in the moonlight. "You remember?"

Regina snorted. "Hardly. Since I was, like, four at the time." She plucked the wet silk from her breasts. She'd have to make a trip to the mainland now. There was no dry cleaners on the island.

"Here." A flash, like a white flag in the dark, as he pulled out his handkerchief. A real gentleman.

And then his hand was on her chest, his fingers spanning the tiny gold cross that lay beneath her collarbone, the heel of his palm pressing the handkerchief right between her breasts. Warm. Intimate. Shocking.

Regina sucked in her breath. Not a gentleman at all. Asshole.

She knocked his wrist away. "I've got it."

Beneath the wet material, her nipples beaded. Could he see, in the dark? She mopped at her dress with his handkerchief. "What are you doing here?"

"I followed you."

If he hadn't just groped her breasts, she'd be flattered. "I meant, on the island."

"I wanted to see if they would actually go through with it."

"The wedding?"

"Yes." He refilled her flute, emptying the bottle, and handed it to her.

The gesture reminded her sharply of his brother. Despite the breeze off the water, her face felt hot. She felt warm all over. She gulped her wine. "So, you just showed up? After twenty-five years?"

"Not quite that long."

He folded his long body onto the rock beside her. His hip nudged her thigh. His hard, rounded shoulder brushed her shoulder. The warmth spread low in the pit of her stomach.

She cleared her throat. "What about your mother?"

"Dead."

Oops. Ouch. "Sorry."

Let it go, she told herself. She wasn't getting anywhere swapping dysfunctional family stories. Not that she wanted this to go anywhere, but—

"It's pretty strange that you never came back before," she said.

"You only think so because you never left."

She was stung. "I did, too. Right out of high school.

Got a job washing dishes at Perfetto's in Boston until Puccini promoted me to prep cook."

"Perfetto's."

"Alain Puccini's restaurant. You know. Food Network?"

"I take it I should be impressed."

"Damn straight." Pride and annoyance simmered together like a thick sauce. She drained her glass. "He was going to make me his sous chef."

"But you came back. Why?"

Because Alain—the son-of-a-bitch—had knocked her up. She couldn't work kitchen hours with an infant, or pay a babysitter on a line cook's salary. Even after she'd forced Alain to take a paternity test, his court-ordered child support barely covered day care. His assets were tied up—hidden—in the restaurant.

But she didn't say that. Her son and her life were none of Dylan's business.

His thigh pressed warm against her leg.

Anyway, men looked at you differently when you had a kid. It had been a long time since she'd sat with a man in the moonlight.

Longer still since she'd had sex with one.

She looked at Dylan, lean and dark and dangerous and close, and felt attraction run along her veins like the spark on a detonator fuse.

She shook her head to clear it.

"Why did you?" She turned the question back on him.

His shoulder moved against hers as he shrugged. "I came for the wedding. I'm not staying."

Regina quelled an unreasonable disappointment.

So it didn't matter how he looked at her, really. She leaned down to dig the bottom of her glass into the sand.

It didn't matter what he thought. After tonight, she'd never see him again. She could say anything she wanted. She could do . . .

Her breath caught in her throat. *Anything she wanted.*

She straightened, flushed and dizzy. Okay, that was the wine talking. Loneliness, and the wine. She wouldn't ever really—she couldn't actually be considering—

She stumbled to her feet.

"Easy." He caught her hand, supporting her.

"Not usually," she muttered.

His grip tightened as he stood. "What?"

She shook her head again, heat crawling in her face. "Nothing. Let me go. I need to take a walk."

"I'll go with you."

She wet her lips. "Bad idea."

He lifted an eyebrow. He did it beautifully. She wondered if he practiced in the mirror. "Better than you turning an ankle on those rocks."

"I'll be fine."

To anyone watching from the tent, they must look like lovers, standing hand in hand at the surf's edge. Her heart thumped. She tried to tug away.

His gaze dropped to their clasped hands. His fingers tightened. "You are warded."

She scowled at him, aroused and confused. "What are you talking about?"

He ran his thumb along the inside of her wrist, over her tattoo. Could he feel her pulse go wild? "This."

Regina swallowed, watching his thumb stroke over the dark lines, the pale skin. "My tatt? It's the Celtic sign for the triple goddess. A female empowerment thing."

"It is a triskelion." He traced the three flowing, connected spirals with his finger. "Earth, air, and sea, bound together in a circle. A powerful ward." He looked up at her, his eyes dark and serious.

Too serious. She felt a jolt in her stomach that might have been nerves or desire.

"So, I'm safe," she said breathlessly.

His beautiful mouth curved in the moonlight. "As safe as you want to be."

Goose bumps tingled along her arms. She shivered, as exposed as if she stood naked by a window.

"Safe works for me," she said. Or it had until recently. "I have responsibilities."

"Not any longer. Caleb told you not to work tonight."

Regina blinked. He'd heard that? He was watching her with his brother?

Caution flickered. She hadn't been aware of an audience. She hadn't been aware of him at all except as Caleb's brother, a tall, dark presence at the back of the wedding, on the edges of the celebration.

Her toes curled into the sand.

She was aware of him now. He was barely touching her, only that light grip on her wrist, and yet she felt the heat of him all along her body. His eyes glittered black in the moonlight, absorbing the light, absorbing the air, growing bigger, darker, enormous as he leaned close, closer, tempting her with that well-cut mouth, teasing her with the promise of his kiss. His breath skated across her lips. She tasted wine and something else—dark, salty, elusive—heard a rushing in her ears like the sea. She opened her mouth to breathe, and he bent over her and covered her mouth firmly, warmly, with his.

2

HE TASTED SO GOOD, HOT AND GOOD, LIKE salt and sex and brandy. Or maybe that was the wine she'd been drinking.

Regina rose on tiptoe, straining for more of his taste, as his teeth scraped her lower lip, as his tongue plundered her mouth. Nerves and need danced together in her belly. Warning pulsed in her head.

If she were smart—if she were sober—she would end this right now.

Dylan's hands stroked down her back and settled on her hips to draw her closer. His erection nudged between her thighs, and she lost her breath because he felt so good, hard and real against her, filling up the empty places, driving away the lonely thoughts.

She wanted this. Needed it.

She wrapped her arms around his neck, tangling her tongue with his, grinding their hips together. His hands moved lower as he rocked against her. He was so hot, and she was burning up inside, everything inside her melting and flowing toward him. He kneaded her buttocks, pressing below, between, and when she spread her legs to give him better access, his fingers dug into her thighs, and he lifted her, positioned her against him.

Sensation shuddered through her. She closed her eyes at the irresistible pressure, the unbearable temptation.

Stupid, stupid.

She tore her mouth away. Her heart slammed in her chest. Anyone could see them from the tent. Her mother, anyone.

Okay, not her mother, Antonia had left with Nick. But—

"No," Regina gasped.

Dylan's arms tensed. His grip shifted. "No?"

Her head spun. Her blood pounded. She was wet and open and aching as a wound, and if she didn't get some relief, she would scream.

"Not here," she amended.

His low chuckle vibrated through her belly. If she knew him better, she would have slugged him. Regina scowled, her brows drawing together. Of course, if she knew him better, she wouldn't be groping him in full sight of a wedding reception.

Before she could follow that line of thought, Dylan hitched her thighs higher around his waist and carried her down the beach, over the shale.

Barefoot?

He splashed through water. Slabs of granite lay like tumbled building blocks where the land plunged to the sea.

Regina clutched his shoulders. "What are you—"

Dylan rounded a tall outcrop of rock. "It's all right. I've got you."

"Not yet."

His smile gleamed in the twilight. He set her down on dry rock, smooth and warm with residual sun, and took her mouth in another deep, drowning kiss.

His kiss swamped her thoughts. Dizzy with wine and lust, she staggered as if the tide dragged at her knees. Her heart pounded—hard, fast, reckless. She felt alight, alive, her mouth as hungry, as greedy, as his.

His skin was hot, his body taut. She burrowed beneath his jacket, yanked at his shirt, desperate to grab as many sensations as possible to take back with her into the long, celibate nights. "Touch me," she demanded.

Anywhere. Everywhere.

He did.

His hands were strong and lean like the rest of him, rubbing her through her dress, cupping and caressing, until the fabric scraped her nerves and her knees trembled. He shaped her breast, weighed it in his palm, before tugging the neckline aside, freeing her to the cool, moist air.

She sucked in her breath at the sight of her pale breast in his dark hand, his fingers working the tight nipple.

His arm was a warm band at her back. He bent her over it and suckled her hard. And she went off—just like that—in a series of swift, light bursts, her orgasm rising through her like the bubbles in her wine.

"*Oh.*" Oh, God.

Her blood fizzed. Her face heated. She stared down at his dark head, her fingers still tangled in his hair, her mind a mess. She had never . . . She couldn't possibly . . .

She gulped. Obviously, she could. She had.

"Well." Her voice sounded insanely cheerful. "That was . . ." *Embarrassing.* "Quick."

He slid to his knees in front of her, his hands hard on her hips. "I'm not done with you."

Oh. Regina pressed her thighs together. Or tried to. He was in the way. She had to tell him, politely, she was done.

Not that she wasn't grateful. He'd just touched off her first male-induced orgasm in years. She owed him.

He slid up her dress, making her shiver.

Really, she should say something.

His hair brushed her stomach as he pulled her panties down, his breath hot against her, and she flushed.

"Uh, listen, you don't need to—"

He licked between her thighs and her mind went blank. She didn't say anything. She didn't have to do . . . anything. She was trapped between his warm, insistent hands and his urgent, clever mouth. He kept at her, on and on, while the stars wheeled and the sea whispered and the rocks shifted under her feet. She strained against him as the pressure built inside her, as the tension coiled tighter, until she couldn't stand it, until she twitched and twisted to escape, until she came, over and over again, between his hands, against his mouth.

She was limp and loose and reeling when he surged up between her thighs. He was breathing hard, his chest warm and damp. She spread her fingers against his shirt-front, against his pounding heart. Dimly, she registered the rasp of his zipper, and then he put himself where his mouth had been.

She thought, *Oh, yes.*

And then, *Oh, no.*

And then, as he plunged thick and hot inside her, *Oh, shit.*

She panted. "Stop."

He withdrew and thrust again. "No."

She bit her lip to keep from screaming. He felt so good, hard and good, filling her, stretching her. *There.*

She whacked his shoulder in time with his thrusts. "I won't . . . you're not . . . I could get pregnant!" The last word was a wail.

His head reared back. His black eyes glittered. "So?"

She smacked him again. "Get *out!*"

With mingled relief and frustration, she felt him pull out.

He turned her, so that she faced the cliffs, and grabbed her hips.

She braced her palms on the cold, rough rock face for balance. "What are you doing?"

Stupid question. She could feel him, his erection, rubbing her, pressing her from behind, wet with her moisture, sliding and gliding along the cleft of her buttocks.

She stiffened, her mouth dry with panic and excitement. "Uh . . . no. I don't—"

His arm was hard around her waist, his chest solid at her back. "Quiet."

She set her teeth. Okay, she owed him. But not—

His hand worked between their bodies, pumping once, twice, before he gripped her hips with both hands. He ground himself against her, his fingers digging into her flesh. She felt him jerk, felt his hot exhalation in her ear, and then the warm stickiness at the small of her back.

Oh. Thank God he had pulled out.

He shuddered, his body warm and heavy against hers.

An odd tenderness stirred under her heart. Peeling one hand from the cliff face, she stretched back her arm to pat his hip. His thigh. His leg was hard with muscle and rough with hair. He turned his head to nuzzle her hair, and the unexpected sweetness of the gesture made something turn over in her chest.

She closed her eyes, willing away thought.

Gradually, her body cooled. His breathing evened. She became aware of tiny, separate sensations: the gritty stone beneath her feet, the rising mist around her bare legs, the rich salt smells of sea and sex . . .

And then he let her go.

She heard him behind her, adjusting his clothing, and shivered, suddenly cold.

"You lost something." His voice was deep, polite. Caleb's voice.

Regina opened her eyes, leaning her forehead against the rock. "My self-respect?"

He didn't laugh.

Okay, not funny. She swallowed against the tightness in her throat, sobriety creeping in like the tide. Not funny at all.

"Your panties," he said.

"Right." Flushing, she turned. There they were, dangling from his fingers. She snatched the scrap of nylon from him without quite meeting his eyes. "Thanks."

He inclined his head. "You are welcome."

If he smirked, she would kill him.

But he continued to watch her with an unnerving lack

of expression, as if he'd never been inside her, as if they'd never—

Oh, God. Her insides contracted. Her knees wobbled. No way was she pulling on her panties under that flat black gaze.

Regina balled the damp nylon in her fist. Now what?

"Are you going back to the party?" she asked.

"I have no reason to."

Right.

Regina bit her lip, relieved and disappointed. "You could say good-bye."

Not to her. She didn't care if she never saw him again.

His shoulders shrugged under his well-cut jacket. "Margred will not notice my leaving."

"Your brother will."

Dylan's black eyes glittered. "I did not come for my brother."

An awkward silence fell, broken only by the whisper of waves on the rocks, the stones tinkling and tumbling like wind chimes. Strains of music drifted from the tent, too faint for Regina to distinguish words or melody. She opened her mouth to say something, anything. *That was fun. Let's never do it again.*

"You knew Maggie?" she asked. "Before she got married?"

"Yes."

Regina sucked in her breath. Not her problem, she reminded herself. None of her business.

But Margred was her employee. Regina had hired her to help out at the restaurant after Caleb found her on the beach, naked and bleeding from a blow to her head. Margred claimed not to remember anything of her life before she came to the island. Regina always suspected the other woman was fleeing an abusive relationship.

But if Dylan knew her . . .

Regina scowled. "How?"

His brows rose. "I suggest you ask her."

"I will."

As soon as she gets back from her honeymoon with your brother.

Maybe not.

"Or you could tell me now," Regina said.

"No."

She folded her arms, her underwear still wadded in her hand. "Are you always this chatty after sex? Or is it me?"

"Maybe I don't like gossip."

"Or maybe you're protecting somebody."

He didn't answer.

"Her?" Regina guessed. "Or yourself?"

*   *   *

Human women.

Always wanting something.

Dylan regarded this one with frustrated resignation. He had liked the look of her, the straight, cropped hair, the angular body, the contrast of those soft, sensitive lips in that sharp-featured face. Her differences drew him, all that tension and energy confined in a tight, feminine little body. He had enjoyed unwrapping her and watching her fly apart.

But the big dark eyes had sharpened to points, and her chin was at a militant angle. Now that he'd had her, she thought that he owed her—attention, answers, some damn thing.

Not so different, after all. He supposed her attitude was only human.

Too bad for her he wasn't.

"Let me take you back," he said. "You must have work to do."

The chin rose a notch. "You don't need to take me anywhere. I can get where I'm going by myself."

Almost amused, he stepped back to let her pass. She marched to the edge of the water and stopped.

Of course. She would not be able to see in the dark. Dylan remembered how it had been before his first Change. These rocks would slice her narrow human feet to pieces.

She edged forward.

He frowned. He wasn't going to waste the breath or effort to argue with her. But neither could he stand by while she cut herself stumbling around in the surf.

Jeering at himself for caring, he picked her up.

Regina yelped. Jerked. The top of her head connected with his chin, snapping his mouth shut. Pain shot through his jaw.

He unclenched his teeth and growled. "Hold still."

She glared, her nose inches from his. Her hair was soft against his cheek and smelled like fruit, strawberries or—

"You surprised me," she accused.

"I surprise myself," he murmured.

"What's the matter? Never swept a girl off her feet before?"

"Not usually." Apricots, he decided. She smelled like apricots, tart and ripe. She was heavier than he expected, muscle wrapped around a tensile steel frame. The skin behind her knees was soft and smooth. To distance himself, to bait her, he said, "Mostly they just lie down."

Her smile sliced knife-sharp through the twilight. "That explains why your technique needs work."

He laughed softly. "And you?"

Water splashed around his ankles.

Her grip tightened on his neck. "What about me?"

"Do you often get, ah, carried away?"

"Are you asking if I sleep around?"

He did not know what he was asking. Or why. "Your sexual history is no concern of mine."

She snorted. "Obviously. Or you would have used a condom."

In truth, she was no more likely to get him sick than he was to get her pregnant. But Dylan could not be bothered to explain that to her. She would not believe him if he did.

He walked out of the water and set her on the beach, keeping his hands on her forearms while she found her balance.

She sighed. "Look, you don't need to worry. You're the first in—oh, a long time."

He felt a tinge of satisfaction, a twinge of guilt, and scowled. He should not feel anything. His kind did not. They sought the sensations and the physical release of sex. They did not blind themselves with emotion or bind their partners with expectations.

"Your shoes." He jerked his head toward them.

They lay on their sides just out of reach of the water, the flirty heels and skinny straps totally unsuited to this stretch of rock and sand.

"Right." She scooped them up. "Thanks."

"You're welcome." He met her gaze, warm and wary,

and felt heat curl in his belly. He wanted her again. But that flash of feeling had alarmed him.

He should have learned by now not to fuck with humans.

He was too close to being one of them.

This one hadn't even been that good, he told himself, ignoring the intensity of her response, his satisfaction at making her come. Oh, she was acceptable by human standards. But he was accustomed to partners who knew what pleased them and how to please him. He was fourteen and grieving for his mother when he had his first lover, a lush selkie female who had honed her skills and her lust over a millennium of practice. Nerienne had been nothing at all like this uptight, argumentative human.

Her words pounded in his temples. *"You're the first in—oh, a long time."*

His chest tightened.

The air was too warm. Warm and close. It dragged on him like a fisherman's net, constraining his lungs, cutting off his air. He could not breathe. He was wild to go, to run, to return to the freedom of the sea.

He stood immobile at the cliffs while the woman—Regina—fumbled with her sandals.

"Well." She straightened and pinned him with a bright smile. "Have a nice stay on the island."

"I am leaving tonight."

Her smile faltered; set. "Oh. Then I guess I won't see you again."

Her casual pat on his flank, that tender, careless touch on his thigh, burned like a brand. The mer did not touch. Only to fight, or to mate.

His hands curled into fists at his sides.

"No," he said.

She turned away without another word.

He stood without moving as she wobbled up the beach, toward the lights and the music, leaving him alone.

3

THE TOWER OF CAER SUBAI WAS VERY OLD, mortared with mists and magic. The prince was older still, weary with the weight of years and responsibilities. But as long as he stayed within this tower on the selkie isle of Sanctuary, he did not age. He would not die.

Conn ap Llyr, prince of the mer, lord of the sea, gazed west out his windows, listening to the sea song rise from the rocks below and the north wind pry through the stones like a knife. He could feel the demon's presence from half a world away, swirling like an oil slick, dark and corrosive, lapping at the island the humans called World's End.

Conn did not give a damn if the humans were overrun with demons and their island sank into the sea. For millennia, the children of the sea had maintained an uneasy peace with demonkind, a peace struck from pride and self-interest, cobbled together with compromises and broken promises, defended through centuries of violations and encroachments. A peace he believed would hold.

Until six weeks ago, when a demon had murdered one of Conn's people on World's End.

He gripped the edge of his desk, a massive slab of iron and carved walnut salvaged from a Spanish galleon wrecked off the Cornish coast. Everything that dwelled in and under the sea, everything that fell below its surface, was his to claim or dispose of. Nine tenths of the earth was in his realm. But the demon eluded him.

He reached outward, his thoughts eddying, circling the darkness, seeking its source, its threat. He might as well have tried to sieve a drop from a current. The demon slipped his grasp, lost in a moving tide of humanity.

Conn bowed his head, failure bitter in his mouth. The hound sleeping at his feet twitched and whined. Beyond his tower windows, the bright sea rolled, wild, wide, and deep, beyond his reach, taunting his control.

There was a time—the whales sang of it—when the sea lords' power ran high and full, when the mer were attuned to every creature in and over the sea, when they could summon glaciers or transport themselves in a shower of rain. Even Conn's own father, Llyr, before he abandoned human form and all responsibility—

But Conn could not think of the absentee king without anger, and anger was something else he had learned to deny himself. Deliberately, he uncurled his hands, splaying them against the map on his desk.

In recent centuries, the sea kings' gifts had dwindled as their people's numbers declined. All that was left for the sea king's heir was to safeguard what remained with whatever tools he could find.

Footsteps sounded from the tower stairs.

Conn glanced up as Dylan emerged, the top of his head nearly brushing the arch of rough cut stone.

Here was a tool. A weapon, rather. Dylan was ambitious and resourceful, a son of the sea witch Atargatis and her human husband. After her death, Conn had taken the boy under his own protection. Dylan had yet to demonstrate any power beyond what every selkie possessed, sexual glamour and a little weather magic. But he had proven his courage and his loyalty; and in the current situation, Conn must use what lay at hand.

"You sent for me, lord?" Dylan asked.

"Yes." Frustration had made him abrupt. He leashed his tone. "I have something to show you."

Dylan surveyed the chart covering the surface of the desk. "Since when do we depend on human maps?"

"It suits my purpose," Conn said.

"Which is?"

Instead of replying, Conn spread his hands over the desk. He concentrated his gift, adding his little findings to the information already imbued in the map. Gradually the image came alive, colors winking into being like stars in the night sky, forming streams and clusters of light.

Dylan's brows flicked up. "Impressive. What is it?"

Conn closed his fists, ignoring the faint, residual headache that exercising his magic always gave him. The map pulsed and swirled with color. "The gray"— great swathes of it—"indicates human habitation. The blue represents our people."

A few, too few, thousand scattered points of light, almost lost in the vastness of the oceans.

"The children of earth are here." Conn's finger followed the trail of green along the mountain ranges, tapped the sacred places of the sidhe. "Demons here." A sweep of his hand indicated the children of fire, spattered like blood across fault lines and land forms.

Dylan stepped closer to the desk, narrowing his eyes in concentration. "I do not see the children of air on your map."

"Because they are not there. Angelic intervention is less common than most humans believe. Or would welcome," Conn said dryly. "Besides, it is the demons' activity that concerns me."

"Because of Gwyneth."

Conn's rage welled, deep and slow as ice. Six weeks ago, the selkie Gwyneth of Hiort had been lured to land, stripped of her pelt, tortured, and killed by a demon in human form.

"Because they murdered one of us," Conn agreed, "and because they attempted to cast blame on the humans. I will not be tricked into taking sides in the demons' war on heaven and humankind."

Dylan frowned at the map. The darkness Conn had sensed earlier was a red blot off the coast of Maine. "You may not have a choice. If the demons upset the balance—"

"Margred restored the balance when she bound Gwyneth's murderer in the sea."

Dylan raised one eyebrow. "A life for a life?"

"After a fashion." Elementals were immortal. The selkie would be reborn in the sea; the demon was trapped for eternity. A fair enough exchange, in Conn's view. "But Margred's action carries its own consequences."

"You think she is in danger?" Dylan asked sharply.

"I think she could be."

"Revenge?"

Conn considered. The demons understood justice; they were not ruled by it. Revenge would certainly play a part in their response. But they were driven by more practical considerations. "Say, rather, that Margred's demonstration of power may have put her at risk."

"Why are you telling me this?"

"She married your brother."

Dylan's lips pulled back from his teeth. "Unfortunately. She is human now. Which means her choices and her fate are really none of my business."

Or yours. The implication hung in the air, unspoken.

"Unless she carries your brother's child," Conn said evenly.

Dylan's pale face turned white. There were feelings there, Conn thought. Feelings he would not hesitate to use for his own purposes.

"What difference would that make?" Dylan asked.

"Your mother's blood was strong. Her gift was powerful. There are songs—" *Prophecy or history?* Conn wondered. Impossible to tell from the whales' song. The great mammals had even less concept of time than selkies. "There are stories that a daughter of Atargatis's lineage could forever change the balance of power and the destiny of her people."

"A daughter." Dylan's eyes were black. "Not a son?"

Conn sympathized with his disappointment. Better for them both if Atargatis's power had devolved to a son. To Dylan.

"The songs say a daughter."

"Then . . ." Dylan scowled, still regarding the red-tinged map of Maine. "My sister?"

Conn shook his head. "Both your brother and your sister are human. So far the demons have considered them unworthy of notice. But if your brother were to have a child—"

"Or if I did."

"Yes. I had hoped—" Conn broke off. He did not indulge in hope any more than anger. "The combination of your mother's blood and Margred's gift might be regarded as an advantage for our people. Or as a threat by the demons."

"So what do you want me to do? Tell my brother he shouldn't fuck his wife?"

Conn thought about it. "Would he listen to you?"

"No."

Conn shrugged. "Just as well. Our numbers are declining. We need children. We need this child."

Dylan sneered. "Assuming he can get Margred pregnant."

"Assuming their child is selkie. And female. Yes."

"You assume a great deal."

Conn's mouth twitched in a rare smile. "True." And few of his court dared to speak the truth to him. "Yet something draws the demons to World's End. I need you to find out what."

*   *   *

Dylan stared at his prince, his heart thundering in his ears. For a moment he wondered if he'd heard Conn correctly. "That's a warden's job."

The prince's gaze was clear and light as frost, deep and measureless as the sea. "Do you refuse me?"

"I—No, my lord." He was startled, not stupid. "But why not send one of them?"

The wardens were Conn's confidants, his elite. Chosen for their loyalty and the strength of their gift, they kept the prince's peace, defending his realm from the depredations of human and demon kind.

Since he was fourteen years old, Dylan had burned to be counted as one of them, to wear the wardens' mark around his neck.

It had been a bitter realization to accept he was too nearly human to have either their power or the prince's trust.

"They do not have your knowledge of the island," Conn said. "Or your connection to it."

For some reason, Dylan's brain presented him with a picture of the woman, the prickly one with the ward on her wrist and the tight body humming with energy.

They were not connected, he thought. He had merely had sex with her. He had sex with many women.

And banished the memory of her voice saying, *"You're the first in—oh, a long time."*

Conn must have taken his silence as dissent, for he said, "You grew up there."

Dylan dragged his mind back to the tower and the present discussion. "Many years ago."

"Your family lives there."

A touchy point. "They are not my family any longer. I am selkie now."

The prince regarded him with cool, light eyes. "And yet you keep a human habitation not three miles east of them."

Dylan flushed. How much did Conn know? And how much did he hold against him? "The island was my mother's."

"Your father built and furnished the house."

He had not known. He told himself it did not matter. "It's a convenient stopping place, that's all," Dylan said.

"Certainly it will be," Conn agreed. "You may need to live among them for a time."

Dylan's stomach sank. "After more than twenty years, the islanders are likely to question my sudden reappearance."

"Not so sudden," Conn pointed out. "You were at your brother's wedding."

Something Dylan regretted now. "That's hardly the same. I didn't have to talk to them."

Or his father. Or his sister.

Sweat broke out on his lip and under his arms.

"They will want to know why I am there."

"The humans have a story, do they not? Of the prodigal son?"

"I do not think my brother"—*the older brother, the good son, the one who stayed with his father*—"will buy that explanation for my return."

"Then you will have to offer him another one," Conn said coolly. "You can think of some excuse that will satisfy him."

Unbidden, the woman appeared again in his mind's eye, her chin raised in the moonlight, her panties balled in his fist.

"Yes," Dylan said slowly. "I can."

* * *

Regina counted the twenties under the tray of the cash register drawer. *Forty, sixty, eighty . . .*

The lunchtime rush was over, the tourists gone to catch the two thirty ferry to the mainland. The afternoon sun slanted through the restaurant's faded red awning, warming the vinyl booths and scratched wood floor. Be-

yond the plate glass window, the harbor sparkled blue
and bright, boats at anchor in the quiet water.

Margred loaded glasses from an empty table into a
dish pan, her movements languid and graceful as the res-
ident cat's. She and Caleb had returned from their two
nights in Portland yesterday.

"So." Regina snapped a rubber band around the pile
of bills. "How was the honeymoon?"

Margred showed her teeth in a slow, satisfied smile.
"Too short."

Regina laughed, ignoring her own wistfulness.
"That's what you get for marrying the only cop on the island in the middle of the tourist season. If you'd waited
until September, he could have taken you on a real honeymoon. Hawaii, maybe. Or Paris."

"I do not want Paris." Margred's smile spread. "And
Caleb did not want to wait."

Regina fought a pinch of envy. Had she ever been that
happy? That desired? That . . . confident?

"I was surprised to see his brother at the wedding,"
she said.

"Dylan?" Margred cocked her head, leaning forward
to wipe the table. "Did you like him?"

"I barely talked to him."

No, she'd just had sex with him on the beach. Really
excellent sex. But no meaningful conversation.

Her face burned.

She wasn't looking for meaningful, Regina reminded
herself. And neither, obviously, was he. At least, not with
her.

"He seemed to know you, though," she added.

Margred's rag paused. "He is Caleb's brother."

"From before." Regina wiped her sweating palms on her apron. "He said he knew you before."

"Did he?" Margred continued her slow, even strokes on the table. "What else did he say?"

Regina had a vision of Dylan's face, black and bitter. *"I did not come for my brother."*

She cleared her throat. "Nothing, really. I just found it interesting. Since you, you know, lost your memory and all."

"Ah."

Let it go, Regina told herself. *Not your problem. None of your business.*

"So, how did you meet him?"

Margred straightened, rag in hand. "Curious?"

Regina scowled. "Concerned. Damn it, you're my friend."

My employee.

Cal's wife.

"So I am. And as your friend, I am telling you to leave this alone."

Regina closed the register drawer with a short *cha-ching.* "Fine."

Margred's expression softened. "I promise, there is nothing in our relationship that Caleb could object to."

"Does he know?" Regina asked before she could stop herself.

"Oh, yes. I have no secrets from Caleb."

"Bet the memory loss thing helps with that," Regina muttered.

"Excuse me?"

The bell over the door jingled. Jane Ivey, the owner of the island's gift shop, entered wearing a lumpy cardigan and the determined look of a woman on a mission.

"What can I get you?" Regina asked.

"Here's the bride!" Jane exclaimed as if she hadn't spoken. "You looked real good on Saturday, honey."

"Thank you," Margred said.

"That whole wedding—it was real nice," Jane said.

Margred smiled. "Regina did it all."

Jane's tight brown perm quivered as she nodded. "Well, I know that. That's why I stopped by. The girls are coming home for Frank's birthday in September," she said to Regina.

"That's . . . great," Regina said. Was it great? She couldn't remember how well Jane got along with her absent children. Sons stayed on the island, took over their fathers' lobstering business or bought boats of their own. But daughters moved Away, seeking education, opportunities, husbands.

Sometimes they came back.

"We never thought when Frank had that episode last winter that he'd make it to his sixty-fifth," Jane said, clutching her purse. "But he did, the old coot. Anyway, they're all coming, Trish and Ed and Erica and the grandkids. We're having a big party. And I want you to cater it."

Regina felt a spurt of satisfaction, warm and sweet as biting into pastry filling. She knew her food was good. But she didn't get many opportunities to show what she could do. "Um, I'm not really set up for—"

"We don't do catering here," Antonia said from the kitchen pass through. "We do take-out. You can look at a menu, if you want."

"Oh." Jane's face folded. "Well . . ."

"How many guests?" Regina asked.

"I don't—thirty?" Jane guessed.

She could do thirty, Regina thought, excitement balling in her stomach. She could feed thirty in her *sleep*. As long as Margred was willing to help with setup . . .

"Talk to the inn," Antonia said. "The chef there can probably—"

"I already asked at the inn. Forty-eight dollars a head, he wanted, and twenty-four for the kids, who won't eat nothing but chocolate milk and hot dogs anyway." Jane's soft jaw set. "I want you to do it."

"So take a menu," Antonia said.

"Frank really liked those little crab cakes," Jane said to Regina.

He liked her *food*.

She could *do* this.

"Why don't I put together some ideas," Regina said, already reviewing appetizers in her head. Tiny grilled sausages, that was easy, the kids could snack on those. Canapes. Maybe Gorgonzola with pine nuts? Roasted asparagus wrapped in proscuitto. "I can come by the shop later to talk. Thursday?" Thursdays she worked from lunch until close. "Thursday morning?"

Jane beamed, relieved and triumphant. "Thursday morning, sure."

"Is that all you came in for?" Antonia asked.

"Yes." Jane's gaze flickered to Margred; lingered on her belly. "And to see the bride, of course."

"Well, you've seen her. Now we can all get back to work. Real work," Antonia added as Jane sailed out the door. "Not wasting time and money on Frank Ivey's birthday party."

"It's not a waste," Regina argued. "We can do this. We should do this."

"We don't have the staff," Antonia said.

It was an old argument, one that started the headache behind Regina's eyes. They alternated shifts now, mornings and evenings, both of them on during the lunch and dinner hours and Margred filling in as needed. "So we hire—"

"Who?" Antonia demanded. "Anybody around here wants to pick up extra cash, they get it working the stern on a lobster boat, not scrubbing pots or serving fancy appetizers."

"I'm just saying if we developed a catering business—just as a sideline—"

"We're doing fine without it."

"We could do better."

Catering would give her a shot at an expanded menu and more flexible hours. But what Regina saw as an opportunity, her mother saw as a rejection of everything she'd worked for.

"So now you have a problem with the way I'm running the restaurant?"

Regina's head pulsed. "No, Ma. It's business."

"It's bullshit. Jane only came in here because she wanted to get a good look at Maggie."

Regina pressed her fingers to her temples. "What the hell are you talking about?"

"I'm only telling you what everybody's saying."

"What are they saying?" Margred asked.

"You got married in an awful hurry. Could be—" Antonia paused uncharacteristically before plunging on. "Some folks figure you must be pregnant."

"Ma!" Regina protested. Instinctively, she looked for Nick, but he was upstairs in the apartment they had shared since she brought him home over seven years ago: four small rooms with mice in the walls and the smell of garlic and red sauce rising from the kitchen below.

"What?" Antonia folded her arms across her chest. "Some people find out they're expecting, they actually marry their baby's father."

Oh, God. Regina's stomach flipped. Like this day didn't suck enough already. Her mother couldn't be content with control of the restaurant, she wanted to run Regina's life as well.

"That doesn't always work out, Ma."

Antonia glared. "What's that supposed to mean?"

Margred had abandoned wiping tables to listen.

"You married Dad," Regina said. "How many years did he stick around? Two? Three?"

"At least you got your father's name."

"And that's all I got. You did everything. Paid for everything. He never even sent child support."

"Oh, and you did so much better with the Greedy Gourmet."

Frustration closed Regina's throat. She had never been able to talk with her mother. They were like oil and vinegar, too different to ever really understand one another.

Or maybe they were too much alike.

"I wasn't—" She worried the crucifix around her neck, running it back and forth along the chain. "I'm trying to tell you I appreciate—"

"He loved us. Your father. Not everybody is suited for island life, you know."

"I know. *Jesus.*" Did they have to exhume every skeleton in the family closet just because Jane Ivey liked

Regina's crab cakes better than her mother's lasagna? "I'd leave myself if I could."

The words hung on the air, thick as the grease smell from the fryer. The hurt on Antonia's face registered like a slap.

Regina bit her tongue. *Crap.*

"I am not pregnant," Margred said.

Antonia rounded on her. "What?"

"You wanted to know. I would like a baby. But I am not pregnant yet."

"You want a baby?" Regina repeated. Remembering her own pregnancy with Nick, when she was sick all the time and tired and alone. "You just got married."

Antonia snorted. "Married, hell. They only met six weeks ago."

Margred arched her eyebrows. "I was not aware of a time requirement. How long must you know someone before you can get pregnant?"

Memory swamped Regina: Dylan, plunging thick and hot inside her, filling her, stretching her. Her own voice panting, *"I could get pregnant!"*

Her stomach dived. *Oh, God.* She couldn't be pregnant. Nobody could be that unlucky twice.

The bell jangled as a scarecrow figure pushed through the door: thin face, thin beard, dingy fatigue jacket over layers of sweatshirts.

Not a camper, Regina thought, despite the backpack. The patina of wear, the dirt embedded in the creases of his knuckles and his boots, went deeper than a week in the wild. Homeless, maybe.

"Can I help you?" Antonia asked in a voice that meant something else. *Get out. Go away.*

Regina understood her hostility. World's End barely had the social services to support its own population. The ferry and the local businesses catered to residents and tourists, not the homeless.

The man eased the pack from his broad, bony shoulders to thump on the floor. "I'm looking for work."

"What's your name?" Regina asked.

"Jericho."

"Last name?"

"Jones."

At least he had a last name. It was more than Margred had offered when she first came to work for them.

"Do you have any restaurant experience, Mr. Jones?"

His gaze slid to meet hers, and her breath caught in her throat.

Alain used to say the eyes were windows to the soul. Regina figured it was mostly a line to get her into bed, but she knew what he meant. You could tell when nobody was home. But this guy ... His eyes were crowded, haunted, like he had too many people living in his head, jockeying for position at the windows.

Schizophrenia? Or substance abuse?

She didn't care so much if he was using. Half the staff at Perfetto's had been addicted to something, booze or drugs or the adrenaline rush of a perfectly performed dinner service. But she wasn't hiring a crazy to work in her mother's kitchen, her son's home.

"Call me Jericho," he said.

She cleared her throat. "Fine. Do you have any—"

"I washed dishes in the Army."

Margred set her bus tray on the counter. "You were in the Army?"

He nodded.

"Iraq? My husband was in Iraq."

"Yes, ma'am."

Regina bit back a groan. Of course he would say that. He'd probably say anything to get a job. Or a handout.

"We're not hiring," Antonia said.

Margred frowned. "But—"

Jericho picked up his pack. "Okay."

That was it. No resentment. No expectations. His flat acceptance got under Regina's skin, made them kin somehow.

She scowled. Nobody should live that devoid of hope. "You want to wait a minute, I'll make you a sandwich," she said.

He turned his head, and she did her best to meet that haunted, eerie gaze without a shudder.

"Thanks," he said at last. "Mind if I wash up first?"

"Be my guest."

"He trashes the restroom, you clean it up," Antonia said when the door had closed behind him.

"I can clean," Margred said before Regina could bite back.

Antonia sniffed. "We can't feed everybody who walks in off the street, you know."

Regina was irritated enough to shove aside her own misgivings. "Then maybe we're in the wrong business," she said and stomped into the kitchen to make the man a sandwich.

She glanced up the apartment stairs as she passed. Nick had already visited the kitchen to eat his lunch and punch holes in the pizza dough. But she could call him down for a snack, shoo him outside to play. Summers were tough on them both. School was out while the restaurant stayed open longer hours. Nick had more free time, and Regina had less.

This summer for some reason had been worse. Maybe because Nick was old enough now to chafe at his mother's restrictions. Regina rubbed the headache brewing between her eyebrows. She ought to be able to sympathize with that.

"Nick," she called.

He was silent. Sulking? She'd been short with him this morning.

Distracted, Regina thought guiltily, trying hard not to remember Saturday night, Dylan's hands on her hips as he moved slickly, thickly inside her.

No sex on the beach was as important as her son.

"Nicky?"

The restaurant cat, Hercules, meowed plaintively from the top of the stairs.

No answer.

Worry trickled through her. On World's End, everybody knew everybody's business. Every neighbor kept an eye on every child. Children here still walked to the store alone, still played on the beach unsupervised.

But she'd told Nick and told him not to leave the restaurant without telling her. There were dangers on the island, too, tides and fog and gravel pits, teenagers in cars, strangers with haunted eyes . . .

Regina shook her head. She was not letting herself get spooked because some homeless guy had wandered into the restaurant looking for work and a sandwich.

Knowing she was overreacting, however, didn't keep her palms from sweating, didn't stop her heart from hammering in her chest. When you were a single mom, there was nobody to share the worry or the blame, and so the worry doubled and every danger assumed terrifying proportions. Anything could threaten this tiny person who had been entrusted to you, your baby, your son, the best and most inconvenient thing that had ever happened to you, and it would all be *your fault* because you hadn't been taking care, you hadn't wanted him in the first place.

Regina forced herself to release her grip on the stair railing. Okay, definitely overreacting now.

She opened the unlocked door to their apartment, Hercules darting between her ankles into the empty living room.

"Nick?" She cocked her head, listening for the sound of the television, the gurgle of water from the bathroom.

But he was gone.

4

NICK BARONE EYED THE LITTLE BLUE SKIFF
hauled up on the rocks with longing. He could take it out.
He was old enough; he could handle it.

And if he went out on the water alone, his mom would
probably kill him.

She was already mad. Not with him. With Nonna.
Nick had heard them arguing, his grandmother's raised
voice, his mother's low tones. The sound made his stomach hurt until he couldn't stand it, couldn't stand being
cooped up in the boring apartment with nothing to do but
listen to the two people he loved best in the world fighting with each other.

So he got out.

Nick hugged his knees and stared at the flat, bright
water, waiting for his stomach to settle. His best friend,
Danny Trujillo, was sterning on his dad's lobster boat, so
Nick couldn't hang out at his house, and a bunch of summer people had taken over Nick's favorite sitting-and-

thinking spot. He watched them: a couple of moms and a half-dozen kids, from almost his age to a baby.

No dads. Probably the dads were fishing. Or maybe they worked on the mainland and joined their families on the weekends. Nick's father worked on the mainland, but he never came on weekends. Or ever.

Nick kicked at the rocks and wondered if his mom and Nonna were still fighting. Probably not. Their fights never lasted long, but sometimes for hours afterward his grandmother would be grumpy and his mom's face was all stiff. Nick's stomach tightened just thinking about it.

After a while, the summer people packed up their lotions and towels and hunted for their shoes, and Nick had the beach to himself.

There was a sailboat coming in, bigger than the little sunfish Nick had learned to sail, almost too big for the one man Nick could see on deck. The sailor didn't look like he was having trouble, though, even with both sails up. And that was another weird thing, those full sails, because there wasn't any wind where Nick stood.

The boat slid past the orange buoys that marked shallow water. Too fast, Nick thought. Too far. He opened his mouth to yell a warning, but then the sails collapsed like a big old gum bubble and the boat just stopped. Nick had never seen anything like it. He watched as the guy in the boat—he was tall, with long, dark hair—secured the lines and dropped anchor. The splash slapped the sides of his boat.

The guy looked at the distance between his boat and the beach and then at Nick. With a slight shrug, the man stepped off the boat and into water up to his wiener.

Nick giggled. He couldn't help it. Man, oh, man, that must be cold.

The guy tossed back his wet hair and looked right at him.

Nick covered his mouth with his hand.

But instead of getting mad, the man grinned, too, a real grin, guy to guy. He sloshed toward shore.

Nick held his ground and waited to see what the dude would do next.

He came out of the sea, water streaming from his shorts and squishing in his shoes.

"You could have rowed a dinghy," Nick said. "From your boat."

"I could."

Nick couldn't tell from the man's voice if he was agreeing or asking a question.

He sat on a rock to take off his shoes. Ordinary boat shoes, curled at the seams from repeated wettings. He emptied the water from one and wriggled his toes back inside.

Nick frowned. Something about the man's toes . . .

He jammed his other foot into wet leather.

"Or you could have tied up in the harbor," Nick said.

The man grunted and stood. He was very tall and not very old, for a grown-up. "I am looking for someone."

Nick's heart jumped and slammed into his ribs, because it was the sort of thing he used to imagine his father might say if his father ever showed up looking for him. It was a dumb dream; Nick knew it would never happen. His father didn't care about him.

Besides, Nick knew what his father, his real father, looked like. He was on TV, for cripe's sake. Nick used to tell people that, but then they asked him stuff, and Nick didn't know anything about his father, not really. But he knew what he looked like. He didn't look anything like this guy.

Still, Nick's mouth was dry as he asked, "Who?"

"A woman."

Nick swallowed. Okay. He hadn't really figured—He hadn't actually hoped— "What's her name?"

The man's dark eyes went blank. "Her name."

Some of Nick's disappointment escaped in exasperation. "She has to have a name."

"She cooks," the man said. "She cooked for a wedding."

His mom. Nick stuck out his chin. This guy was looking for his mother. "Were you at the wedding?"

"Yes." The man looked him over and then offered, "I am Caleb's brother."

Nick's shoulders relaxed. That was okay, then. Chief Hunter was totally cool. He came into the restaurant all the time. Sometimes he let Nick play with his handcuffs.

"That's my mom," he said. "She cooks."

The man's eyes narrowed. "Your mother."

Jeez. Did he have to repeat everything?

"Yeah. Regina Barone."

"Where is your father?"

Nick sighed. Sometimes he wished his father was dead. No, that wasn't right. Sometimes he wished his parents were divorced, like normal kids' parents, so he didn't have to explain them.

"In Boston." His father's restaurant was in Boston. "We left him." Years and years ago, when Nick was a baby.

"Ah." The man's eyes were real dark, pupil and iris together, like a dog's.

"I am Dylan," the man said, using his first name like

an islander would, not "Mr.," like most grown-ups from Away.

"Nick." He stuck out his hand, the way his mom said you should.

The guy looked at his hand a moment, and then he shook. His hand was dry and warm.

"Will you take me to your mother?" Dylan asked.

* * *

"Nick's not here," Brenda Trujillo said over the phone. "He called, but Manuel took Danny out on the boat today."

Regina took a deep breath, trying not to panic. "When?"

"I don't know. Early this morning, five or—"

"No, I meant, when did Nick call?"

"Oh." A long pause. "Is everything all right? You sound—"

"Everything's fine," Regina said through her teeth. "What time did you talk to Nick?"

"An hour ago?" Brenda guessed. "Two? It's not like I was looking at my watch, I—"

"Okay, thanks. If you see him, will you let me know? Or if he calls again—"

"I told him not to call until after five."

Regina was silent.

"It's not my job to keep track of everybody else's children," Brenda said defensively.

Regina gripped the receiver as if she could throttle Brenda through the phone. "I'm not asking you to watch him. Just to call me."

"Well, of course I will, but—"

"Thanks," Regina said and hung up the kitchen phone.

She rubbed the cross around her neck, threading it back and forth along the chain, struggling to focus. Nick had the same freedom she did at his age. Living on an island, you knew which houses were safe and which ones to stay away from. Even the summer people—most of them—were known quantities, returning year after year.

Of course, it was only a month ago that Bruce Whittaker went off his nut and murdered some poor stranger on the beach. Bad things could happen, even on an island. But at least Nick couldn't get lost, couldn't run away, could never go more than three miles from home.

Unless he took a boat.

Some of his older friends, ten- and twelve-year-olds, already had their own outboard skiffs; ran their own lobster lines.

And swiped their mothers' cigarettes and their fathers' beer, Regina thought grimly, but she didn't think her son was vulnerable to those temptations yet. He wanted a boat, though. He wasn't supposed to go out on the water without telling her. But then, he wasn't supposed to leave the house without telling her either. The ball of worry in her gut formed a hard lump.

"I'm calling Cal," she said.

Her mother looked up from shucking clams for the night's dinner service. The restaurant served shellfish only two ways, steamed or fried. At the moment, Regina couldn't bring herself to care.

"Why?" Antonia asked.

"To keep an eye out for Nick."

"Nick's fine. Leave the boy alone. Leave them both alone." She shot a glance at Margred, refilling salt and pepper shakers on the other side of the pass-through, and lowered her voice. "Caleb's married now."

Regina flushed. She hadn't thought her crush was that obvious. Bad enough that on the island everybody knew everybody's business. She'd prefer to keep her feelings private. Who else had observed or guessed she was carrying a torch for the chief? Cal himself?

She winced. Margred?

She opened her mouth to say something, anything, when the bell over the door jangled and they walked in.

Nick. Relief rushed to her head, making her dizzy.

And Dylan.

Another wave of emotion hit her, just as hard and not nearly as clear as the first.

She wasn't going to see him again. Everything she'd done that night, everything they'd done, was based on that certainty. He was leaving, he'd said. He hadn't even asked for her phone number. The bastard.

Setting her jaw, she pushed through the swinging door. "Where have you been?" she demanded.

"The beach. I met this guy." Nick flashed her a hopeful smile, as if he'd brought home a handful of shells for her instead of a potential disaster. "He says he knows you."

Dylan smiled, showing the edge of his teeth. He looked different by daylight, harder, more threatening. "Hello, Regina."

At least he remembered her name.

She glared at him, betrayed by circumstances and the leap of her own pulse. "I thought you left."

"And now I am back."

She crossed her arms, aware of her mother's sharp look from the other side of the pass-through, of Margred's frank interest. "What do you want?"

"I haven't decided," Dylan said silkily. "What are you offering?"

Her breath hissed through her teeth. If he stuck around, she was going to have to kill him. And then possibly herself.

But she had Nick to deal with first.

"You're too late for lunch. Dinner specials are on the chalkboard. You." She jabbed her finger at Nick. "Upstairs. We have to talk."

"It's always trouble when they say that," Dylan murmured.

Nick grinned.

"You shut up," Regina said. The last thing she needed was her one-time beach hookup coaching her son in irresponsible behavior. She jerked her head toward the kitchen door. "Upstairs," she repeated.

"Aren't you glad to see me?" Dylan inquired.

Regina's stomach lurched. She scowled. "Not particularly."

"You're Bart's boy," Antonia announced suddenly. "The older one. What are you doing here?"

"Yes, Dylan, what *are* you doing here?" Margred asked.

Regina's headache had grown until her neck wobbled with the weight of it. For eight long years, she'd lived like a damn nun. Eight years of silencing the gossips, of living down her past mistakes. One lousy screwup in eight years, and it followed her home like a puppy.

He followed her home.

Life was so unfair.

Dylan smiled into Regina's eyes, arrogant and confident and cool. "Exploring the local . . . attractions."

"Go explore someplace else," she said. "I'm working."

"There's no need to be embarrassed," he said softly.

Antonia's eyes narrowed. "Why should she be embarrassed?"

Regina ground her teeth together. "I am not embarrassed. I'm busy."

Dylan looked around the empty restaurant; raised one eyebrow. "I can wait."

"You'll wait a long time." She ruffled her son's hair, ignoring a pang when he ducked from her touch. "Come on, Nick."

"I'll come back, then," Dylan said.

Their eyes clashed. His were very dark. She felt a catch in her chest like a hiccup while her mind blanked with lust. That was bad. She needed to breathe, she needed to think, and she couldn't do either while he watched her with those dark, unsmiling eyes.

"Whatever," she said, dismissing him. "It's been real."

Too real, she thought as she escaped upstairs to lecture Nick about house rules and responsibility.

She'd liked Dylan better when he was a fantasy.

*   *   *

Like a fantasy, Dylan continued to haunt her, popping up at inconvenient moments, distracting her from her work.

He dropped by the restaurant every day for a whole damn week, wanting things: a cup of coffee, a few words with Margred, a sandwich. Never at the same time, so Regina could brace herself against the little fizzle she felt each time she saw him, so she could find something else to do in the back.

Besides, she refused to be chased around her own damn restaurant. Her mother's restaurant.

She could take care of herself. She was eighteen when she ran away to Boston, fresh meat to the wait staff who were always hungover, horny, or high. She'd learned to ignore the busboys' liquid looks and comments in Spanish, to use her elbows and once a boning knife when she'd been crowded against the stove or cornered in the walk-in refrigerator.

Dylan didn't touch her. He barely spoke to her. Regina wondered if he came to see her at all or if he was really sniffing around his sister-in-law. That thought didn't sit well with Regina for a variety of reasons.

But it wasn't Margred he watched.

Regina would be doing her job, writing specials on the board, say, or bringing plates to the pass-through, and she'd look up to find him staring at her with dark-eyed intensity, like the brooding hero of some romance novel. Regina shivered. It was perversely arousing. Annoying. People were beginning to talk.

"Don't you have anything better to do?" she demanded, keeping her voice low.

By the door, a middle-aged couple hung with cameras and water bottles perused the menu. Nick was under one of the tables, playing with the cat.

Dylan studied her a moment. A corner of his mouth quirked. "No."

"Someplace to go? A job?"

"I have a job to do here."

"You're not a lobsterman." The lobster fishermen, the good ones, were all on the water by five o'clock. It was after ten now.

"No," he acknowledged.

She set her hands on her hips and waited.

"Salvage," he offered finally.

Her brows drew together. "You mean, shipwrecks? Like, *Titanic* stuff?"

"What lies in the sea belongs to the sea."

"I heard it belongs to the government."

He shrugged. "Most exploration is done by private divers."

"Grave robbers."

The edge of his teeth showed in a smile. "Treasure seekers."

Nick poked his head from under the table. "Did you ever find treasure?"

He was stuck indoors, grounded, until Regina's shift ended at three. Antonia told Regina she was overreacting, but she didn't care. She had enough problems without worrying about Nick's whereabouts ten times a day.

Dylan reached into his pocket and pulled out a coin. Regina caught the gleam as he flipped it to her son.

"Wow." Nick's eyes widened as he turned the coin over in his hand. "Is it real?"

Dylan nodded. "Morgan Liberty Head silver dollar."

"Cool."

"Keep it."

"No," Regina said.

"It's only a dollar," Nick said.

"And not in mint condition," Dylan added.

"I don't care what kind of condition it's in. He doesn't take gifts from strangers."

Nick thrust out his lower lip. "But—"

She pinned him with her I-mean-it-Nicky-now look. She didn't want her son romanticizing this guy. Even if Dylan did look a little like a pirate, with that long dark hair and sexy stubble . . .

She pulled herself up. She wasn't going to romanticize him either. He was just an island boy who'd gone away, no different and certainly no better than any of the men she had considered and rejected over the years.

Men she hadn't had sex with.

Shit.

"Sorry, kid," Dylan said.

"Yeah." Nick dropped the coin into Dylan's palm. "Me, too."

Regina sighed as her son stomped into the kitchen.

Dylan turned toward the door, stretching his legs into the room. Long legs, Regina noticed. No socks.

"Who is that?" he asked.

Regina jerked her attention from his corded legs and followed his gaze to the front window, where Jericho waited on the sidewalk. "Jericho Jones."

She gave him the islanders' wave, lifted fingers, an almost-nod. The vet shouldered his pack and disappeared around the corner of the building.

"What does he want?"

"Nothing. A sandwich."

He came by once a day, or every other day. She slipped him food through the back door when Antonia wasn't watching.

"I meant here, on the island."

Regina shrugged. "Maybe he can't afford the ferry back to the mainland."

"Is that what he told you?"

"I didn't ask. It's your brother's job to question people. I just feed them."

Dylan's gaze narrowed on her face. "You are kind," he said, almost accusingly.

"Not really. The way our country treats its returning

soldiers sucks. He shouldn't be living on the streets, he—"

"—could be trouble."

"Look, he doesn't bother the customers, and he's not a registered sex offender. That's all I need to know."

"And how do you know that much?"

She flushed. "Your brother told me."

"Where does he sleep?"

"Jericho? I don't know," she said irritably. "Around. I don't know where you sleep either."

"Would you like to see?" he asked softly.

Her pulse jumped. "N-no." She cleared her throat. "No. It's just . . . The inn's full up, and most places were rented months ago. Unless you're staying with your family?"

Dylan's brows rose. "With the newlyweds? I think not."

She wiped her hands on her apron. "What about your dad's place?"

His face closed like a poker player's. "My father and I do not speak."

"But your sister—"

"Lucy was a baby when I . . . left."

He had Margred's habit of pausing before certain words, as if English was his second language or something. Regina wondered again where he'd lived and how they'd met. "All the more reason to get to know her now," she pointed out.

"You're suddenly very interested in my personal life."

"I—" Oh, shit. "I'm thinking about Lucy. She was Nicky's teacher for two years, you know. First and second grade."

"I did not know." He caught her eye and for a second looked almost embarrassed, like the boy he must have been before his mother took him away. "We do not have much sense of family."

But that wasn't true. Bart Hunter had been devastated by his wife's desertion. Lucy had turned down a post in Cumberland County to teach on the island and keep house for her father. Caleb was a thoughtful and devoted brother. Since his return from Iraq, he had even begun a painful reconciliation with his dad.

"You mean, *you* don't have much sense of family," she accused.

He shrugged. "If you like."

She didn't like it at all.

*   *   *

The next morning, Regina sat on the toilet, counting the days in her mental calendar, controlling panic.

Her period wasn't even due yet, not for another—she counted again—two days, she wasn't late, she couldn't possibly be pregnant.

Her throat closed.

Well, technically, she could.

She could take a pregnancy test. Regina thought about walking into Wiley's Grocery and requesting a pregnancy kit from the Wileys' teenage daughter and shuddered. That would certainly liven up the discussion in the checkout line.

Regina swallowed. Okay, no test. Not yet. Not until she could get to the mainland, Rockland or someplace, to buy one. In the meanwhile, she would count the days and pray and stay as far away as possible from Dylan "No Family Ties" Hunter.

5

~

LIVING IN HUMAN FORM AMONG HUMANS
was like being dragged naked over rocks.

Dylan stood motionless on the wharf outside the lobster cooperative, itching for the coverage of his pelt,
craving the rush and freedom of the sea.

His hands flexed and fisted. He had dallied in human
form before, sometimes for sex, most often alone on the
island his mother had bequeathed to him. But never for
so long. Never surrounded by other beings who claimed
a share of his space, a portion of his attention. He felt assaulted, abraded, by the constant human contact.

No wonder the old king, Llyr, had gone "beneath the
wave," the polite selkie term for those who had withdrawn so deeply into themselves and the sea that they
lost the desire and ability to assume human shape.

The smell of diesel and oil, the tang of coffee, sweat,
and cigarettes, rose from the saturated planks, overlay-
ing the rich brine of the ocean. Fishermen came into the

low wooden building to sell their catch, to buy bait and fuel and rubber bands, to share complaints or gossip. Dylan felt their glances light like flies against his skin, but no one questioned his presence. He was accepted—not one of them, but still of the island.

He listened to their conversations, trying to fathom from their talk of weather, traps, and prices what the demons could possibly want from World's End.

"He's got no right to set traps on that ledge," one man told another. "So I cut his line and retied it with a big knot up by the buoy."

His companion nodded. "That'll teach him."

"It better." The rumble of an incoming boat underscored the threat. "Or next time I'll cut his line for good."

Dylan smiled to himself. Apparently humans could be as territorial as selkies.

The engine behind him throttled down. Another fisherman, Dylan thought. He turned. And froze, his casual greeting stuck in his throat.

The boat was the *Pretty Saro*. He recognized her lines even before he registered the name painted on her side. And the fisherman was Bart Hunter.

His father.

He was old. Dylan had seen his father before, of course, at the wedding. But out of a suit, out in the sunlight, the realization struck with fresh force.

Bart Hunter had always been a big man. Dylan had his height; Caleb, his shoulders and large, square, workingman's hands. But the years or the drinking had whittled the flesh from his bones, weathered his face, bleached his hair, until he stood like an old spar, stark and gray. Human. Old.

How had Dylan ever been afraid of him?

They stared at each other across the narrowing strip of water.

They had barely spoken at the wedding. Dylan had nothing to say to the man who had held his mother captive for fourteen years.

But before he could clear out, Bart tossed him a rope.

Dylan caught it automatically. Old habits died hard. He was eight or nine when he started sterning for his father, hard, wet, dirty work in oversized boots and rubber gloves.

Dylan tied the line, cursing the memories that dragged at him as hard as any rope.

And then he turned and walked away without a word.

"Don't judge me, boy," Bart called after him. The words thumped like stones between his shoulder blades. "You can't judge me."

Dylan did not look back.

He climbed the road away from the wharf, the need to escape swelling inside him, coiling in his gut, clawing under his skin.

He sucked in the cool ocean air in a vain attempt to placate the beast in his belly. He burned with need, for a woman, for the sea, the two hungers twining and combining, eating him up inside. He fought the urge to run back and plunge off the pier, to merge with the dance beneath the waves, the life lurking, darting, swaying, streaming, in the flowing moss, in the forests of kelp, in the cold, deep dark. To blot out thought with sensation. To wash the taint of humanity from his soul.

How did Conn stand it?

Within the confines of Sanctuary, the prince had held

to his human form longer than any selkie living. But he would not leave the magic of the island. He could not risk aging.

Dylan gulped another mouthful of air. He was young by selkie standards—not yet forty. He could spend weeks, years, on land and still not approach his chronological age. At least he would not die from this experience. Unless the frustration killed him.

He raised his gaze from the asphalt. At the top of the winding road, the restaurant's red awning gleamed like a sail in the sunset.

The slippery knot in his gut eased. There was one hunger he could satisfy.

He went to see her only because it suited his purpose, Dylan told himself as he passed the ferry road. His very public pursuit of Regina provided him with an excuse to keep an eye on the humans' comings and goings, to listen to their gossip. If a demon *did* possess an islander, chances were good that his neighbors would be discussing his strange behavior over coffee at Antonia's the next day.

And yet . . .

He wanted to see her. Looked forward to the wary light that came into her eyes when he walked through the door, the challenge in her chin, the annoyance in her voice. Liked watching her through the pass-through into the kitchen, her quick, neat movements, her small, strong hands, the impatient press of her lips. He smiled, picturing her. Always busy, always in motion, like a bird at the edge of the tide.

He pushed open the restaurant door, making the bell jangle. The restaurant cat raised its head from its window perch, regarding him with sleepy golden eyes.

Margred paused in the act of untying her apron. "Oh, it's you."

Dylan raised an eyebrow, nettled by her obvious disappointment. Selkie or human, married or not, Margred had power, a purely female magic that would always draw men's eyes. But this time the sight of her did nothing to blunt the edge in him.

His restless gaze moved past her to the kitchen. "Where is she?"

"Regina? She went to the dock to meet the ferry. I am waiting for her to come back."

"Why?"

"So I can go home."

He bared his teeth. "Who is she meeting at the ferry?"

"No one. They're off-loading supplies for the restaurant. Dylan . . ." Margred's eyes were troubled. Seeking. "What are you doing here?"

She had faced a demon before, Dylan reminded himself. They had faced a demon together. He did not need to pretend with her. And Conn had not instructed him to lie.

"Conn sent me."

"Why?"

"He believes the fire spawn are seeking something on World's End."

Margred went very still. "Seeking what?"

Your child. Yours and my brother's. But Dylan could not say that. He did not know it to be true.

"That's what I'm here to find out."

"Vengeance?"

"It's possible."

"Then why did you not come to me?" She crumpled

her apron between her hands. "Why did you not *warn* me?"

"Because we do not know."

"And because I am human now," she guessed.

Possibly. Probably. Guilt made him stiff. "By your own choice."

"Yes. *My* choice. Being human pleases me." She added deliberately, "Caleb pleases me."

"Till death do you part," Dylan sneered.

She tossed her head. "Better a lifetime with him than eternity without him."

"And when you both are old, will he still please you then?"

"Yes," she said with absolute certainty.

"How do you know?"

"Why do you care?" she shot back.

The back door slammed.

"Idiot supplier sent me iceberg," Regina said. "Four crates of—Well." She stopped, her gaze flicking from Dylan to Margred and back again. She set a big cardboard box on the stainless steel counter; crossed her arms. "Don't let me interrupt."

"You're not interrupting," Margred said. "I am leaving."

The bell over the door jangled in her wake.

"Shit," Regina said wearily. She ran her fingers through her straight, cropped hair. "I was going to ask her to give me another twenty minutes."

"Why?" Dylan asked.

"Ma's doing mayor stuff—waste committee meeting," Regina explained. "I'm covering the dinner shift by myself. Which isn't a problem normally, but there wasn't room for the truck on the morning ferry, and now I've got to unload the delivery myself."

She was already moving as she spoke, sliding the carton, wedging open the back door. There was no rest in her, no peace, only this slightly nervous, crackling energy. And yet for the first time all day, Dylan felt his shoulders relax.

He walked into the kitchen as she returned from the alley carrying another big box. Through the open door he could see an old white van, its rear doors open to reveal stacked crates and cartons.

"You are alone?"

"I just said so, didn't I?" She sidestepped to avoid him.

He followed. "Where is Nick?"

"At Danny Trujillo's, playing Ultimate Alliance. Get out of my way."

He took the box from her instead, dumping it on the counter.

She bit her lip. "Listen—"

The front bell jingled. Regina glanced toward the door and back at him, her dilemma plain on her face.

He showed her the edge of his teeth. "Deal with it."

The customers? Or him helping her? He wasn't sure.

Maybe she wasn't either, but she didn't have much choice. She shot him a look and stalked through the swinging door. He heard her voice. "How's it going, Henry? What can I get you tonight?"

Dylan unloaded two more cartons while she boxed Henry's dinner—one lasagna to go—and took an order for four lobsters, steamed, with a side of slaw.

She bumped a hip against the door, grabbing up the

lobsters on her way to the cook top. "Thanks." She dismissed him. "I'll get the rest in a minute."

Dylan ignored her. Each case of tomatoes must weigh sixty pounds. How had she gotten them into the van in the first place? "Where does this go?"

"Walk-in refrigerator. On your left. But—"

"What's wrong with iceberg?" he asked, to distract her.

She dropped the lobsters into boiling water. Dylan restrained a wince. "Other than being colorless, tasteless, and relatively lacking in nutritional value, not a thing."

"Then why buy it?"

"I don't. So either my mother did, or the supplier switched the order."

She snapped the lids on various containers: lemon, butter, cole slaw. By the time she rang up the lobsters, Dylan was setting the last case on the floor.

Regina blew out her breath. "Thanks. I guess I owe you."

"I'm sure we can work out some form of payment," he said silkily.

She snorted. "I'll cook you dinner."

"That's not what I had in mind." He moved in, trapping her against the stainless steel counter, watching awareness bloom in her big brown eyes.

"Too bad, because that's all I'm offering."

He stepped between her thighs, sliding his hands into her hair, beneath her bandana. The pulse in her throat leaped against the heel of his hand. "Then I won't wait for you to offer," he said and took her scowling mouth.

She tasted sharp and earthy, like sun-warmed tomatoes and olives and garlic. She smelled like apricots. She flooded his senses, filled his head, *good, yes, this, now.*

Her arms wrapped around his neck. Her mouth was warm and eager. He felt the tension in her tight little body as she pressed against him, slight breasts, narrow waist, slim thighs, all fine, all feminine, all his, and the hunger in him developed claws that raked his gut.

He wanted . . . something. The release of sex, yes. More. He wanted to feel her tremble and come apart again, wanted her wet and soft and under him. Craved her tenderness. Her touch.

He hitched her up on the counter. She hooked her legs around his waist. He pictured himself stripping the jeans from her and pushing his way inside, *now*. He fumbled for her waistband.

Her hands came up between them, flattened against his chest. *Good, yes, touch me,* he thought.

She pushed, hard.

He raised his head, confused.

Her lips were full and wet, her eyes dark. The tiny gold cross on her chest moved up and down with her breath.

"So, what's the deal with you and Margred?" she asked.

"What?"

"You were talking to her when I came in."

His blood roared in his head. "That has nothing to do with you. With this."

"Yeah?" She attempted to close her legs. He didn't move. "Because I won't be used to make her jealous. Or to cover whatever thing you two have going on from Caleb. What do you want, Dylan?"

"I'd think that was obvious."

"Not to me."

He took her hand and pressed it to his crotch, where

he was hard and aching for her. "You," he said. "I want you."

Her lips trembled; firmed into a sneer. "Very nice. Excuse me if I'm not flattered. Or convinced."

He pulsed against her. "What would it take to convince you?"

Blushing, she tugged her hand away. "I don't know. More than being groped against the kitchen counter. Been there, done that."

"I did not grope you," he said, irritated. She'd pushed him away before he'd had the chance.

"It's not always about you, handsome."

Some other man, then.

He narrowed his eyes. "Who?"

"I don't want to talk about it."

"Then you shouldn't have brought him up. Who was he?"

"Like you really want to know." Her head came up, almost connecting with his jaw. "It's not me you care about; it's who else had what you want. Well, fuck you."

"You ruled that out. So talk to me."

Her snort of laughter took them both by surprise. "It was Nick's father, all right? I worked in his kitchen."

"In Boston."

Her eyes widened. "How did you know?"

"Nick told me. That first day, on the beach."

Her hand went to the chain around her neck, to the totem of her murdered Christ. Dylan had noticed the gesture before. Did she call on Him for help? Or was the gesture merely nervous habit?

"Nick talked to you about his father?" she asked.

He was still looking at her chest, the gold chain, all

that smooth skin above the scooped neckline of her tank top. "He said you left him."

"Yeah. After Alain made it really clear he didn't want anything to do with me or the baby."

Babies, well . . . Babies were a serious commitment. No wonder the guy was scared off. Dylan raised his gaze from the slight slope of her breasts to her mouth, sensitive and a little sad.

"There are worse things than growing up without a father," he offered.

"I wouldn't know."

Dylan raised his brows.

"Mine took off when I was three years old," Regina explained.

"But you had your mother."

"When she wasn't working. I wanted different for Nick."

The shadows in her eyes disturbed him. "It wasn't your choice," Dylan said.

"Not then. It is now."

He didn't follow. He was still hard, his brain still blurred with lust.

Regina sighed. "I can't give Nick a mother who's around all the time. The least I can do is spare him some guy who won't stick."

Dylan frowned. "You knew all along I would not stay. It did not stop you on the beach."

Her pointed chin came up. "I was drunk. Anyway, that was before I knew you. Before Nick knew you. I can't risk him getting attached."

"I'm not asking to move in with you." Frustration sharpened his voice. "Nothing has to change. I just want sex."

"Sex changes things." Her eyes met his. Warm, brown, honest eyes. "Maybe I can't risk me getting attached either."

His heart tightened like a fist. He was selkie. It was not in his nature to form attachments. And yet . . .

"You underestimate yourself," he said.

"What the hell does that mean?"

"Perhaps you are more like me than you acknowledge."

Or perhaps she had more power over him than he dared admit, even to himself.

"I have a kid. You don't." Regina hopped down from the counter, brushing him aside. "You try being responsible for somebody besides yourself sometime, and we'll talk."

6

❦

"I CAN'T EAT IN THE KITCHEN." JERICHO TOOK a step back from the kitchen door, clutching his take-out bag. The aroma of potatoes and onions followed him into the alley, mingling with the smell of grease from the fryer, a whiff of rotting lobster from the Dumpster. Regina's gorge rose.

"It would be different," he said, "if I wasn't taking charity."

Regina scowled. It pissed her off that she couldn't do more for him. Didn't want to do more. "It's not charity. It's a sandwich."

Jericho's thin lips twitched in the ghost of a smile. He'd made an effort to wash, she noticed, even to shave. She could see the line on his neck where his beard ended and the dirt began. Despite that dubious demarcation, she had to admit he looked more approachable without the stubble. Not as scary.

"I could help out maybe," he offered, not quite meeting her eyes. "In return for the food."

Oh, no. She wasn't looking to take on another responsibility. Although, maybe . . .

Her relief when Dylan showed up yesterday had been a revelation and a warning. She couldn't count on his help with every delivery. She couldn't count on Dylan, period.

What had he said yesterday? *"Nothing has to change. I just want sex."* Predictable guy response.

Not reliable. But predictable.

"Sorry," she said. "We're not hiring."

"I'm not asking for money." A hint of the South flavored Jericho's voice like bourbon in branch water. She wondered again what demons drove him so far from home. "Just sometimes . . . I thought I could help out," he repeated with quiet dignity.

Her head hurt. She didn't know what to do. When Perfetto's needed a dishwasher, Alain used to drive to the corner where the day laborers hung out and hire a guy right off the street. But then, Alain didn't have a kid on the premises to worry about. Hadn't wanted a kid to worry about. Rat bastard.

But after all these years, the words no longer had the power to energize her. Thinking of Alain only made her tired.

"I'll let you know," she said.

"Yes, ma'am." Jericho tugged on his cap, shading those clear, haunted eyes. "Appreciate it."

He turned to go, almost bumping into Margred as she rounded the corner. They circled without touching, like fighters looking for an opening. Finally, Jericho stepped back, and Margred entered the kitchen.

She reached for her apron, her cheeks flushed. "What was he doing here?"

Regina raised her brows, surprised by the faint hostility in her tone. "I'm thinking of hiring him."

"What for?"

"Scrub floors, unload deliveries, stuff like that."

Antonia sniffed without turning around from the cook top. "We don't need some man around to do our work for us."

They hadn't needed a man eight years ago, when Regina showed up on Antonia's doorstep with Nick in her arms. Whatever her faults, whatever her feelings about providing for her estranged daughter and a three-month-old grandson, Antonia had done everything that needed to be done. But her mother wasn't getting any younger. Regina watched her mother's hands on the spatula as she turned hash on the griddle—strong, veined hands, the knuckles growing knobby with age, the nails yellow with smoke—and felt a surge of love and panic tighten her throat. Antonia would never admit it, but she couldn't do as much as she used to. Margred was great with customers, but she went home to her husband at night. And Regina . . .

"Things change," Regina said shortly.

"Sex changes things," she'd said to Dylan.

Oh, boy, did it ever.

Her period was late. Only a day late. One day.

Maybe she wasn't knocked up. But she felt the weight of worry like a live thing pressing on her abdomen, burning beneath her breastbone.

"It's those damn catering jobs," Antonia told Margred. "She took on another one, family reunion, week after Frank Ivey's birthday party. Now she wants to hire help."

Regina grabbed a knife and started chopping scallions for the pasta salad, ignoring the ball in her stomach. "Six bucks an hour, a couple hours a day, a few days a week. Big deal."

"We can't afford him. Not once the season's over," Antonia grumbled.

Chop chop chop. "He won't last that long. He won't want to stay here in the winter."

"He could. He looks crazy enough."

Maybe he did at that. Her knife faltered.

"I don't like him," Margred said.

Regina glared at her, feeling betrayed. "You were okay with him before. He's a vet. Like Caleb."

"He smells bad."

Regina remembered Jericho's freshly scraped jaw, the line of dirt around his neck, and felt an uncomfortable prickle of guilt. "So would you if you didn't have a place to take regular showers."

Margred shook her head. "Not that kind of bad. He smells . . . wrong."

Antonia slapped a plate on the pass. "As long as he doesn't touch the food or scare off the customers, I don't care how he smells."

Regina gaped at this unexpected support from her mother.

Antonia set her hands on her hips. "You going to stand there jawing? Or are you going to serve this hash before it gets cold?"

The next few hours passed in a haze of work and steam. At eleven o'clock the menu changed from eggs, hash, and home fries to sandwiches, subs, and pizza. The tables filled with summer people who didn't want to cook, campers in search of a hot meal, yachters ashore for shopping or some local color.

No Dylan. Regina caught her gaze wandering to the pass, watching the door for his tall, lean figure, and pressed her lips together.

"Shit, oh, shit." She jerked her hand from the cutting board.

Her mother looked over. "You all right?"

"Fine," she said, examining her white fingers. She'd only caught a nail this time, under the knife's edge. No blood, no foul.

No blood.

She'd run to the bathroom three times to check, as if the act of pulling down her underpants could somehow transform the sweat of the kitchen into good news: *Not pregnant.*

She needed to go to Rockland and buy a damn test.

She needed to keep her mind on her work. She loved cooking, took a deep satisfaction in feeding people. But there was no challenge in it anymore. No distraction. She could prepare this menu blindfolded.

"If I never fried another clam or made another lobster roll, I could be happy," she muttered.

"You'd be happy, and we'd be out of business," Antonia said. "Order up."

Eventually, the line of tickets shortened. The dining room cleared as customers returned to their boats, vacations, lives.

"God, I need a cigarette," Antonia said and went out by the Dumpster to smoke.

Regina garnished the last two orders: lettuce, tomato, a slice of red onion. As she set the plates on the pass, she glanced again at the door. *Tall man. Dark hair.* Just for a moment the pressure eased. *Dylan?*

But it was only Caleb, standing with his weight on his good leg, talking to Margred.

"Get you anything?" Regina asked. "Cup of coffee?"

His smile crinkled the corners of his eyes. "Coffee would be good."

She carried the mug out to him while Margred served the last table.

"Thanks." Caleb took the cup; watched her over the rim. "Maggie tells me you hired that homeless guy you've been feeding."

Regina jerked her mind from one set of worries to another. "I'm thinking about it. You said he checked out."

"He doesn't have a record. He still has issues."

She cocked her chin, on the defensive. "You mean, besides needing a job and a place to live?"

Caleb sipped his coffee. "There's an encampment," he said abruptly. "Homeless guys, vets mostly, out at the old quarry."

Her mouth opened. Shut without a sound. A camp? Of homeless vets. On World's End?

Margred finished her table.

"I've been by there once or twice," Caleb continued. "Keeping an eye out. Took one of them to the clinic this afternoon to see Doc Tomah."

"So?"

"He had headaches. Delusions." Caleb's gaze locked with his wife's. "Claimed he was possessed by the devil."

Margred sucked in her breath.

"Uh-huh," Regina said. Why was he telling her this?

"What did you do?" Margred asked.

"The doctor prescribed Haldol. And I drove him back to camp."

"You have to tell Dylan," Margred said.

"I plan to." Caleb's voice was grim.

"Where is Dylan?" Regina wanted to know.

Caleb's gaze switched back to her face, but she got the impression he didn't actually see her. Story of her life, really. "Damned if I know."

Typical. Unreliable, typical male.

"Reggie." Caleb's eyes sharpened. His voice was gentle. "Is there something going on? Is there a reason you want to hire this guy, this Jericho?"

Yes. No.

I could be pregnant. With your brother's child.

Definitely, *No.*

She shrugged. "We're really busy right now. I could use some help."

"Lucy," Margred said.

Caleb frowned thoughtfully.

Regina shook her head. "I don't need a waitress. I need somebody to do the dirty work."

"Lucy's not afraid of work," Caleb said. "Or dirt."

Margred nodded. "And she's strong."

"On her college track team," Caleb said with pride.

"She'd make more money sterning for your father," Regina felt obliged to point out.

"Lucy hates the water," Margred said.

"Talk to her," Caleb said. "I'll tell her to stop by."

"That would be . . . good," Regina decided. She smiled. "Thanks."

Caleb did not smile back. "Just take care of yourself."

Regina fingered the cross at her neck. "I'm trying."

With one eye on the clock and the other on the entrance, she tackled the evening prep, chalked the day's specials on the board, boiled and boxed a dozen lobster orders for pickup.

And every time a tall, dark man crossed the threshold, her heart jangled like the bell above the door.

But it was never Dylan.

Customers came and went, picking up orders of lobsters and pizza, lingering to chew over gossip or pasta in the dining room. Antonia came and went during the height of the dinner rush to help on the line. Nick came downstairs to bolt a meatball sub between the first and second features of a Chuck Norris movie marathon on TV.

Dylan did not come.

Maybe his conversation with his brother took longer than expected, Regina thought as she shut down the grill.

Or maybe she had finally driven him away. She walked through the silent restaurant, her own words echoing in the empty space. *"You try being responsible for somebody besides yourself sometime, and we'll talk."*

Well, fine. She flipped the sign on the front door from OPEN to CLOSED.

She didn't expect anything else. From him, from anybody. If you learned not to expect things, you couldn't be disappointed. She and Nick were fine on their own.

Or they would be with a little help. Tomorrow she would talk to Lucy about working out the summer.

She closed the register, counted bills and receipts. *Twenty, forty, sixty, eighty* . . . Counted: *September, October, November, December* . . .

Her baby would be born in April. If there was a baby.

If the pressure deep in her abdomen was more than nerves and water weight.

She lost track of the numbers, had to begin again. *Twenty, forty, sixty . . .*

Wipe the tables, clean the case and counters, haul out the garbage, mop the floor. The routine should have steadied her, but her mind kept racing like a hamster in a wheel, circling round and round without getting anywhere.

She was accustomed to planning and preparing, more comfortable with "What next?" than "What if?" Even the gamble of going to Boston at the age of eighteen had appeared to her practical mind as the next logical step in her chosen career.

Yeah, and look how that had turned out. Every risk she'd ever taken, no matter how calculated, had ended in dead ends and disaster.

Except for Nick. She was glad she had Nick.

But God, oh, God, she didn't want to be pregnant again.

Fatigue pulled her muscles, settled in her bones. She returned from the Dumpster and headed for the mop sink, a cramped closet in an out-of-the-way corner.

She flipped on the light. The mops jumped out of the shadows, skinny monsters with clumped and stringy hair. Regina leaned against the tiled wall, listening to the water hiss into the bucket and trickle down the drain.

She couldn't say what made her turn. A noise. A shadow. A tickle at the base of her spine . . .

"Jericho!" The name whooshed from her, an explosion of breath, of annoyance and alarm.

He blocked the work aisle behind her, skinny and

stringy as the mops, and close. Too close. She could smell him, his clothes, damp with the outdoors, sour with sweat and the smoke from too many campfires.

"He smells . . . wrong," Margred had said.

Yes.

Her heart beat in her throat. "You scared the shit out of me."

"I'm sorry," he said.

But he did not move out of her way. She could shove past him. But touching him didn't seem like a good idea. She didn't want to commit herself to physical contact, to push him into violence. Skinny or not, he was bigger than her.

The taste of adrenaline was flat in her mouth. "What do you want?"

The job, she thought with sudden hope. Maybe he'd come about the job. Although now, with him looming between her and the door, didn't seem like the best time to tell him she was thinking of hiring somebody else.

He didn't answer.

"Listen, it's late," she said in what she hoped was a calm, rational voice. As if her tone could tug him back from whatever brink of crazy he was on. "Why don't you come back tomorrow—" She wet her lips. *In daylight, when there are people around.*"—and we can talk about that job?"

He shook his head. "I'm sorry," he repeated.

He sounded sincere. Which, for some reason, made her knees tremble. Her knives were on the other side of the kitchen, like the phone, like the door.

She couldn't run away. Nick was upstairs.

Should she scream? But if she screamed, Nick might hear and come down to investigate. Please, God, don't let him come down, her boy, her baby. *"Take care of yourself,"* Caleb had advised, but he didn't have an eight-year-old depending on him.

Regina gulped and eased her hand around a mop. The handle was smooth and reassuring in her grip. "So, uh, can I get you something? A sandwich?" If she could reach the counter, if she could get to the phone . . .

Jericho lunged.

She jerked back. Swung. But she was too close, he was too close, the mop crashed into the wall and slid uselessly off his shoulder. She did try to scream then, but his hands closed hard and bruising around her neck, and it was too late.

Nick, she thought. *Nick.*

Too late.

Jericho's fingers pressed. Her vision grayed. She slammed her foot into his instep, tried to bring up her knee, clawed at his hands, his wrists. He grunted, his fingers slackening. She lashed out with hands and feet. He snarled and grabbed at her chest.

Burning. She smelled burning. Spots spangled the darkness behind her eyes. Something stung the back of her neck. Jericho roared and threw her into the wall. Her head thumped once, and then his forearm pressed, an iron bar against her throat. Smoke filled her head, cut off her air.

Air. She raked his arm. She needed . . .

More sparks swam in the roaring dark, and then blackness swallowed everything.

*   *   *

Nick woke in front of the TV. His legs were cold. His cheek pressed against the carpet. Chuck Norris was gone, replaced on the flickering screen by some guy with a bunch of cars behind him, promising the best deal in town.

Nick sat up slowly, rubbing his face. It felt late. His mom never let him stay up this late. Where was his mom?

His mouth tasted funny. He stumbled to his feet and into the bathroom, took a pee, drank some water from the plastic cup.

In the living room, he flopped down on the couch and thumbed the remote. Nothing was on. Just grown-ups, sitting and smiling, selling things. It must be really late. He squinted at the little blue numbers above the TV. 3:37.

Nick got a funny feeling in his stomach. Had his mom just gone to bed and left him lying on the floor? Without a blanket?

He got to his feet, more slowly this time, and shuffled to her bedroom door. She slept with it cracked. So she could hear him, she said, if he woke in the night.

"Mom?" he whispered.

No answer.

So he said it louder. "Mom."

And again, *"Mom."*

He pushed the door open. The covers on her bed were flat and smooth. She wasn't in it. Wasn't there.

"Mom?" Real loud, this time, which was stupid, she must be in the restaurant, she couldn't hear him.

Nick didn't like to go downstairs at night, didn't want to go out on the landing in the dark and the cold, down the iron stairs to the alley. The kitchen was really big and dark, all corners and shadows, and the windows out front didn't have any curtains, so anybody walking by could see in.

But his mom should be upstairs by now.

He was mad at her because she wasn't, and now he had to go downstairs, past the Dumpster, in the dark.

What if something bad happened? What if she fell and couldn't get up, like the old lady in the commercial, and he had to call for help, call Nonna or 9-1-1. Nick didn't like to think about that, didn't want to think anything could happen to his mother. But she should *be* here.

He was shaking a little as he unlocked the door, as he crept out on the landing. He wasn't afraid. He was cold. He stood on the landing a minute, getting up his nerve to go down the stairs, when a shadow slunk from the deeper shadows around the Dumpster.

Nick's toes curled on the rough, cold metal. Oh, jeez. Oh, shit. A rat. Nick hated rats.

But then the shadow crossed into the moonlight of the graveled parking strip, and he recognized the bushy tail, the golden eyes. *Hercules.*

So . . . okay. Nick drew a deep breath and ran down the steps to the cracked concrete, hopping from one foot to the other as he fumbled with the handle, as he yanked on the door. All the lights were on. Good. That was good.

"Hey, Mom!"

The kitchen was empty.

His heart pounded in his chest, making it hard to breathe. "Mom? Mom?"

But she wasn't there.

7

CALEB STILL HAD NIGHTMARES.

From Iraq, and from seven weeks ago, when he'd tangled with a demon. The Army shrink said the dreams would get better over time. In the meantime, he wrote Caleb a prescription.

Caleb never filled it. He swallowed enough pills to handle the pain of his shattered leg; he wasn't taking more to deal with nightmares. Now when he woke, heart pounding, brain searing, drenched with sweat, he reached for Maggie.

But it wasn't a dream that woke him this time.

He rolled away from his wife and fumbled for the phone. "Hunter," he said, keeping his voice low.

Margred was already stirring, her warm, rounded body shifting under the covers, her hand finding the small of his back as he swung his legs out of bed.

Antonia's voice pierced the fog of sleep. Caleb listened grimly, a bad feeling in his gut.

"I'll be right over. Take him upstairs." He sat up straighter. "No, don't touch anything."

"What is it?" Margred asked as he crossed to the dresser.

"Regina Barone." Caleb tugged on a shirt. "She didn't come home last night."

"She—But—" Margred's eyes widened. "What happened?"

Caleb sat on the edge of the bed to tie his shoes. "That's what I'm going to find out."

*　*　*

More than an hour after his phone had rung in the dark, Caleb still didn't know if he'd been called to a crime scene.

Nothing in his initial walk-through suggested Regina was the victim of violence. No mark of forced entry, no sign of a struggle, no ominous note to suggest suicide or kidnapping. No vandalism, no robbery. The previous day's receipts were neatly totaled, the bank deposit bag in plain sight beside the untouched register. Everything was clean, everything—except for a mop lying flat in the work aisle—in its place. That was the good news.

The bad news was that Regina was simply gone. Vanished. And until the state's evidence team arrived to process the scene, Caleb had almost nothing to go on.

He stood in the middle of the missing woman's living room, a shabby space brightened by the red blanket over the back of the couch, the bits of green and gold sea glass hanging in the windows. The sun was just beginning to rim the edges with light.

Caleb rubbed his face with his hand. It was going to be a long day.

Antonia scowled. "I'm not taking that boy anywhere. I just got him down fifteen minutes ago."

"I doubt he's sleeping," Caleb said.

He had spoken to Nick only briefly before going downstairs to rope off the perimeter, stretching yellow crime scene tape across the sidewalk in front and around the parking strip out back. *And wouldn't that give the early morning fishermen something to talk about.*

The boy had been crying but clear. He remembered the apartment door had been locked and the kitchen door unlocked but closed. No, he hadn't seen his mother since dinnertime. After the movie. Seven? His big eyes sought Caleb's for confirmation. Reassurance. *"She's okay, isn't she?"* he'd asked. *"You'll find her."*

Caleb didn't have the answer the boy wanted. *"That's my job,"* he'd said gently.

Antonia's mouth set in a stubborn line. "Boy's better off in his own bed."

"He would be," Caleb agreed. "If I didn't have to process the apartment."

"Why? You heard Nick. She never came home last night."

"We think she never came home. That doesn't mean we can't learn something from her things."

"What things?"

He owed her an explanation. If not as Regina's mother, then as his boss the mayor. "Address book. Cell phone records. Credit card statements. If we have a record of who she knows—"

"Christ Jesus, Cal, we know everybody she knows. And we know who did this. That homeless guy, Jericho something. You need to go after him."

"I will," Caleb promised. "As soon as I leave here.

Right now I need you to take Nick back to your place and wait."

"Who's going to open the restaurant?"

"Nobody. You're closed until I can release the scene."

Antonia's hard mouth trembled. "You think she's dead."

"I'm not assuming anything at this point," Caleb said evenly. Kinder to keep what he hoped, what he feared, to himself. "Maybe she took a walk. Visited a friend. But I've got to process the scene while the potential for evidence is still there."

He didn't tell her that anything he found was unlikely to narrow the field of suspects. There wasn't a soul on the island who didn't eat at Antonia's, whose prints or presence couldn't be explained away.

"And what am I supposed to do? Besides go crazy?"

"Make me a list. Anybody she talked to, girlfriends maybe, anybody who might have called her up in the middle of the night—"

"Regina wouldn't leave Nicky."

That's what Caleb figured, too. "Can you think of anything else that might explain her disappearing for a couple hours? Drugs, alcohol, anything like that?"

Antonia made a visible effort to pull herself together. "She drank in high school. Same as you and everybody else. I don't know what she did in Boston. But if she got up to anything now, I'd have heard."

Caleb nodded. On the island, you started working young and drinking young. But if you had a problem, your neighbors talked about it. Caleb knew. He'd grown up the son of a drunk.

"What about men? Boyfriends?"

"She won't have anything to do with the island boys."

"That could cause hard feelings. She complain about anybody hanging around, giving her a hard time?"

Antonia crossed her arms. "You mean, besides your brother? Why don't you ask him where she is?"

Their gazes locked.

"I'll talk to him," Caleb said grimly.

If he could find him.

Caleb didn't think his brother would hurt a woman. Not physically, at least. But the fate of one human female wasn't likely to concern him too much either.

Margred claimed Dylan was really here on some kind of fact-finding mission for the selkie prince.

Fine. If there were demons on World's End, Caleb hoped the merfolk were prepared to deal with them. Because in any selkie-demon skirmish, humans were bound to lose.

Caleb couldn't ignore the possibility that Dylan's presence and Regina's disappearance were connected somehow. But neither could he let speculation drive his investigation. People did shitty things to each other all the time. They might blame the devil, but it was mostly human nature.

Caleb was damned if he knew why a demon would target a twenty-nine-year-old restaurant cook.

Dylan could tell him.

Too bad his brother was never around when Caleb needed him.

* * *

Dylan plunged into the wet, salty womb of the sea, felt the water stroke his thick fur pelt and surround him like a lover. Here he was alive in every strand and cell.

Here he was free.

He swam through the great green darkness, the cold salt tang. Through streamers of light and pennants of kelp, past colonies of steely black mussels and milky moon jellies. The beat of the surge was his pulse, the rush of the waves better than breath. He spiraled down, drifted up. No gravity. No responsibility.

Regina's words hooked him like a barb, ripping at his peace. *"You try being responsible for somebody besides yourself sometime, and we'll talk."*

He dove deeper. He was responsible, damn it. He was here, wasn't he? Doing his job, obeying his prince.

Dylan exhaled in a cloud of silver bubbles. Not that he could tell Regina that.

Not that she would understand or believe him if he did. Hard-headed, sharp-tongued Regina, with her quick laugh and hair-trigger temper, was completely human.

And he was . . .

He had been human once. The thought was another barb. Had believed himself human. Had imagined himself part of a family.

A memory pulled at him, strong as any current: his mother, posing them for a picture, ten-year-old Caleb with Lucy smiling on his lap, and Dylan, already standing a little apart. He had known even then that he was different, that things were about to change.

He hadn't guessed how much.

He never thought he would be the one responsible for tearing their family apart.

He raced through water dense with light and life; broke the surface into the sharp, bright air of morning. The sea was his refuge, the place where he could feel and move and breathe and be. But today he could not outpace his thoughts. Could not escape Regina's image, the smooth skin of her arms and chest, the gold cross glinting below her collarbone, her scowl. *"I can't give Nick a mother who's around all the time. The least I can do is spare him some guy who won't stick."*

Dylan blew out a noisy gust of air. He would not stick. His kind never did. If he cared for her . . . His thoughts tangled like seaweed. He did not care for anyone. It was only fair for him to leave her now, before—how had she put it?—she became attached to him.

Only, of course, he could not go.

He rode the rolling waves toward the deserted shore. Conn had charged him to discover what the demons wanted on World's End. For the past two weeks, Dylan had eavesdropped, observed, and tramped all over the island, hoping to find some trace of demonkind, some clue to their purpose.

To the immortal seaborn, the time was nothing. But Dylan was dying by minutes, trapped in his human body, trapped by his human family, trapped on this fucking island, forced to watch Regina joke and work behind the counter, her long slim legs, her strong firm arms, always in motion, always just beyond his reach.

Frustration drove him onto the rocks. He hauled himself onto the stony beach as the surf exploded around him. The water drained away, and Dylan stood naked in the foam, his webbed toes gripping the sand, his sealskin swirling around his ankles.

He stooped to drag his pelt from the sea; froze.

Something was wrong. He could sense it. Smell it. He straightened slowly.

The air was thick and still. Under the August sun, the

island gave off heat like a beast breathing. Dylan tested and tasted the wind, feeling the tickle of ash in the back of his throat.

His hackles rose. *Demon.*

In the air.

On the island.

Among humans.

Dylan's lips pulled back from his teeth. Retrieving his clothes from their hiding place, he began to dress.

Finally, he could hunt.

* * *

Regina lay cold and curled on her side, clinging to sleep like a blanket. Pain in her head, in her cramped legs and shoulders. Burning in her throat. Her mouth was dry, her tongue thick and swollen. She tried to swallow, and the fire in her throat woke her.

Oh my God, oh my God . . .

And then, *Nicky.*

Instinct surged, quicker than memory. Her muscles tensed. She had to run. To fight. To protect Nicky.

The thought jolted her eyelids open.

Dark. She was somewhere dark and gritty, damp and cold. She began to shake. Basement? No. There was an outside feel to the air, an outside smell, earth and rock and water. She could hear it, water lapping.

Where was she? Where was Jericho? Why was it so dark? She blinked, straining her eyes against the blackness. Even on a cloudy night, she should see a hint of moon, the reflection of the water.

She struggled to sit, pushing herself upright with her palms against the cold, flat surface, taking cautious inventory. She wasn't tied up. That was good. She had all her clothes on. Even better. Despite various scrapes and bruises, she didn't think she had been raped. Yet.

She swallowed convulsively. *Agony.*

Her cracked lips parted without sound. Her heart pounded.

Must not cry out. Must not scream. Jericho might be nearby. Sleeping? What if he was only waiting for her to wake up before he came back to do—

Her mind stumbled, teetering on the edge of panic. He could do whatever he wanted to her. Unless she found a way to stop him. To escape.

A tiny sound escaped her bruised throat. Her scrapes burned, bloody in the dark. She bit her lip hard, digging her nails into the gritty floor, curling her hands into fists, shuddering against the cold.

Think of Nick. Don't panic. Think.

She was hurt in the dark. She was alone. For now.

So. She better make the most of the time she had.

She crawled shakily to her knees.

*   *   *

As Caleb drove inland, the oversized cottages of the summer people gradually gave way to the older, smaller houses of year-round residents.

Detective Evelyn Hall, State Criminal Investigation Division, rode shotgun beside him. Hall, square and weathered as a barn, had come with the evidence team. Caleb's surprise at seeing her step off the ferry must have shown, because she'd said, "Seems women on your island can't catch a break."

Caleb had smiled grimly, acknowledging the dig. Only months after he accepted the position of police chief on World's End, Maggie had been attacked and the selkie Gwyneth's naked, dead body had been discovered on the beach. Now Regina was missing.

Evelyn Hall had suspected Caleb in the earlier attacks. But she was the only female officer available to him, and if—when—they found Regina Barone, Caleb wanted a woman with him.

Hall nodded out the Jeep window at a soaring A-frame perched above a rock face. "Nice little place."

Her tone was still dry, but Caleb recognized and responded to the olive branch. "The old quarry's a swimming hole now—or a skating pond, in winter. Lot of vacation homes around here."

"You said we were headed to a homeless camp."

Caleb nodded. "On the other side. Used to be a waste dump for the mining company."

They passed more homes, the McMansions ceding ground to dilapidated cabins, the terraced landscaping replaced by abandoned appliances and rusting pickups. Not all the island had benefited from high lobster prices and rising property taxes. Here, Caleb knew, were households that had fallen off the beaten track and out of the mainstream, adults inclined to drink or drugs, children subsisting on deer meat and short lobster.

Which brought them to the homeless encampment, strewn like garbage between the boulders. Waste disposal was a problem on the islands. Anything transported on had to be hauled off or burned. As a result, there were plenty of materials lying around for reuse. Caleb counted several structures built of plywood, cardboard, and scrap metal, and one honest-to-God tent pitched under the pines, its faded blue nylon spotted with mildew.

The men around the fire—five, six, seven, not bad odds—were as ragged and seedy as their shelters.

Caleb got out first. Evelyn Hall waited by the Jeep, the door open and the shotgun within easy reach.

A fat, muscled man sporting a red bandana and a graying ponytail stood as Caleb approached.

Caleb greeted him. "Bull."

"Chief. You checking up on Lonnie?"

Lonnie, the clinic patient, who claimed he was possessed by the devil.

"How's he doing?" Caleb asked.

Bull shrugged. "See for yourself."

Caleb found Lonnie in the ring around the fire, his elbows on his knees, his eyes on the smoke. He didn't look up. In the good news department, he didn't levitate off his boulder and start spitting pea soup either.

"Make sure he takes his meds," Caleb said.

"I'm not his fucking nurse," Bull said.

"Me either," Caleb said evenly. "I want to speak with Jericho."

"He's sick."

Caleb's gaze traveled over the encampment. "Mind if I look around?"

Bull crossed his thick arms over his massive chest. "Got a search warrant?"

"Got a camping permit?" Caleb asked evenly.

"Fuck," Bull said.

"I'll take that as permission to search," Caleb said.

He regarded the dark opening of the nearest shelter, sprouting from the shadow of the trees like a giant fungus, and his mind flashed back to hot white streets and sharp black shadows, blank doorways and blind windows, snipers on rooftops. His belly tightened. He was glad to have Hall and her shotgun at his back.

He ducked inside the structure, a finger of sweat tracing down his spine.

A stench compounded of beer and urine, sweat and mold, hit him. No Jericho. Nobody at all. No body. Caleb didn't know whether to be sorry or glad.

He wiped his face. And heard a rustle in the leaves outside, a crackle in the stillness. Squirrel? Deer? His instincts jumped on high alert. His hand as he reached for his gun trembled. *Shit.*

Light slanted beneath the rear wall where plywood rested on an exposed root. Caleb eyed the crack. Barely room for someone there to crawl out the back while he came in the front. Not two someones, not a man dragging a woman. *(Bound, unconscious, dead.)* But that rustle . . .

He backed out of the structure—there wasn't room to turn around—and signaled to Hall to hold her position. Would she understand? She nodded without speaking and leveled the shotgun to her shoulder.

"Hey," Bull protested.

"Shut up," she said.

Caleb eased around the side of the shelter, his gaze sweeping the woods and slope behind. Tough going if he had to give chase. Leaves crunched. A bush rattled. He raised his weapon.

And came face to face with his brother, Dylan.

Caleb exhaled. "What the fuck are you doing here?"

Dylan's black gaze lifted from the muzzle of the gun to Caleb's face. "Your job."

Caleb's job was protecting the island. He didn't have time for this shit. "Where is she?"

"Who?"

"Regina Barone. Have you seen her?"

There was an instant's utter stillness. Some expression flickered on Dylan's face and was gone too quickly to be identified. "Two days ago," he said coolly. As if it didn't matter. As if she didn't matter. "Why?"

"She's gone."

Dylan was rigid. "Where?"

"I wish to hell I knew," Caleb said, more honestly than he intended.

Dylan's face was white, his mouth a thin, grim line. "Hell has more to do with this than either of us could wish."

Caleb frowned. "What are you talking about?"

"I must find her," Dylan said.

8

"YOU'RE NOT GOING ANYWHERE," CALEB SAID.

Dylan raised his eyebrows, fighting the pressure in his chest. "Obviously not. Since I came back."

He could hardly breathe. The urgency that had driven him from the sea surged back. Only now the stink of something wrong, the stench of evil, was sharper. Stronger.

Regina was gone.

He made himself like stone, like flint, like the prince's tower at Caer Subai. Cold and immovable. Emotion would not bring her back.

"What are you doing here?" Caleb asked bluntly.

Dylan relaxed his fists; forced himself to speak coolly. "I followed the demon spoor here. If they have her, I will find her."

If they held her . . . He did not like to imagine what the demons could do to her smooth skin, her strong spirit.

"What would demons want with a twenty-nine-year-old cook?" Caleb asked skeptically.

Dylan shook his head, frustrated. "I don't know. They should not have taken her in any case. She is warded."

"Warded?"

"She wears the triskelion on her wrist—the wardens' mark. It should have protected her."

"From demons maybe," Caleb said. "A tattoo won't stop a human kidnapper. She could have been grabbed by this Jones character."

"Have you found him? Questioned him?"

"Not yet."

"Then I will."

"Forget it," Caleb said. "This is a police investigation. You can't interfere."

Dylan suppressed the snarl in his throat; stared down his nose instead. "And if he is possessed, you can't help. You need me, little brother."

Caleb didn't like that. Dylan could tell. *Too bad.*

"Right," Caleb said tersely at last. "Let's go."

Dylan followed him around the corner of the ratty shelter. Stopped. The half-dozen humans collected around the fire did not concern him. However, the large woman with the gun standing beside Caleb's Cherokee could be a problem.

She swung the long barrel toward him. "Who's that?"

"Don't say anything," Caleb said to Dylan.

Fine with him. He had had enough of humans and talking in the past two weeks. But there was that gun . . .

"Detective Hall," Caleb said. "My brother, Dylan."

Dylan met her gaze and smiled at her slowly, deliberately, watching in satisfaction as the barrel of the shotgun wavered and dipped. Not quite enough.

"What's he doing here?" she asked.

"Assisting in the investigation," Caleb said.

Dylan could see from the woman's uniform that she was some kind of law enforcement officer. Wouldn't she recognize official bullshit? Object to it?

He continued to smile, concentrating his power until he saw her pupils dilate and the square line of her shoulders relax.

"Oh," she said in a soft, faraway voice. "Well, that's . . . Dylan, did you say?"

Dylan nodded, still smiling faintly.

"Very nice to meet you, Dylan," Hall said and giggled.

Caleb shot him a sharp look. "Shit. What did you do to her?" he muttered.

Dylan shrugged. She was human and female and therefore susceptible. Perhaps more susceptible than most, nothing at all like— But thinking of Regina caused a spasm of something like panic in his chest. "We're looking for Jericho," he said.

"Yeah." Caleb shook his head. "This way."

The men around the fire watched—curious, predatory, or indifferent—as Dylan and Caleb picked their way through the littered camp.

Caleb stopped in front of a lean-to with a rusting metal roof. A sheet of cardboard blocked the entry. He bent, tugging a flashlight from his belt. "Stay here."

The beam of light preceded him through the rough opening. Dylan waited until both disappeared before he stooped and followed.

The smell assaulted his nostrils. Not demon. Not all demon. Human vomit, piss, and sweat. Corrupted flesh. Charred meat. Dylan gagged.

Caleb, kneeling over a pile of rags at the back of the lean-to, appeared immune. Inferior human senses? Or superior self-control?

Dylan set his teeth and took a shallow breath.

The rags moved. Moaned. Dylan distinguished a boot, the shape of a leg under a thin green army blanket, the corner of a sleeve, a hand. He frowned, his attention caught by more than smell or sight. Something about that hand . . .

He took a step forward.

"Stay back," Caleb ordered.

"Who is it?"

"Jones." The beam from Caleb's flashlight played over a thin face gleaming with sweat. "Where's Regina Barone?"

The man twitched, turning his head away.

"Regina," Caleb repeated inexorably. "Where is she?"

Jericho stared at him a moment, his mouth working. And then his eyes rolled back in his head.

"Damn it," Caleb snapped. "Jones? *Jones.*"

No answer.

"Drunk," Caleb said in disgust.

Sweat broke out on Dylan's forehead. His father's gray and ruined face rose in his mind. *This* was what he came from, he thought in revulsion, what had sired him, what he could return to if he became entangled in human affairs: mortal flesh, human corruption.

He forced himself to think logically. To observe dispassionately. There were differences, after all.

Unlike their father, this man was not drunk.

"No," Dylan said.

Caleb stiffened; turned. "You think he's possessed?"

"I—" Dylan allowed the fetid air through his nose. Smells thick as sewage rushed in on him, clogging, choking . . . He cleared his throat. He could discern a charred odor, an acrid taint burning his sinuses. Demon, yes, faint but unmistakable. And . . .

"I think he is burnt."

"What do you mean, burnt?"

Dylan could not explain. He just knew. He surveyed the man lying under the blanket. Reaching for his bony wrist, he turned over his hand.

Caleb hissed. "Holy Christ."

* * *

The dark was worse than the cold.

Regina could keep warm—well, warmer—by moving. But nothing could help her see, and her blindness hobbled and terrified her. She could not stumble more than a few feet without slipping and tripping over things. Rocks. Walls. She could not stand upright for more than a few steps in any direction. She was trapped underground. Buried alive. The blackness dragged on her, pressed on her, weighted her chest, swallowed her up. She was sweating, heart racing, throat tight, and she had to take long, slow breaths to keep from screaming, crying, battering her hands bloody against the cold stone walls in the dark.

Swallow. Breathe. There was a way in. She was here, wasn't she?

Another breath.

There had to be a way out.

She just had to find it. On her hands and knees. In the dark. Her heart thumped uncomfortably.

She explored her prison, fumbling, crawling with a

hand or hip always pressed to the rough rock wall on her right so she could find her way back, so she wouldn't get lost. *Lost.* She swallowed a sob. What a joke.

She remembered a long-ago shopping trip to Freeport, the mall full of shoppers, and her kneeling to unzip Nick's coat outside a store. *"If we get separated, I want you to stay put, okay? Don't move, and Mommy will find you."*

She would have torn the mall apart looking for him.

But who would be looking for her? How would they even know where to begin to search?

I'm sorry, Nick. Ma, I'm so sorry.

The heel of her left hand was bruised from supporting her weight. Her knees ached. The fingers of her right hand were cracked and bleeding. But she figured out she was in some sort of—tunnel? chamber?—in the rock, bounded by water at one end. She sniffed. It smelled fresh. She lifted a cautious finger to her lips. The moisture was cool and welcome on her parched mouth and burning throat. But the drop left a mineral aftertaste, a warning hint of brine. With a sigh, she abandoned it and crawled the other way.

The passage meandered up and down, over boulders and around curves, gradually getting narrower. Tighter. She bruised her knees; bumped her head; inched forward on her stomach until she was blocked, stopped, squeezed in the rock like a roach in a crack.

She laid down her head, resting her cheek on the cold, damp grit, and cried. She gasped and keened and whimpered until her nose ran with snot and her throat was on fire. Water. She needed water. She wanted to get out. She wanted to go *home*. To Nick. To her mother.

Hot tears leaked from her eyes. Regina wiped her face on her shoulder. It was so quiet. So dark. She could feel her heart beating in the darkness, hear each wheezing breath. The silence was a weight like the rock, pressing down on her.

Slowly, she began to inch backward, pushing herself with fingers and toes, hissing and gasping when the rocks scraped her hands, when she bumped her head.

When the tunnel widened again, she curled into a ball with her back against the wall, listening to the soft lap of the water. Gradually, her sweat dried. Her breathing evened. She no longer worried Jericho would come back for her. She worried he would not.

Not a good thought.

Let him come. She'd kick his ass. Bastard.

Of course, she hadn't done so well in their first round. He'd practically killed her. She swallowed against the pain of her abused throat.

Why hadn't he killed her?

Maybe he was coming back after all. She'd seen a news story about a guy who kept a woman locked in his basement. For years.

Regina shivered, wrapping her arms around her knees to hold in her body heat. The air was cold and moist. The floor was cold and damp. Her butt was numb.

She heard a slither and a soft plop as something slid into the water. A rock? A rat? A snake? What kind of animals lived down here in the dark, in that water? Things without eyes. White, slimy, hungry things. Maybe Jericho was still there in the dark, watching her. Waiting for her.

She shook herself. She ought to get up. Get moving. In a minute.

She was so tired, her muscles cramped and aching.

How long had she been down here? Hours? It felt like hours. The quiet stretched on forever, like the dark.

Was Nick awake by now? He would be worried when he awoke and she was gone. And her mother . . . *Please, dear God, get me out of here, and I'll never fight with my mother again.*

How long had she been down here? She wished she wore a watch. A luminous dial would be really nice right now. But kitchen workers didn't wear watches. She strained her eyes against the darkness. Nothing to tell her whether it was day or night, no hint of light or anything else. Only her body warned her time was passing. She was thirsty and cold and she needed to pee. Her limbs were shaking. Her whole body was shaking.

Okay, she really had to get up. Nobody was coming to get her out of this one. Not Alain, not her mother, not Caleb, not . . .

She didn't want to think about Dylan. Dylan was gone, like her father, like Nick's father, like every other man in her life. *"You knew all along I would not stay."*

Her anger was good. It warmed her, a hard little lump smoldering like a coal in the pit of her stomach. So she didn't have a knight in shining armor riding to her rescue. She still had a life waiting for her somewhere in the sunlight. She had a son.

She climbed to her feet.

There was a way in. There had to be a way out.

* * *

"Holy Christ," Caleb breathed.

The unconscious man's exposed palm was orange, raw and swollen; the fingers blistered dirty white; the skin puffing, sloughing off. And black in the center like a brand was the oozing sign of the cross.

"Yes," Dylan agreed simply. "If he was possessed, he is not now."

"You can't know that."

"Demons would not inflict such a mark."

"You think he did this to himself?"

Dylan shrugged. "It would protect him. No demon would willingly stay for long in a host branded by the cross."

Caleb sighed. "I hate this woo-woo shit. Okay, say a demon possessed Jones. You're sure about that?"

Dylan nodded. "The fire spoor is all over him."

"I'll take your word for it. Jones gets burned, we don't know how. Demon . . . jumps?"

"Probably not at once," Dylan said. "The mark would gradually grow more and more unbearable. But it would take time for the demon to relinquish its host."

"Or to find a new one?" Caleb asked. His voice was steady. His hand holding the flashlight was not.

Dylan watched the trembling beam of the flashlight and felt a rare sympathy for his human brother.

Caleb had experience with possession. The demon Tan had tried to take him over. Caleb had been willing to die, had died, had drowned himself, rather than submit to the demon's control. Dylan had dragged Caleb's body from the ocean bottom.

This could not be easy for him.

"Yes," Dylan said.

"Shit," Caleb said again, wearily. He rubbed his face with his free hand. "So we've got some time."

"We have time. Regina may not." A deep and unfamiliar fear settled in his bones. Dylan forced his mind away from it, struggled to focus on the next step. "We don't know what this Jericho did with her before the demon left him. Or where it went. You must arrest the men outside, the ones he had contact with."

"I can watch them. I can't arrest them. I need proof. Probable cause."

"I can scan them," Dylan offered. "If any of them are possessed, I will know."

"It doesn't matter a rat's ass if they're possessed. Not unless or until one of them breaks the law."

"I don't care about human laws. Or humans either."

Only Regina.

He shied away from the thought.

"That was always your problem, bro." Caleb slid an arm under the unconscious man.

Dylan's brows drew together. "What are you doing?"

Caleb raised Jericho to a sitting position. "Getting him out of here."

"He won't lead us to Regina. He can't even answer questions."

"Not now," Caleb agreed. "Maybe when he wakes up."

"Not then either." Dylan watched in annoyance as Caleb staggered to one knee—his good knee—cradling Jericho in his arms. "The demon probably wiped his memory."

"He's still a human being. He needs help. Medical attention."

Dylan scowled. He was not his brother. He did not think about others' needs.

"That was always your problem, bro."

Caleb lurched and grunted in pain as his bad knee took the brunt of Jericho's weight.

Dylan's mouth tightened. "Give him to me."

"I've got him."

Dylan blocked his brother's way.

Their gazes locked.

Caleb's eyes narrowed. Dylan didn't know what his brother saw in his face, but after a moment Caleb sighed and surrendered Jericho's body. "Don't drop him."

"Thanks," Dylan said dryly and took his brother's burden.

*   *   *

Regina sucked in her breath. The water was *really* cold. It soaked her sneakers, swirled around her ankles, saturated her pant legs.

She steeled herself to wade forward, ducking her head to avoid contact with the sloping ceiling. Her hands groped blindly, clutching at the rough rock with torn, tingling fingers. She was afraid of the water, of what might live in the water, unseen in the dark.

She felt the tremors start deep in her bones. She was already freezing. The water would drop her body temperature even faster, like a turkey defrosting in the sink. She could get hypothermia. She could die.

Of course, she could die sitting on her ass in the dark waiting for somebody who never came.

She gritted her teeth against the bone-biting cold and slid her feet forward over the uneven bottom. *Holy Mary,*

Mother of God, don't let me fall into a hole. Twist an ankle. Trip over a rock.

Her feet were numb. She couldn't feel her toes at all. The water crept up her knees, her thighs. How deep was it? She wished she had a stick to test the way, to probe the cold black void. If Jericho had come this way, he would have had a light. Boots. A hard hat.

Maybe he hadn't brought her in this way at all. But she'd already tried the tunnel on the other side. What was left?

The cold hit her crotch, and her bladder couldn't take it anymore. A cloud of pee released into the cold water. Regina shuddered in relief, standing in her own pee, warm around her freezing thighs. She forced herself to shuffle deeper into the water and the dark.

The water level rose to her waist. To her ribs. She could feel a cold current around her ankles. Hope trickled in her chest. There was an opening somewhere. The water went somewhere. She strained her eyes in the dark. Silver spots and red webs floated on the face of the water, in the moist black air. The darkness was a thing, a barrier like the water, cold and choking. She waded through it, pushed against it, and smacked her head into the stone ceiling.

Ow ow ow. Pain exploded, white stars and yellow bolts of pain. She doubled over and her face splashed in the water. She could not breathe. Panicked, she sputtered, gulped, gasped. She was pressed between the low hard ceiling and the cold flat water. Trapped. She flattened her palms against the rock face, reading the passage like a blind woman learning Braille. The tunnel dropped. The ceiling touched the water. She was trapped.

She went a little crazy then, beating the walls and the

water with her hands, croaking and crying out. She wanted out. Oh, God, she needed to get out of here.

Breathing hard, she stood shuddering, chest deep in the freezing water. Her face was wet, her hair was wet, her clothes glued to her body. She bit her lip, tasting blood and salt and defeat.

Tasting salt.

She brought her trembling hand to her lips, sucked on her fingers. The salt taste was definitely stronger. Or was she simply thirstier? She held herself still, listening to the echoes bounce and fade, and felt the surge moving between her legs. Her heart pounded. In or out? She could not tell. When the tide dropped, would the passage open? Had she found a way out?

Shaking with cold and a desperate hope, Regina fumbled her way back to the black chamber in the rock to wait for the tide to turn.

*   *   *

Dylan waited outside the yellow tape stretched along the sidewalk in front of Antonia's, his hands in his pockets and every muscle tensed. Through the plate glass window he could see busy humans with brushes, bags, and bits of tape moving systematically through the dining room. They were wasting their time. They had no idea what they were looking for. What they were up against. Fingerprints and carpet fibers would not get Regina back.

Caleb had mobilized volunteers to search the ten square miles of island in a carefully coordinated grid, concentrating first on the areas around the restaurant and the homeless encampment. Dylan wanted to plunge after them, to run around screaming her name. Futile human activity, he told himself. Useless human emotion.

But at least they were doing something.

His hands clenched into fists. Conn had directed him to observe, not to act.

His inactivity was killing him. Regina was gone. Missing. And Dylan was desperately aware that his inactivity could be killing her, too.

He wanted to take his fists to Jericho, to beat him bloody until the man confessed what he had done with her. Jericho, however, was under guard at the clinic, awaiting medevac to a hospital on the mainland to have his burn treated. Even if the unconscious man were here and in his right mind, he could not tell Dylan anything the selkie didn't already know.

Regina was gone. Dylan had to find her.

She was only human, and yet he felt . . . connected to her. They had a sexual bond. If his power were stronger, if their connection were stronger, he might have used it to trace her.

But their attachment was too tenuous for him to follow. The memory of her wide brown eyes, her wry smile, haunted him. *"Maybe I can't risk me getting attached either."*

He felt the bite of frustration and, worse, a lick of guilt. He could have changed her mind. He could have told her, promised her . . . What? She was human. He was selkie.

She was gone.

He had to find her.

"Nonna says you know where my mother is."

Startled, Dylan looked down. Nick Barone scowled

from beside the yellow tape, his chin cocked at a kiss-my-ass angle and his eyes full of raw misery.

Dylan's stomach lurched. "Is that what she told you?" he asked carefully.

"I heard her talking to Chief Hunter. Do you?" Nick persisted. "Know where my mom is?"

"No." Such a flat, bald word. "But I will find her."

The promises he had not made to Regina were somehow easier to make to the child. Her son.

Nick looked skeptical. "How?"

"I don't know yet," Dylan admitted.

Nick's face closed into a smooth, polite child's mask. "Yeah. Okay. Thanks."

The boy did not believe him. Why should he? Nick did not need some stranger to tell him everything would be all right. He needed his mother.

Dylan's gaze went past him to the quiet street. The yellow tape had drawn as many people as it kept away. As hours passed without a break in the case or the gossip, however, most of the islanders who weren't assisting in the search had gone on with their grocery shopping or their work or their lives.

"You shouldn't be alone," Dylan said, sounding, even to his own ears, like a well-meaning and clueless adult. He tried again. "Where is your grandmother?"

Nick hunched a shoulder.

"Does she know you're here?"

The boy's gaze dropped. "Chief Hunter said he wanted to talk to me," Nick mumbled.

Dylan had a sudden image of himself at fourteen, fearful and alone, waiting at Caer Subai for his mother to come home from the sea. Only she never had. Conn had taken Dylan under his wing. Nick needed someone like that, someone he could trust to provide him with assurances and answers.

Someone like . . . Caleb.

"I'll get him for you," Dylan said and ducked under the crime scene tape.

The bell jangled overhead as Dylan pushed open the door of the restaurant. A man wearing the navy windbreaker of the state police was on his knees by one of the booths.

He looked up in annoyance. "What do you want?"

"Caleb."

"Do you have information pertaining to the case?"

"No."

"Then get the fuck out of the crime scene."

Dylan strode past him.

"Hey!" The man's shout followed him into the kitchen.

He found Caleb standing at the stainless steel counter watching another man slide a shiny object into an envelope.

Every muscle in Dylan's body went rigid. "Where did you get that?"

"Do you recognize it?" Caleb asked.

Dylan stared at the small gold cross glittering from a nest of fine chain. His mouth went dry. His head buzzed. "It's Regina's. She must have been wearing it when he grabbed her. That's why his hand is burned. Where did you find it?"

"Mop bucket," Caleb answered shortly. "I missed it on the initial walk-through."

The other man's quick brown gaze shifted from Dylan to Caleb. "Who is this guy and why are you confiding details of the case to him?"

Caleb stiffened. "My brother, Dylan, Detective Sam Reynolds of the Maine CID."

Dylan didn't care who he was. The noise in his head drowned out everything else. He held out his hand for the chain. "Give it to me."

"Why?"

"Is he crazy?" Reynolds asked.

"She wore it all the time," Dylan said to Caleb. The totem of her murdered Christ, bright across the smooth skin of her breast, a ward as personal and more powerful than the triskelion inked into her skin. It should have protected her. Perhaps it even had. But now that protection had been stripped from her, and she was out there somewhere, defenseless.

Not quite defenseless, he thought, recalling her strong will, her sharp tongue. But still only human and alone.

He hoped she was alone. Because if she were in demon hands . . .

"It's a connection," he explained, aware of the urgency surging in his veins, pushing into his voice. "I can use it to find her. Give it to me."

"I can't," Caleb said regretfully. "It's evidence. We'll send the necklace to the crime lab for testing, and then—"

"The necklace won't tell you a damn thing you don't already know," Dylan said.

Caleb raised his eyebrows. "And it will you?"

Dylan held his gaze. Held out his hand. "Yes."

"No," Reynolds said. "We're not using some crazy

psychic, even if he is your brother. Get him the hell out of here."

Dylan ignored him, his gaze locked on his brother's, his heart pounding in his ears.

"Right," Caleb said.

He dropped the necklace into his brother's hand.

* * *

Regina huddled in her silent chamber in the rock. The dark *wasn't* worse than the cold. The darkness couldn't kill her. The cold might.

Time passed. Minutes? Hours? She hadn't dried one bit. Water still saturated her hair, T-shirt, and jeans. The chill penetrated her clothes. Her blood. Her bones.

The oppressive quiet, the unrelenting void, sapped her energy. Weighed on her spirits. Messed with her mind.

She dozed. Sometimes she dreamed—of her son's face, her mother's voice, the baby inside her—and woke to find herself with tears sliding down her cheeks, alone again. Always alone.

"I'm sorry, Ma. I didn't mean for you to raise another kid on your own."

"It's all right. It doesn't matter."

But it did. It mattered a lot.

She raised her head from her knees, roused by the sound of dripping water. At least she wasn't shaking so hard. She wanted to think that was a good sign. Her body, however, knew differently. Her breath wheezed. Her joints ached. Her head felt like a lead balloon, heavy and hollow. It would be so easy to put her face back down and escape into sleep. She didn't even have to close her eyes. So dark . . .

Regina jerked back her head and swore. Time to get up. Get moving.

She listened to the drip become a gurgle, the gurgle grow to a rush, and felt a faint, warming flicker of hope. The tide must have turned. Time to try the passage again.

So cold. She forced her body to uncurl, her body trembling in protest. Painfully, she stood, biting her lip against the stabs of returning circulation. She could not see her feet. She couldn't feel her toes. She shuffled forward, one hand on the wall.

Splash.

She froze, bewildered, her sluggish mind struggling with the message her feet were sending. She had already reached the water. She was standing in the current. The tide had turned.

The water was rising.

9

~≈~

THE TIDE WAS COMING IN. DYLAN STOOD ON the headland where the island fell down in a tumble of rocks and spray. Below him was a line of dark spruce and then the shore, black rock breaking white water, and then the ocean glimmering as far as the horizon, the white caps' plumes running before the wind like the horses of Llyr.

The wind drummed in Dylan's ears. Doubt ate at his heart.

He was not anyone's choice to stand against the power of Hell. He should summon a warden, send for instructions, ask for advice.

Assuming Conn would hear and answer.

Assuming help would come in time.

The wind snickered, snatching at Dylan's clothes and hair. The waves raged like his heart.

He didn't need this. He didn't want her. He had witnessed firsthand the wreck of his parents' marriage, the tangled net of love and obsession and resentment that had dragged his mother from the sea. He would never give a woman that kind of power over him.

That did not mean he could not use his own power to find Regina. To save her.

He had always been adept at small magics. He could summon a wave, a woman, a breeze. For convenience, for amusement, for spite. But no significant outcome, no significant other, had ever depended on his skill before.

"You try being responsible for somebody besides yourself sometime, and we'll talk."

Indeed.

The cross was in his hand. He spread his arms against the wind, annoyed to notice his hands trembling.

He gazed down on the sea, polished and pocked as a sheet of hammered silver. The waters of the ocean ran through him, his mother's blood, his mother's gift. The magic of the ocean was his birthright.

He planted his feet on the rock. He stretched his arms, opened his mind, and invited the sea in.

Power rose like fog from the surface of the water, moist, heavy. He felt it envelope him, stream over him and into him, pour down his throat like wine and pool in his loins like lust. His mind spun as the power surged, seeking an outlet. It filled him to overflowing; spilled from his throat on a cry: *"Regina."*

So he called her, by her name and by his knowledge of her, her flesh and her spirit, and by the power of the totem in his hand.

Regina.

The wind in the trees replied. A bird soaring over the waters replied. The quickening of his own heart answered him.

Clenching his hand on the burning gold of the cross, Dylan plunged from the sunlit hill and into the shadow of the trees. He was already loosening his belt when he reached the shore.

*   *   *

Regina stumbled in the dark, at the limits of her strength, driven by terror and the rising water. The cold current dragged and hissed at her knees, soaked her jeans, weighted her sneakers. If she took off her shoes, she would cut her feet. If she didn't take them off, she could drown.

A whimper escaped her. She set her teeth. She couldn't drown. She had to get home to Nick. *Oh, Ma, I'm so sorry. Nick* . . .

She had to keep her head above water. She had to find the chamber's highest point. If only she could *see*. She sloshed through icy water, patting and slapping the cave ceiling, her fingers like frozen sausages.

The ceiling rose away from the wall. She followed its slope, dazed with cold, disoriented in the dark, her fingers fumbling, sliding, touching . . . nothing.

She bit back a scream. There was a— She groped. A hole overhead. She patted. A passage, a chimney in the rock, wider than her shoulders, wider than her whole body, on a level with her wrists. Her heart pounded. If she could pull herself up there, if she could climb . . .

She scrabbled at the edges of the hole, clawing frantically at the rock. Stones dislodged, sliding and striking her head and shoulders. The water lapped and sucked at her legs. She jumped, grabbed, and slid. Jumped and slid. Jumped, grabbed, and caught a handhold in the passage above.

Her arms screamed. Her shoulders protested. She hung there for long moments, a dead weight with battered, bleeding hands. Her feet dangled in the water. She felt it churning around her ankles, cold, cold, coming for her. Her breath sobbed. *Come on, come on. Think of Ma; think of Nick.* She kicked with her feet, twisting like a kid in gym class under the pull-up bar. *Please oh please oh please oh* . . .

Up. She scraped her elbow, wedged her ribs on the edge of the hole. Her blood drummed in her ears. She did it. She made it. She was gasping, huffing, sweating, although she couldn't move her fingers or feel her toes. She pulled in her stomach, struggled to bring her knee up—

And fell.

A cry ripped from her broken throat, a squawk of rage and despair. *No.*

Cold water, cold, closing over her head.

She thrashed, flailing at the water, bumping her hip, her knees, her elbow against the rocks.

The rocks. She located bottom; pushed off, dragging her feet under her; and stood in water up to her waist.

Water streamed from her hair, streamed in her eyes. She drew great, gasping, shuddering breaths, wrapping her arms around her waist as if she could hold in her heat, hold herself together.

She shivered violently, her teeth clacking together. *It wasn't fair, goddammit.* Nick was growing up without a father. He needed his mother.

She could not control her shaking. She stretched her arms over her head and groped again for the edge of the chimney. Had Jericho brought her down this way? Lowered her down? How much time had she wasted feeling her way in the dark?

She was disoriented, dizzy from her fall. The water was deeper. She set her teeth and waded, feeling the rock ceiling overhead.

Something brushed against her leg. *A rock.* She ignored it. *Again.* Something large and long and low, moving fast through the water. The surface churned.

She screamed and stumbled backward, windmilling her arms for balance. *Oh, God, oh, no, oh—*

"Regina." Dylan's voice, warm in the dark.

She was hearing things, imagining things. Nick's face. Her mother's voice . . .

She turned her head wildly, frightened, freaked out, straining her eyes against the blackness. Her teeth chattered.

"Regina?" Closer now, questioning.

She was losing her mind. She was losing it.

Something touched her shoulder. She jerked and struck out.

Whatever, whoever it was, simply pulled her close, trapping her sluggish, useless arms between them, wrapping her in a strong, warm embrace, murmuring, "It's all right now. It's all right."

Dylan's voice. Dylan's scent.

She was hallucinating. Had to be. But he felt solid and warm and real against her, and she was cold, so cold, and alone. She buried her face against his chest, wet and slippery smooth, burrowing against him. He was strong and warm, close and . . . naked?

She jolted as he held her, as he stroked her hair. "Where—" Her voice was a croak. She coughed and tried again. "Clothes?"

He was silent.

Maybe she'd offended him.

Maybe he wasn't there. Like her mother. Like Nick.

"Sorry. Dumb question. My fantasy," she babbled, holding on to him. *Don't leave me alone.* "Why wouldn't you . . . be naked?"

"Regina." His voice was shaken with laughter or something else. "Are you all right?"

"Lost . . . my mind." The words ripped her throat. "Unless . . . you're here?"

"I'm here." His voice flowed over her, deep and reassuring. "You're fine. We're going to get you out."

Her head wobbled. She let it drop against his chest. The relief of having someone here, someone warm to lean on, was unspeakable. "How?"

"We're going to swim through the tunnel."

His words roused her to doubt. If he were really here, if he were really real, wouldn't he be wearing . . . Her confused mind stumbled among options. Diving equipment?

"How did . . . you find me?"

Another moment of silence. "It doesn't matter."

He sounded like her mother. Her dreams of her mother. But maybe that didn't matter either.

"Regina." His tone was sharper now.

Her arms were tight around his waist, absorbing his warmth. "Mm?"

"We need to go. You need to hold on to me."

He was so warm. If he were a figment of her imagination, would he feel so warm?

"Am holding you," she slurred.

"Not like that." He broke the circle of her arms, mak-

ing her murmur in protest, her body bereft at the loss of
his heat.

She heard splashing and then he thrust something
into her hand. Wet, soft, flowing . . .

Seaweed? She pulled her hand away.

He caught her wrist; forced it back to the thing between them.

Her fingers splayed. Flexed. "What . . . ?"

"A sealskin. I need it to take you through the tunnel."

She stroked the wet fur. She could not feel an end to it
in the dark.

"—go underwater," he was saying. "Not a long way,
but it will be quicker if I Change. Can you hold on?"

Her limbs felt too heavy to move. Her fingers were fat
and numb. Regina took a deep breath and thought of
Nick. *Hold on.* She just had to hold on a little longer.

She nodded, forgetting Dylan couldn't see her in the
dark.

"Good girl," he said, taking her cooperation for
granted. "This way."

He put his arm around her waist to lead her forward.
And maybe he could see after all, she thought dazedly,
because he guided her without any trouble deeper and
deeper into water up to her breasts. Up to her neck. She
began to shake against his arm, hard, deep tremors that
hurt her bones. She was so cold now that the water felt
warmer than the air, but she felt its pressure in her chest
as if she were already underwater. Her womb contracted.
He was taking her into the water. Under the water. She
couldn't breathe.

She stopped, her hands curling protectively over her
stomach.

"It's all right," Dylan said.

"I'm not . . ." But she was afraid. Horribly afraid. "The baby."

"Baby," he said without inflection.

She didn't, couldn't, answer him. She stood there, her teeth chattering, shaking like a dog in the dark.

He turned her into his body. His fingers stroked her cheek. He cupped her face in his hands. Was he going to kiss her? Now? Why not? She wanted him to. Either he was here—the only man who had ever showed up when she needed him—or she was dreaming. Let him kiss her before the water took her.

His breath skated over her eyelids, over her lips, hot, drugging, salty sweet. She stood a little on tiptoe, wanting to be closer to him, but he slipped away. She felt the sealskin again, in the water between them, moving with the current, heavy against her legs.

"Hold on," he said.

And then he was gone.

She cried out in shock and loss, reaching for him, stretching her arms through the black water. The sealskin flowed under her hands, thick, soft, fluid. Her fingers curled reflexively. *Hold on.* His voice? Hers?

The pelt rolled with the water, assuming weight and form, muscle and mass. Her hands dug deeper in its folds. It was huge. Warm. Pulsing with life. The sleek fur glided under and against her like a dog nudging for attention. A really big dog. She caught her breath at the feel of the solid body under her hands, and it pulled her off her feet and under the water.

A confused rush filled her ears, filled her head. She couldn't think. She barely had time to be afraid. She was weightless, warm, buoyed up and supported by the powerful body surging under hers, by the water streaming and bubbling over and around her. Her mind churned. Her grip tightened. The darkness grew gray and then gold and then erupted in dazzling light.

Sunset spilled over the rocks, and Regina sprawled beached on a block of granite with the day going down in banners of pink and gold on the horizon and a massive thing . . . shape . . . warm, black, sleek . . . beside her. She blinked. Gasped. Raised her head. Pushed up on her elbows.

A violent fit of coughing seized her. Helpless, she heaved, spasms squeezing her chest. Her head exploded. Her lungs rattled. Tears leaked from her eyes.

When she forced her lids open again, Dylan knelt naked at her side, and the sealskin lay empty on the rocks.

She passed out.

*　*　*

"You can go in now," the doctor said.

Finally. Dylan stood.

He hadn't known when he carried Regina into the clinic that he would be barred from her bedside. But he had known she needed more help than he could give. Medical help. Human help.

He'd stripped off Regina's wet clothes and wrapped her in his shirt before carrying her to the nearest house. One look at her, unconscious in his arms, and the woman living there had called 9-1-1.

Caleb came, lights flashing, to drive them to the clinic and stayed past the clinic's offical closing at five to hear the doctor's report. Out of concern? Or to question Regina when she regained consciousness?

Antonia Barone came to smoke and pace on the sidewalk just outside the front doors.

Nick came with his grandmother. He hunched over some kind of video game, his thumbs busy, his face fixed and white, his attention completely focused on the glowing screen. As if the future of the world depended on his ability to punch and kick the tiny bad guys into oblivion. He had barely looked up the entire time they waited.

At the doctor's announcement, however, he lurched to his feet, the game system sliding unnoticed onto the chair.

Dylan followed the boy forward.

The doctor—female, sixtyish, with a round, brown face and salt-and-pepper hair—frowned over her clipboard. "Family only."

"But he saved her," Nick protested.

Dylan looked down in surprise.

"I'm sure your mom will thank him," the doctor said. "Later. Right now she just wants to see you."

Antonia took Nick through the door to the exam room.

Caleb stopped the doctor as she turned to follow them. "How is she?"

"Better. Tired," the doctor said. "The warmed IV brought her body temperature back up. I'm keeping an eye on her toes."

"What about the baby?" Dylan asked.

"What baby?" Caleb's tone was sharp.

Dylan's shoulders tensed. "There's a possibility she is pregnant," he said stiffly to the doctor.

The doctor glanced down at her clipboard and then up at him. "And you are . . . ?"

Dylan set his jaw. "The father."

"I'll talk to the patient," the doctor said and disappeared through the door.

"You son of a bitch," Caleb said.

Dylan winced. Emotions seethed and bubbled inside him: worry, responsibility, guilt. He covered them, as he had learned to cover all emotion at the selkie court, with a sneer. "Why? Because you weren't the only one to enjoy himself on your wedding night?"

Caleb's punch snapped back his head and rocked him on his heels.

Dylan ran his tongue around his teeth and tasted blood. "One," he snarled. "I'll give you one." He deserved it. "But hit me again and I'll take you down."

"You can try," Caleb said.

"If you were really eager to defend Regina, you would ask me why she was taken."

Caleb hooked his thumbs into his pockets. "I'm listening."

It was one thing to confide his mission to Margred; quite another, Dylan discovered, to discuss family matters with his brother. The Hunters had never been big on communication.

"There are . . . stories about our family. About our mother."

"Yeah, I heard most of them. After she took a hike."

Dylan shook his head. "Not gossip. Legends. Prophecies, if you will. The stories say that a daughter born of the lineage of Atargatis will one day change the balance of power among the elementals."

"Atargatis."

"Alice Hunter. Our mother."

Caleb's eyes narrowed. "So?"

Dylan spoke carefully, in the even tones he'd learned

at the prince's court. "If Regina is with child, a female child, that offspring could fulfill the prophecy. It would be regarded by Hell as a danger to the present order."

"Regina's child," Caleb repeated.

"Hers. And mine." He felt a lurch of something—possessiveness? pride?—as he said the words.

"You think the demons decided to take her out?"

"To eliminate the threat of the child. Yes."

His brother eyed him grimly. "So, before you knocked her up, did you tell her she was going to be a demon magnet?"

Dylan's lips thinned. "I did not know she was a target."

"You didn't know she was pregnant?"

It chafed him to admit it. "No."

"You still had no business putting her at risk."

"Remember that," Dylan said, "when you go home to your wife tonight."

10

❧

"I WANT TO GO HOME," REGINA CROAKED.

Warmth seeped from the hot water bottles packed along her sides; dripped from the IV attached to her arm. She was still cold all over. Except for her throat. Her throat burned. She wanted desperately to feel normal again. For everything to be normal.

"Don't be stupid," Antonia snapped. Her mother's way of expressing concern.

Nick's hand tightened on Regina's through the blankets. He'd stuck his arm through the metal bars on the other side of the clinic bed, holding on to her bandaged hand as if he never wanted to let go. Regina knew how he felt. She wiggled her fingers, tickling his palm, until his tight, pinched face relaxed.

Donna Tomah folded the blanket back over Regina's feet. "Actually, I can discharge her in a couple of hours. As long as she gets lots of rest and plenty of warm fluids, there's no reason we can't all go home tonight."

"I can make tea," Nick volunteered.

Regina smiled at him, so full of love she thought she might burst with it.

"You're spending the night at the Trujillos'," his grandmother said.

Regina's heart dropped.

So did Nicky's expression. He tightened his grip on her hand.

"Not tonight," Regina said.

Last night Nick had woken up in front of the TV to find her gone. Tonight he needed to sleep secure in his own bed with his mother safe in the next room.

"I already talked to Brenda Trujillo," Antonia said. "It's all arranged. She's giving the boys dinner."

"Dinner, fine," Regina said. "But Nick needs to be home tonight."

They needed to be home. Together.

Her eyes clashed with her mother's.

"Fine," Antonia said. "I guess I can stay with him until you get out of here."

The tension eased from Nick's bony shoulders.

"Thanks, Ma."

Antonia's mouth trembled. She bent it into a scowl. Her face resembled a wooden mask, the lines carved deep, the eyes dark and devastated. "I was going to spend the night at the restaurant cleaning anyway."

This had been an ordeal for her, too, Regina realized. And she was trying, the best way she knew how, to restore her restaurant and their lives, to make things right again.

Sudden tears pricked Regina's eyes. She widened her gaze, staring up at the stained acoustic tile. She didn't want Nick to see her cry.

Antonia reached through the bars on the other side to pat her hand. "Don't you worry. They arrested that guy. Jericho."

"Where . . ." Regina's throat hurt too much to continue.

Antonia understood. "The hospital in Rockport. Caleb's out front, waiting to take your statement."

Regina swallowed painfully. *Caleb.* Of course. He was the chief of police. She thought she'd dreamed . . . She must have imagined . . .

"You don't have to see him now," Donna Tomah said. "You don't have to see either of them until you're ready."

Either of them?

Regina's heart began to pound. "Dylan?" she croaked.

Donna glanced from the monitor to her face. "Mm. He hasn't budged from the waiting room since he brought you in."

Regina opened her mouth. No sound came out.

"He rescued you," Nick said.

Dylan's voice, deep in the dark. "It's all right." The water surging, swishing, bubbling around her, and her fingers flexing, cramping. "You need to hold on to me," he'd said. "Hold on."

Yeah, and then he'd turned into a giant seal.

Regina closed her eyes, cold and hot at once.

"Are you all right?" Donna asked.

He'd said that, too. Or had she imagined it, the way she'd imagined everything else?

Regina moistened her lips. Her hand crept under the blanket to her stomach. "Fine," she said hoarsely.

She was fine. Everything was fine, as long as she ignored the persistent ache in her throat, the pain of returning feeling in her toes, the panic fluttering at the edges of her mind.

Antonia left to take Nicky to the Trujillos' for dinner, promising to pick him up later and put him to bed. Rare hugs and more reassurances. *"I'm fine. I love you. I'll be home soon."*

Regina lay back, exhausted. With one hand she stroked the change of clothes her mother had brought: black sweatpants, a tank top, a hoodie. She needed to get dressed. In a minute. Just . . . one . . . minute . . .

She slept.

Donna came back with Regina's discharge instructions and scrawled something on her chart. "I want you to come back tomorrow for more tests."

Regina struggled to sit. She didn't want more tests. She wanted to go home, back to her real life and her regular routines, Nicky running up and down the stairs to the apartment and her mother driving her crazy in the kitchen.

"Can't we . . . get them over with now?"

"I'm afraid not. All the fluids you've had will affect your hormone levels." The doctor's voice was brisk and professional, her eyes sympathetic. "Although if you'd prefer to take a home pregnancy test tomorrow morning, the results should be fairly accurate."

Regina's breath caught painfully. *Pregnancy test.*

Donna knew.

Dylan knew.

"I'm not . . ." she'd said to him. *"The baby."*

Realization crashed through her careful pretense.

Things were never going back to normal again.

* * *

Regina hobbled into the waiting room on Donna's arm, clutching a plastic bag full of her old, wet clothes.

She stopped dead at the door. They were both there, waiting for her, Caleb, wearing his uniform and a thoughtful, guarded expression, and . . .

Dylan.

Her heart pumped. He was taller than his brother, darker, leaner. Younger, until you looked in his eyes. His eyes were flat black and dangerous.

She moistened her lips and looked away. "Where's Ma?"

Caleb moved forward. "I told her I would bring you home."

Regina tightened her grip on Donna's arm.

"She can't answer questions now," the doctor said. "Her throat's bruised. She needs to rest."

"Understood. I can take your statement in the morning," he said to Regina. "Tonight I'm just your taxi driver."

Her gaze flicked back to Dylan, black and brooding beside him. "What's he? My bodyguard?"

"Yes," Dylan said. He wasn't smiling.

Regina drew a shaky breath. O-kay. She didn't feel up for an argument. Besides . . .

"Should . . . say thanks," she croaked.

"No, you shouldn't," Dylan said, relieving her of the bag. He hesitated and then put his free arm awkwardly around her waist. "You're not supposed to talk."

She snuck another glance at his hard profile. Was he kidding? She didn't know him well enough to tell. She didn't know him at all, really. The thought depressed her.

Donna unlocked the clinic doors. The evening air blew in, cool and moist. In mid-August, the days were already shortening, the sunset almost an hour earlier than a month ago. Regina shivered, grateful for Dylan's warmth as he helped her out to the curb and into Caleb's Jeep.

She eyed the grill separating the front and back seats and tried not to feel like she was under arrest. She didn't need a police escort. Or a bodyguard.

Why was he here?

"He rescued you," Nick had said.

And now he wouldn't even look at her.

Caleb glanced in the rearview mirror, like a cop, like a father driving his fourteen-year-old on a date. "All set back there?"

Regina nodded. Dylan had withdrawn to his side of the car. Fine. She hadn't asked for his company. She wasn't going to cling. She pressed her lips together, pressed her hands together, keeping them warm between her legs.

They rode to the restaurant in silence.

*   *   *

Dylan gazed out at the unlit streets, his heart a live coal in his chest. He needed to talk to her. He had to explain, to win her over somehow, to make her accept . . .

Not *him*. Dylan scowled. His experience with his own family, with his father and his brother, made him despair of Regina ever accepting *him*.

But she had to accept his protection, the necessity of it. For the sake of the child she carried. Whether she liked it or not.

His hands closed into fists. When he had led her to the Jeep, she had leaned on him. Just for a moment. He could still feel her slight weight against his side, the pressure of her arm.

He glanced at her, her clasped hands nestled between her thighs as if she sought to warm them, and fought a completely uncharacteristic urge to cover them with one of his own.

The merfolk did not touch. Yet as the road wound down and around toward the harbor, he was conscious of her upright and fragile beside him, every shift of her body, every rasping intake of her breath.

The Cherokee rumbled to a stop in front of the restaurant. The yellow crime scene tape was gone from the sidewalk. The lights of the dining room glowed through the wide plate glass windows.

Caleb half turned in his seat; cleared his throat. "I've got to write up some kind of report that will satisfy the state guys. I'll leave you two to . . ."

His eyes met Dylan's. *Talk.*

"Get settled," he said.

Dylan nodded.

Regina fumbled with her door handle as if she couldn't wait to escape them both. Uneasiness tightened Dylan's stomach. How much explaining would he have to do? What did she remember?

His own door was locked. Before he could get out to assist her, Caleb had opened her door and helped her to the curb.

Dylan's jaw set. He pulled his duffel from the back of the Jeep and joined them.

Regina's gaze fell on the packed bag and narrowed.

Dylan felt a lick of panic disguised as irritation. Did she think she could send him away? He leaned very close, close enough to see the pale parting of her hair, to inhale the private fragrance of her skin. "I'm staying," he said softly, for her ears alone. "Deal with it."

Her eyes flashed. But whatever reply she might have made was lost as Antonia bustled through the maze of tables to unlock the front door.

She reached to grab her daughter and then crossed her arms instead. Regina stood stiffly under the restaurant lights, all angles and shadows like a black-and-white drawing.

Antonia regarded her daughter and scowled. "The doctor said warm fluids. I made soup." The smell followed her from the kitchen, rich with chicken, vegetables, and garlic. "Sit down, I'll get you some."

Regina smiled wanly. "Thanks. Is Nick—"

"Already in bed. You can see him after you eat."

Dylan saw the indecision flicker on Regina's face. "We'll go up now," he said.

Antonia looked at him. Looked at his bag. Her eyebrows rose. "Will you." Her tone made it not quite a question. "Planning on staying?"

"Just for tonight," Regina said in that rasping voice that sounded so incongruously, so ridiculously sexy coming from her thin, sharp face.

His heart leaped. She wanted him. Or at least she was prepared to tolerate his presence. *"Just for tonight."*

Antonia snorted. "Well, you're too old to need my permission for a sleepover, but I'd like to know what you're going to say to Nick in the morning."

A red flush swept Regina's face.

"I'm helping take care of his mother," Dylan said. "I'll come down later for the soup."

"Hm. Well, go on," Antonia said. "I've got to lock back up."

Dylan followed Regina through the disarranged tables. She still walked with difficulty, he noted with a frown. At the swinging door, she stopped, and the color that had come back to her cheeks faded away.

He thought he knew why. The kitchen was her territory. Her little kingdom. And she had been brutally attacked in there less than twenty-four hours ago.

His chest constricted. He eased the plastic bag from her grip with one hand, and reached around her with the other to nudge the door open. "I suppose you expect me to thank you because you didn't let your mother throw me out."

Regina glanced at him, startled, her lashes dark smudges against her white face. And then her eyes lit with laughter. "Maybe I wanted the pleasure of doing it myself."

He grinned down at her.

Her slim shoulders straightened, and she marched—hobbled, rather—under his outstretched arm. She went down the kitchen work aisle like a gauntlet and out the back door.

She needed his assistance up the metal stairs. Or he told himself she did. Perhaps it was simply pleasant to touch her.

When she fumbled with the plastic bag digging for her apartment key, he took it from her and fished the key from her wet jeans pocket. He was in control of the situation and himself.

Until he stepped over the threshold of her apartment and the walls closed around him like a trap.

She lived in a . . . *home*. The kind of home he had not
known in nearly twenty-five years. Comfortable. Messy.
The litter of human life was everywhere: pillows on the
floor, a child's artwork on the fridge, photos on the tables, a red blanket on the couch. Regina in a cap and
gown smiled beside a dark-haired Antonia. Nick's much
smaller handprints were preserved in a frame on the
wall.

The children of the sea were magpies. Their sea caves
and the court at Caer Subai were furnished with rich
and shiny things—whatever fell beneath the waves that
pleased their humor or caught their eyes. But their selec-
tions were not personal. They did not bear the weight of
memory, the patina of sentiment. They did not cause this
tightness in his throat, this howling in his chest.

Nothing at Caer Subai ever changed. Gold and iron,
sea and stone, would outlast these human keepsakes. But
now, here, surrounded by the mementos of Regina's life
and her son's childhood, Dylan was achingly aware of
all that would change.

And all that had been lost.

He stood rooted on Regina's shabby carpet, frozen
with desire and despair.

Regina saw him standing like a pillar of salt in the
center of her living room and raised her chin a notch. "I
wasn't expecting company."

"No," he agreed.

She had bits of sea glass strung on fishing line
dangling in her windows, green and gold against the
darkness outside. Why should that jab at his heart?

"Nick and I will be fine. You don't have to stay."

Her tone drew his attention. Her jaw was at a bel-
ligerent angle, her eyes defensive. She was embarrassed,

he realized. She thought he was critical of her home. Her housekeeping. He could hardly tell her that the sight of Nick's crayon drawings, the fat white candles on the table, the popcorn kernels in the bowl by the TV, made something inside him crack and flow like glacier ice.

He shrugged. "It's all right."

"Right." She waited a moment for some reaction he did not know how to give. "You can have the couch, then. I'm going to say good night to Nick."

A crack of light showed beneath the boy's bedroom door. She opened it and disappeared inside, and Dylan could breathe again.

*   *   *

"Hey, kiddo."

Nick's head jerked up. His comic book slithered to the floor. "Mom!"

He was glad, so glad to see her. Even if she did look like crap. Her face was white and tired. Okay, he'd seen her tired before. But her neck . . . Oh, man. Her neck made him sick to his stomach.

She caught him looking and tugged casually on her collar. "How you feeling?" she asked. She sounded like Nonna when she smoked.

Nick jerked his shoulder. "Okay. You?"

She smiled and sat on the end of his bed, like she used to when he was little. "I'm fine. Everything's going to be fine now."

He wanted desperately to believe her. She wanted it, too, he could tell. But last night's terror was still too real. Too raw. He could see the bruises poking over the neck-line of her shirt. That asshole had hurt her, and Nick hadn't done anything to stop him, didn't even know she was in trouble until it was too late.

"What if he comes back?" His voice broke, embarrassing him.

His mom didn't pretend not to know who he was talking about. "He won't," she said firmly. "He's in jail."

Normally Nick knew better than to argue with that tone of voice. But his anxiety pushed him to ask, "But what if he does?"

Somebody knocked on the door.

Nick's stomach lurched.

The Dylan dude stuck his head in the room and nodded to Nick. "How's it going."

"What are you doing here?" Nick asked.

"We're fine," his mom said. "Do you mind?"

Dylan ignored her. "I'm keeping an eye on your mother," he said over her head to Nick. "Until she feels better. Okay?"

Nick swallowed, some of the burden of worry and guilt lifted from his shoulders. Dylan was cool. He'd said he would find Nick's mom, and then he did. If he wanted to keep an eye on her, that was fine. That was good. Somebody had to.

Nick shrugged. "Yeah, okay."

Dylan nodded again, like they'd come to an agreement. It made Nick feel better than he had since he first saw the bruises on his mom's neck. "Good. I'm getting that soup," he said to Nick's mom.

The door closed quietly behind him.

His mother sat on the edge of the bed, biting her lip.

Something quivered in Nick. "Mom?"

She focused on him then, her eyes and smile quick,

warm, familiar. The quiver went away. "You think you could get some sleep now?" she suggested.

He could, because she was here. Maybe because that guy Dylan was here, too, keeping an eye on her.

Nick snuggled under the covers, and when she leaned over to kiss him good night, he put both arms around her like a little kid. And was able to let her go.

*   *   *

Regina closed the bedroom door behind her and leaned against it, throat tight, pulse jumping. She closed her eyes, flattening her battered hands against the smooth, cool wood. She never brought men to the apartment. Never. Nick came first, always.

She sighed. Which was why she couldn't ignore his very real fear or miss the hero worship in his eyes. If Dylan's presence made Nick feel better, if it eased her son's mind or helped him to sleep, then she was grateful Dylan was here . . . and never mind why.

He was here.

He knew about the baby.

Her mind kept struggling with those two things, worrying at them, trying to make them add up, like she was in seventh grade again and wrestling with an uneven equation. Maybe if she'd been better at algebra, she would have gone to college instead of to work as a dishwasher, a prep cook, a line cook at Perfetto's.

She remembered telling Alain she was pregnant, late at night when the dinner service was over and the rest of the staff had finished drinking and gone home. Alain had teased her because she had stuck stubbornly with club soda all night, and she'd let herself hope because he'd noticed, because he'd been watching her. She'd offered to take him home with her. He wasn't completely wasted, but he'd had enough to make driving dangerous. Enough to make him want her. And she . . . Well, she'd always wanted him.

So she'd told him, standing in her living room, twisting her hands together at her waist, her voice rising and falling with apology and hope.

He never came home with her again. Bastard, she thought wearily, out of habit.

But Dylan was here.

He was bringing her soup.

And even though Regina knew better, even though she told herself she was just prolonging the inevitable disappointment, she set her tiny table for two.

She heard him come up the stairs, and her stupid heart bumped into overtime. She opened the door.

His gaze rested on her face. "We need to talk."

She did her best not to wince. "Which one? You hope we can still be friends? Or it's not you, it's me?"

He gave her a flat, hard stare.

"Sorry," she muttered. "It's been a rough day."

His gaze fell to the mottled collar around her neck. Emotion flickered in those black, black eyes and was gone too quickly to be identified. "Yes," he said.

He followed her into the kitchen and saw the white bowls, the lit candles. One eyebrow arched.

Embarrassment rose under her skin, a faint warm flush. She was annoyed with him for noticing and with herself for caring. "Old restaurant trick," she said, ladling the soup—her mother's minestrone, good for whatever ailed you—into bowls. "Candlelight improves the food."

He carried the bowls to the table. "And the company."

She joined him. "Are you saying I look better in low light?"

"It suits you." His gaze met hers across the table. "Your eyes shine."

Another arrow, straight to the heart. She clenched her spoon to hide her hand's trembling.

"Good soup," Dylan remarked.

"Two compliments in a row. Be careful, or I'll start to take you seriously."

"Why shouldn't you? Your mother is a good cook."

Regina let the soothing broth trickle down her throat. It brought back memories, of being sick, of being sad, of being fed. "More than that. Ma supported herself and me and Nicky on an island where a lot of businesses pack up or die in the winter."

"She is a stubborn woman."

"I'm proud of her." How long since she had told her mother so?

"Yet you left."

Regina sipped her water. This was so not the discussion she expected to be having with him. This was not a conversation she would have with anybody on World's End. Everybody here knew everybody. Knew everything, or thought they did. "Antonia's is . . . Antonia's. It's good. It could be great. It's just not . . . mine."

"Your mother is afraid of change."

She shrugged. "Maybe."

"And you are not." His tone was faintly challenging.

"I . . ." She stopped, struck. Was she afraid? When she'd crawled home eight years ago, exhausted, broke, and defeated, she'd seen few choices and little future for herself. But now . . . it was one thing to settle for her mother's menus. At what point had she begun to settle for her mother's life?

"I try to keep an open mind," she said.

"That is fortunate," Dylan murmured.

She frowned, uncomprehending.

He stood to clear their bowls, carrying them to the sink. She pushed back her chair to help him, but he kept her in place with a quick shake of his head. She'd spent years in the kitchen with men. Yet despite Dylan's obvious grace—or maybe because of it—watching him perform the small domestic chore made her breathless and slightly uncomfortable. He ran water over the dishes before he retrieved his duffel from the floor by the front door and brought it to the table.

Her vocal chords tightened. "What's this?"

In answer, he unzipped the bag, reached in, and pulled out a fur, a fur coat, a . . .

Regina stared at the thick, black pelt gleaming in the candlelight. Her heart moved into her throat and choked her.

A sealskin.

11

DYLAN'S HEART POUNDED.

Regina raised her gaze to his, her brown eyes wide with shock. "It was you," she whispered. "In the caves."

She must have known. She'd seen. She'd even thanked him for rescuing her. But now she knew how.

He held himself stiffly, braced for her rejection, his messy human emotions tucked safely out of sight. "Yes."

"In . . . this." Her fingers flexed in the pelt.

He flinched. "Yes."

Her hands, her gaze, returned to her lap. He watched her fingers twist together. His insides knotted.

Moments passed, measured in the mad drumming of his heart and the slow release of her breath.

"I wondered why you weren't wearing a wet suit."

Dylan scowled to cover his surprise. He was a creature of legend. A fairy tale. A freak. His own father couldn't stand the sight of him. He did not expect Regina—hard-headed, practical Regina—simply to accept him or his explanation. "That's it? You're not going to . . ." *Scream. Run away in horror.* "Demand proof?"

She shook her head. "I saw you. I saw . . . I thought I was crazy. This is . . . Well."

"A relief?" he suggested dryly.

She met his eyes. "Not exactly."

His gut clenched. No, of course not.

At least she wasn't hysterical. At least she hadn't recoiled from him. Not yet.

She moistened her lips. "So, how . . . That is, what . . ."

"I am selkie."

"Well, that explains everything."

Her tart tone almost made him smile. "I am a man on the land and a seal in the sea."

"But how do you do it? Are you . . . Which are you?"

"I am both, and I am neither. Not human or animal. Before God made humankind, He created the heavens and the earth, the water, and the fire. With each creation, the elementals took form, the children of air, earth, sea, and fire. Selkies are the children of the sea."

"Um. That's very interesting. Except I know your family. I know your dad, and—"

"My father is human." He was nothing like his father. "I am selkie by my mother's blood."

Regina's throat moved as she swallowed. Dylan waited rigidly, watching as her practical mind sorted through the implications of his story. "But your brother and sister—"

"Take after our father," he said evenly. "Most human-selkie offspring are human."

Did he imagine it, or did she touch her stomach under her bulky sweatshirt? Did she think about their offspring? Their child. His hands clenched.

"So, when did you know that you were . . ."

"Selkie."

"Different?" she finished.

He didn't like to think about it. He didn't want to remember. "Thirteen."

"Wow." She regarded him thoughtfully. He felt his palms grow clammy. "Like puberty didn't suck enough."

Her humor eased the tight knot in his gut.

"That was right before you and your mother left World's End," she observed.

"Yes."

"Tough on you."

He shook his head. "Leaving was my idea. My choice. My . . ."

Fault, he thought but did not say.

"Oh, please. You were thirteen. Your mother was, what, like, forty?"

His mouth was dry. "Older than that."

Regina looked at him questioningly.

"Selkies are immortal. We do not age as humans do."

"Oh." Another silence, while she absorbed this fresh bit of information and he wished he were somewhere far away in the cool, dark depths of the ocean. "But she died. Didn't you say she died?"

"She was killed. Drowned in a fisherman's net within a year of her freedom." He blamed himself for that, too.

Regina winced. "Well, but that doesn't change my point. Your mother was the grown-up. She could have split with you anytime. Or made sure you stayed."

"She could not leave. Before."

"Why not?"

Black resentment boiled in him. He swallowed it. "We cannot change form, we cannot return to the sea, without our sealskins. My mother used to come ashore to . . . visit my father. Before we were born. Before they married. I think they married." Dylan chose his words with care, but it was impossible to disguise the bitterness in his face. "One night, while she lay sleeping, he took her pelt and hid it."

"She used to visit him," Regina repeated.

He should have known she would focus on the wrong thing. She was human and female. Incapable of understanding the needs that drove his kind.

"Yes."

"So she must have been at least attracted to him at some point."

"That did not give him the right to try to contain her," Dylan said tautly. "To control her."

"She still stayed with him for thirteen—fourteen?—years."

He glared. "She had no choice."

"They had three kids."

Dylan could not answer. He was the one who had found his mother's pelt. He had brought it to her. He had destroyed his family.

He met her gaze, speechless, appalled by the emotions that raged and wept inside him. As if he were thirteen again, mortified and distracted by the changes in his own body, torn between his childhood loyalties and affections and his deep, desperate desire for the sea.

He steadied his breathing. He was not that child, he reminded himself. He was not the victim of emotion or anything else. He was selkie, impervious, immortal.

"Does Caleb know?" Regina asked, plunging him back into the torrent of human feeling and connection again. "That you and your mother are some kind of . . ."

He narrowed his eyes. "Freaks?" he asked softly.

She crossed her arms over her stomach. "I was going to say mermaid, but you can call yourself whatever you want. Does he know?"

"He does now. He's had some recent experience with . . . mermaids."

Her mouth dropped open. "Oh my God," she breathed. "Maggie?"

Margred was her friend, Dylan thought, an odd pressure in his chest. Surely Regina, with her fierce loyalties and her kind heart, would not turn from Margred, who had been selkie. And if she did not turn from Margred, then . . . But he would not let himself complete that thought.

He nodded.

"Wow. That's . . . wow." Regina reached for her water. She took a sip, her hand tight on the frosted glass, watching him over the rim. "What about Lucy?"

"Lucy is human. I told you."

"Yeah, but does she know?"

"There is no reason for her to know. She was only a year old when we . . . left."

"Nick was only three months old when we moved from Boston, but he still knows who his father is." Regina gulped more water. "What his father is."

"The situation is not the same," Dylan said stiffly.

"No?" She set down her glass, her hand trembling. "Then why are you telling me?"

To keep her safe.

Whether the child in her womb was the fulfillment of an ancient prophecy or merely a pawn in the elementals' border wars, the demons would not back off when their first attack failed. The child was still threatened. Regina was still in danger. Dylan's gut knotted.

"You deserve to know," he said coolly.

She hunched in her chair, her eyes bright and challenging in her white face. "So you've told me. Now what? Are you going to visit me, like your mom *visited* your dad?"

He recognized the strain under her flippant tone, the tension hiding behind her casual posture. Hadn't he learned to mask his own fears and uncertainties the same way?

Dylan scowled. It was one thing for him to deny or disguise his feelings. He wasn't human. He wasn't female and pregnant. He hadn't been half strangled and thrown down a hole by a demon intent on his destruction. Her strength of mind, her practicality of purpose, as her world turned upside down awed and annoyed him. Couldn't she let her guard down this once and let him take care of things?

Of course not.

In her eyes, he was one of the things she was guarding against, a threat to the life she had built with her son. She was probably dying to get rid of him. Circle the wagons. Repel the alien invader. *"Nicky and I will be fine on our own,"* she'd said.

But she wouldn't. They wouldn't. They needed him, whether Regina admitted it or not. Whether she liked it or not. Now he just had to figure out how to tell her.

"You should get some rest," he said.

She gave him a disbelieving look. "You think that's going to solve anything?"

"I think," he said carefully, "you need to sleep. We can decide what to do in the morning."

"We don't decide," Regina said. "I decide."

"Not tonight," Dylan said.

He knew she prided herself on her independence. This situation, however, was outside her experience and beyond her control. Eventually, she would have to accept that. Accept his protection.

At least she would be safe tonight. He was here. She was warded. In the morning, he would find some way to confer with Conn, to make arrangements to bring her to the selkie island until her baby could be born. In the meantime . . .

He reached into his pocket. "I have something of yours."

Her eyes rounded as he withdrew the bright gold cross on the broken chain. "Oh." Her hand went to her neck in a habitual gesture. "I thought I lost it. Where . . ."

"In the kitchen." He poured the fine chain into her cupped palm, keeping his hand carefully apart from hers. "The clasp is snapped. You need another."

He should have gotten her another, he realized belatedly. But there hadn't been time.

"Thank you," she said, smiling up at him, her eyes glowing as if he'd brought her diamonds instead of a broken necklace that already belonged to her.

His heart constricted. "You're welcome. You should wear it. For protection."

Her smile turned rueful. "It hasn't done a very good job of protecting me so far."

"More than you know." Unable any longer to resist the temptation of her touch, he closed her hand around the cross. Her fingers were light and cool. He let go before she could notice his own hand trembling.

"It is a ward," he explained. "Like the mark on your wrist."

She looked at the triskelion tattooed on her skin; at the gold cross in her hand. "A ward against what? Vampires?"

He had intended to put this conversation off until morning. He owed her his honesty. That didn't mean he had to batter her with the truth when she was exhausted and he was on edge.

But she wouldn't let it go, he thought in irritation. She kept pushing and pushing at him with her wide eyes and her soft heart and her big mouth.

"Not vampires," he said. "Demons."

*   *   *

Regina's jaw dropped. She inhaled. She exhaled. *Demons.* Well.

"I was kidding," she said weakly.

Dylan didn't say anything. *Oh, God.* Obviously, he was not.

Regina had been baptized a Catholic, but her knowledge of demons was pretty much limited to Halloween and a few episodes of *Buffy*.

She swallowed. "Are we talking horns and pitchforks here? Or *The Exorcist*?"

A muscle bunched in Dylan's jaw. "This is not a movie."

"No, it's my life." Her previously dull and ordinary life. She wanted it back.

"This is crap," she said. "I was attacked by somebody I know. A man. A human. Jericho Jones."

"He was possessed," Dylan said. "Unlike the other

elements, fire has no matter of its own. The children of the fire must take over a host to act on the corporal plane."

She struggled to make sense of his words, to hear him through the rushing in her ears, the pounding of her heart. "Possessed or not, Jericho's in jail. The demon—" Even the word stopped her. She wasn't Buffy. She didn't do demons. She was a twenty-nine-year-old line cook with an eight-year-old son. She forced herself to go on. "It's locked up with him. So I'm safe."

"No. The demon was driven out of Jones by your cross. It will seek a new host to come back. To come after you."

"Why?" The word was nearly a wail. She coughed.

Dylan waited while she gulped her water. When she set down her glass, he said gently, "I do not believe the demon seeks your death."

"Right. It just half strangled me and dropped me down a hole for fun."

His mouth tightened. "I should have said, its primary target is not your death."

"What does it want, then? I don't have anything—"

"The child." Dylan's eyes met hers. "Yours and mine."

Oh, God.

Her breath went. Her vision grayed. For a moment, she was back in the caves again, in the icy dark.

Dylan continued to watch her, his smooth, handsome face like stone, his thoughts and feelings buried. She wished he would touch her or something. Hold her hand.

She forced another breath. Okay. Of all the pregnancy horror stories she'd been told or could imagine, *"de-*

mons seek your unborn child" had to be the worst. At least it explained why she had been attacked. Sort of. And why Dylan was sticking around.

For tonight.

She moistened her lips. "I don't know yet that I'm pregnant. I mean, not for sure."

"When will you know?"

"Tomorrow. I have a doctor's appointment."

"I think you are. You smell . . . different."

Good different or bad different? She pushed the thought away. "Have you smelled a lot of pregnant women?"

"No, you are the first." His dark eyes flickered. "There are not many births among the merfolk."

"So, this baby is important, huh? If it's, you know, selkie."

"Selkie and female."

"You want a girl?"

Dylan's breath was as deep, as deliberate, as hers had been. "There is a child foretold among my people," he began. "A daughter of the house of Atargatis who will change the balance of power between Heaven and Hell. Atargatis was my mother. If you were to carry a daughter, yours and mine, the child would be of the lineage of Atargatis."

She took a moment to work it out. "Then . . . we're on Heaven's side?" That made her feel better. A little.

Dylan did not meet her eyes. "Not exactly."

The lump in her throat was getting too big to swallow. "Then where do we stand? Exactly."

"When God made man, the elementals debated His decision. The children of air supported Him in this as in everything. The children of fire—demonkind—did not. But the majority of the First Creation, earth's children and the children of the sea, concluded His wisdom would reveal itself in time. Or not." Dylan's smile revealed the edge of his teeth. "In either event, they— we—withdrew into the bones of the mountains and the depths of the seas, until mankind should either prove or destroy itself. We do not take sides."

"So you're neutral." Like Switzerland.

"My people are, yes."

Regina heard his distinction. She saw past the thin, sharp smile to the turmoil in his eyes. He was not as neutral or as indifferent as he pretended.

The realization gave her hope.

"Yeah, well, my people are human," she said. "Which means my kid is at least half human."

"That's not how it works. There are no fractions to the Change," Dylan said tightly. "No degrees of difference. You are human or not. You are selkie or not. The child will be one or the other."

She heard his cool, clipped tones and saw the rigid set of his shoulders and ached for him, for the choices his mother had forced on him, for the confusion of the boy he had been, for the isolation of the man he had become.

But he was wrong.

"That's a load of crap," Regina said. "Family is family."

Dylan cocked an eyebrow. "Blood is thicker than water?"

Was it? Wasn't it? Could she love the child within her if it were born . . . different?

"Yes," she said recklessly.

"So sure," Dylan mocked. "And so blind. Can you honestly pretend you don't see me differently now, knowing what I am? My brother and I are not the same."

"Yeah," Regina muttered. "He's not a jerk."

Black laughter sprang into his eyes. "There is that."

"And he didn't find me. He couldn't have rescued me. You did. So your seal trick is actually pretty useful."

"Like Lassie saving Timmy in the well," Dylan said.

Regina narrowed her eyes. She recognized that jeering, defensive tone. She was the mother of a son, after all. Dylan was less certain, less in control of himself and the situation, than he would ever admit. Part of her wanted to reassure him, the way she would have soothed Nick. And another part of her resented having to try. She was tired and battered and pregnant and her throat hurt. He was here not because he wanted to be, not because he wanted her, but because the baby she carried could be part of some otherworldly power struggle.

If it's selkie and female.

And if it wasn't, he'd be gone. Which meant she'd be right where she was before, on her own, raising her child, her children, alone.

She pushed back her chair. "The appointment's at ten."

"I will come with you," he said instantly.

Like he cared.

He didn't, of course. She couldn't let the sweetness of his offer seduce her into thinking she could rely on him.

"I'm not asking you to. But I thought I'd tell you in case there are any tests the doctor could do. Or shouldn't do."

"The child was conceived in human form. It may be human. It will appear human, in any case, until it matures."

At thirteen. Her mind boggled at the thought of guiding a half-human adolescent—boy? girl?—through sexual maturity. How would she manage?

How had Dylan?

"Great." She managed a smile. "I wasn't looking forward to explaining to my mother why I had a fish tank next to the crib."

A shadow chased across his face. His eyes were stormy. "Regina . . ."

She pulled her sweatshirt tighter around her. "Not now. Please. I'm . . ." *Exhausted. Frightened. Overwhelmed.* "Going to turn in. I'll see you in the morning."

* * *

Dylan glared at the blank white door that led to Regina's bedroom. She had accepted his explanation. She was prepared to tolerate his presence and protection. That was enough.

He didn't expect her to seek his company or his comfort. In a matter of weeks, he had destroyed her peace, endangered her life, and strained the limits of her belief. She needed time to recover, recover and sleep. She needed space.

He could understand. Wasn't that what he wanted, too? What he'd always wanted. No human expectations, no messy emotional entanglements. To live forever in the license of the sea with its endless moods and changeable weather and endless, changeable sexual partners.

Never mind that the one he wanted had just gone to bed without him.

He imagined her undressing, taking off her bulky sweatshirt and soft black pants and sliding between the sheets alone. He should be in there with her. If he were in there, he could reassure her. He could put his hands on her, all that smoothness, all that delicate softness, taste the salt of her skin and the tartness of her mouth, slide hard deep inside her, pink, wet, *his* . . .

He broke off, breathing hard, appalled at what he was thinking and thinking it anyway.

Not his.

He was not his father, to lay claim to another living being. He was not his mother, to sacrifice the freedom of the sea for sex.

He was selkie. And he was sleeping on the couch. For tonight, at least.

Satisfied with his decision, he grabbed the blanket from the back of the couch; and heard a whimper of distress from Regina's room.

Hell. He threw down the blanket and went to her door.

She lay with her back to him, curled on her side like a child. Her hair was dark and messy on her pillow. He couldn't see her face or her breasts, not even much skin, only her smooth, slim shoulder, her pale, tender nape, the delicate bump at the beginning of her spine.

Longing shivered through him.

She jerked and muttered. Dreaming, he guessed.

"It's all right," he told her softly, standing in the doorway.

"Nicky," she croaked.

"He's fine. He's here," Dylan said, feeling like a helpless jerk. "I'm here."

She moaned.

He'd had it with being helpless. He didn't even think about staying uninvolved.

He crawled into bed with her and took her in his arms, and she buried her face in his neck.

12

❧❧

DYLAN'S BODY WAS WARM, SO WARM, AND Regina was cold, her toes and fingers freezing, the pit of her stomach an icy lump. She burrowed into him, needing heat, wanting skin, seeking to blot out the memory of pitch-black caves and her dreams of rising water. *Chilling her bones, stealing her breath . . .*

She shivered, fumbling with his buttons, clumsy in the dark. He ripped open his shirt and gathered her against him, mashing her nose against the hard planes of his almost smooth chest.

She shuddered in relief. But even in his arms, her dreams crept in, blanketing her brain like a heavy gray fog, clinging and cold. She hated those dreams. She reached for Dylan's belt buckle instead, feeling the muscles of his stomach jump. *Good.* He felt warm, warm and alive, and—

His hand closed over her shaking hands, holding them still. "What are you doing?"

She was close to tears. She tried to joke instead. "Isn't it obvious?"

"Not to me." He sounded grim.

She felt a hot trickle of humiliation, and even that was better than the cold.

"Bad dream," she explained.

"I guessed." He didn't let go of her hand.

"I can't stop remembering . . . I can't help thinking . . ." She was back in the caves, in the dark again, only now the shadows were infested with demons. "I'm scared."

"You should be. And I am not the one to comfort you."

Because he wasn't human? Or because he would leave? Neither mattered much to her at the moment.

"You're the only one." The only one who understood what she had been through. Who knew what she faced. Who could deliver her from the dark. "You were there. You rescued me."

"So, what's this? 'Thank you'?"

The humiliation spread, a warm flush of embarrassment in her cheeks, in her chest. She hunched a shoulder. "If you want."

"Let's talk about what you want," he said, cool as a priest in the confessional.

"I want to stop thinking," she said, her voice shaking as much as her hands. "I want to feel something besides afraid and alone. I want you."

"I don't want to hurt you."

"I'm already sore all over. Sex isn't going to make me feel any worse. It might even make me feel better." *Make me feel alive.*

"A comfort fuck. How very . . . romantic." There was

an edge to his voice now. Annoyance or amusement? She hardly cared. Either was better than his indifferent calm.

"This from a guy who did me drunk and standing against a rock?"

He did laugh, then, a vibration in the dark. She felt him shift—*not close enough, not nearly close enough*—and rise on one elbow. Moonlight from the window behind her painted the hard line of his cheek. His teeth gleamed. "I thought that was romantic."

She sniffed. "You thought I was easy."

"You?" He combed a strand of hair from her forehead, his touch lingering behind her ear. She felt the faint rasp of his roughened fingertips and shivered all the way down to her toes. Not with cold this time. "You're the most difficult woman I've ever known."

He watched her a moment, his dark eyes swallowing the moonlight, making her breath catch in her throat. He laid his mouth gently, lightly on hers, his kiss teasing, almost tender, almost . . .

She groaned and arched to meet him, craving his taste, his tongue. He gave them to her, feeding her in sips and tiny bites that promised more than he delivered.

She curled her fingers into his shirt front to pull him closer. Still not enough. Her hands wandered under his shirt, learning his shape, hard where Alain had been soft, smooth where Alain had been hairy. Different. She flattened her palm on his chest, where his heart beat hard and fast, and something inside her softened. Sundered.

He was here. He was hers. At least for tonight. Tonight she needed him.

His hands smoothed over her camisole top, shaping her breasts, rubbing the peaks, making her clench with excitement. Her legs moved restlessly between the sheets, twining with his. The scrape of denim against her bare skin irritated and aroused her.

She drew back, touching her tongue to her lips, tasting his kiss on her mouth. "You really want romantic, you could take off your pants this time."

Another breath of laughter. "There you go, being difficult again."

The covers heaved as he shucked his jeans and threw them on the floor. He rolled back to her, eyes gleaming. "Satisfied?"

Her heart pounded. "Not yet."

He came over her in one smooth movement, nudging her legs apart with his knee, fitting himself between her thighs. He was thick and hard and hot against her. So very hot. Her pulse stumbled as he rocked into her, as his lips brushed hers once, twice.

"I want to be inside you."

"Yes."

"Come inside you."

Why not? She was already pregnant. And she wanted this. Wanted him.

"Yes."

He licked into her, taking her mouth, his kiss deeper, wetter, wilder. His hands slid around and under her, under her panties, against her flesh. Fabric ripped. She didn't care. He was pulling her down in the dark again, in the wet, swirling blackness, his body her rock and the darkness like velvet, thick and warm. Sensation swirled behind her closed lids, whispered along her veins, rose in her like the tide. She lifted her hips; opened her mouth to breathe. His hands spanned her buttocks. He gripped her, flipped her, turned her belly down on the mattress and dragged her hips up.

She gasped in protest. In excitement. She wanted to touch him. She wanted to see him, his face, his expressions. There was something vaguely disturbing about having him so close and still out of her reach, beyond her control. Disturbing and—okay, she could admit it—exciting. He came down on her, taking his weight on his elbows, holding her in place with his thighs, and she could feel him, all of him, his naked flesh hot against her back, hard against her buttocks, thick and wide at her entrance.

Her nerves thrummed. Her belly quivered. He looped one arm around her waist, his long-fingered hand skimming her stomach to find her slick, soft folds. She sucked in her breath as that hand explored her with curious delicacy, stroked her, spread her. She was warm now, warm and achingly alive, every nerve, every muscle desperately attuned to his touch. His fingers circled, plucking her response from her, coaxing her open. Her hands fisted on the sheets. Waves of pleasure rolled through her as she pressed upward shamelessly, as she arched to take him in.

She heard him grunt in satisfaction and then he pushed into her a little way, his full head stretching her. Possessing her. Her eyelids slid closed. She'd forgotten how big he was. How good this felt. Too much. And still not enough.

His hair fell forward against her cheek. His breath was hot at her ear, warm against her temple.

"Like this," he said.

She could not see his face, but she heard his need. For now, it was enough.

"Yes."

Anything to ease this terrible want. His. Hers.

With one thick thrust, he filled her. She moaned, overtaken. Overwhelmed. In this position, she could feel everything. The strength of his arms, the sweat on his chest, his sex deep within her, stroke after stroke, driving away the cold inside and out. She had always been self-sufficient, self-possessed. Now he had her, controlled her, and his command of her body, his hold on her emotions, was at once freeing, terrifying . . . and terribly erotic. She bucked and wriggled, trying impossibly to get closer, to take more. She wanted to touch him, needed to reach him, but he was behind her, surrounding her, his legs bracketing her legs, his arm hard beside her head, his face damp against the side of her face.

He reached under her, cupping her snugly, and she felt the darkness build and throb, felt it well and spill, felt it fill her, flood her as she came, over and over, biting the pillow to keep from crying out. His rhythm changed, quickened, each slow drag, each sudden intrusion, almost more than she could bear. He pumped in and out, rigid above her, hard inside her. Again. Again. His fingers clamped her hips. His long, lean body convulsed. She shivered, and he groaned against her hair, burying his face in the curve of her neck.

Well.

Eventually the bed stopped spinning and settled down with Dylan still heavy on top of her, his weight pressing her into the mattress. Regina lay with her nose in her pillow, feeling dizzy, trying to hold on to the leftover warmth. Waiting for her heartbeat to return to normal. For her life to return to normal.

She couldn't move. She couldn't breathe either. She

coughed, and Dylan rolled off her, rolled away, leaving her cold, damp, and alone. She winced. Well, that was normal enough.

But then, without speaking, he reached for her and hauled her into his arms. Arranging her against him, he flipped the covers over them both. Her heart stood still. She froze in sheer surprise, her head on his hard shoulder, glued to his side by sweat and sex and exertion.

"Are you . . . cuddling with me?"

A snort. Or maybe that was a snore.

Regina bit her lip. "That's so . . . romantic," she said, needling him.

"It would be." He sounded annoyed. "If you'd shut up."

She grinned and snuggled into his side. Warmed, comforted, she drifted into sleep, lulled by the rise and fall of his chest and the slow beat of his heart.

* * *

"What is this?" Surprise rippled through Margred's low voice. Her small, warm hand explored him under the covers.

Caleb set his jaw, torn between the pleasure of that exploring hand and the challenge posed by her question. "It's a condom."

"I know what it is. I want to know why you wear it."

"To protect you," Caleb said tightly.

"From what?"

"Pregnancy."

She eased away from him, all that softness, all that warmth, retreating. "But . . . I want to get pregnant. We want to have children. We talked about it."

Caleb winced, her bewilderment cutting him more deeply than her indignation had. "That was before."

"Before what?"

He was silent.

"The prophecy." She answered her own question. "You are afraid that if we have a daughter, she will be in danger."

"Or you will."

"That is a risk I am willing to take."

He had always admired her courage. But he could not, would not, risk her life. Her safety.

"I just think with what happened to Regina . . . Until we know . . . It's not a good idea right now."

"But I want a baby."

Fear for her made him sharp. "You can't have everything you want, Maggie."

His words echoed like a slap in the darkness of their bedroom.

"Yes," she said quietly. "I know."

Ah, shit. Caleb closed his eyes. She had given up everything to be with him, her life in the sea and immortality. All she had ever asked from him in return was his love and a family.

If he denied her the second, would the first be enough for her?

*   *   *

Regina woke to a dented pillow and an empty mattress. Alone again.

That much of her life was back to normal.

She rubbed her face with her hand, wincing from the splinters of sensation in her cracked fingertips, the shard at her heart. Damn. She eased to a sitting position, ignoring the morning chorus of birds outside her window and the hit parade of pain from her various scrapes and bruises. Some of them were turning very interesting colors. Her toes, for instance. She hobbled to the mirror. Her throat.

She stared at her pale, hollow-eyed, battered reflection, blinking away the easy tears that welled in her eyes. She looked like crap. No wonder Dylan hadn't stuck around. Just like a man, she thought, fishing her sweatpants from the floor. Got what he wanted and . . .

But that wasn't fair. Last night was on her. Unlike some people, she knew how to face up to her actions, how to take responsibility. Thinking of the way she'd thrown herself at him, the things they had done in the dark, she blushed. At least she didn't have to worry about making eye contact this morning. This way was easier on everyone. On her. Nick would be getting up soon. Just because Dylan had managed to explain away his presence in their apartment last night didn't mean she was up to explaining his presence in her bed this morning.

She dragged the sweatpants over her hips. It was already after seven o'clock. On a regular morning, she'd have been up two hours ago. She'd just sneak down to the kitchen and—

Her bedroom door cracked open.

She turned and gaped at Dylan standing in the doorway with a steaming mug in his hands.

"I thought you could use this."

"What . . ."

"Tea with honey." He set it on the dresser, avoiding her eyes. "My mother used to make it when one of us had a sore throat."

Her heart slammed in her chest. Her head whirled.

He'd made her *tea*, was all she could think. Like his *mother* used to make. She could smell it, lemon, honey, and a hint of spice.

His gaze narrowed as she continued to gawk at him. "Are you all right?"

"Fine." She forced the word from her tightened throat.

But she wasn't. She was in danger, terrible danger.

Regina was a practical woman. She might have resisted Dylan's sulky good looks and sneering humor. She could have suppressed her sympathy for his wounded childhood, her helpless response to his stormy passion. Over time, she might even get over his talent for showing up in the right place at exactly the right time.

But his awkward consideration destroyed her defenses.

She pressed her trembling lips together. *Shit.* She was at very real risk of falling deeply, hopelessly in love with him.

*   *   *

"We'll be fine," Antonia told Regina brusquely, sounding for a moment so much like her daughter that Dylan's brows twitched together. "Maggie's here. Lucy's here. We'll be open for dinner."

Regina leaned her slight weight against the stainless steel counter, ignoring the knife that flashed like lightning not six inches from her hip, chopping, chopping. "Then you need me to do prep."

"You can do it when you get back. Caleb wants to see you now. To take your statement."

Dylan didn't give a damn what his brother wanted. Caleb could not protect Regina.

"Can't." Regina snatched a piece of red pepper from the cutting board and ate it. "I have a doctor's appointment."

"What for?"

"Oh . . ." She wiped her hands on the legs of her jeans, avoiding her mother's gaze. "Follow-up. I think she wants to make sure my toes haven't fallen off."

Dylan lifted an eyebrow. So she hadn't told Antonia about her pregnancy yet. Only him. And only because she hadn't had a choice. He felt the prod of responsibility like a goad.

"And what will you be doing while Regina is at the doctor's?" Margred murmured.

Dylan's gaze slid past Lucy to find Margred beside a screen of shelves with an ease that was almost . . . troubling. Except that no man, especially a brother, would spare a glance for Lucy when Margred was in the room. Lucy was tall and inoffensive. Human. Insignificant. Margred was . . . herself. Although apparently Caleb wasn't letting his beautiful wife get enough sleep these days. Faint shadows lay like bruises under her eyes.

In the large commercial kitchen, there was enough space and enough noise for them to speak privately. He joined her by the shelves, lowering his voice so the others would not hear. "I'm going with her."

Margred tilted her head. "If what Caleb says is true, Conn will expect you to give him a report."

"I'm giving him more than that."

Dylan had it figured out now. He'd had time to think in the long quiet night with Regina sleeping beside him, holding him in place with the lightest pressure of her palm against his heart. He could feel that pressure now, squeezing his chest until he couldn't breathe. Somehow she had made him feel responsible for her. Made him care. That didn't mean he needed to stay with her forever, tangled in a net of human expectations and emotions, trapped on shore.

"I'm taking her to Sanctuary," he explained. "Where she will be safe."

Where he would be free.

Margred's dark eyes widened. "Have you told her so?"

"Not yet."

"Ah." Margred regarded him steadily a moment. Her full lips curved. "Good luck with that."

*　*　*

"You could have been nicer to your sister," Regina said as they climbed the hill toward town hall.

When Dylan left the island, over twenty years ago, the building had not existed. Most of the weathered gray houses and shops at the center of town were the same. But there were more cars than he remembered, more telephone wires, more flags and flower boxes, more signs and pedestrians crowding the narrow street, cutting him off, closing him in. He could barely see the sky or smell the sea.

Slouching beside Regina, he felt like a ten-year-old boy being dragged clothes shopping or a wild animal being paraded on a leash. They could not walk more than a few yards without someone wanting to stop, talk, exclaim. He didn't want to hear about his sister.

"I was nice to her," he growled.

"Yeah? Considering she—"

A pretty young woman blocked their way with a baby

stroller. "Oh, my God, Reggie, your *neck*! You look terrible. Are you okay?"

Regina sighed. "Thanks, Sarah, I'm—"

The young woman's gaze slid sideways. She smiled and fingered her shoulder-length hair. "You must be Dylan. I heard you carried her all the way to the Mitchells' house."

"Yeah, I was pretty out of it," Regina said. "Look, we—"

"It was just so awful. I mean, you don't expect anything like that to happen here." Sarah smiled again at Dylan. "Do you?"

"Actually, I do."

"Okay." Regina grabbed his arm. "Great seeing you, Sarah. Come by the shop sometime."

Dylan regarded the small, strong hand on his arm as she hauled him away. He liked having her hold on to him. And he resented that he liked it.

"So, about your sister . . ." she said.

"What about her?"

"It was nice of her to help us out."

"Why nice? You're paying her."

"Yes, but—"

"Hey, Regina." A ruddy, round-faced man carrying a hard hat and a repair bucket hailed her from the street. "That was some excitement at your place yesterday. Everybody all right?"

More cars crawled by. More people stopped to stare. Dylan was overcome by the smells and press of bodies.

"Just fine, thanks, Doug."

His gaze switched to Dylan. "You the guy that found her?"

Dylan stared down his nose. "Yes. And you are . . . ?"

"Doug does cable repair on the island," Regina explained. "Eats at Antonia's two, three times a week."

"That's right." Doug shifted his weight and the bucket. "Hoping to eat lunch there today, as a matter of fact."

"We won't open until dinner," Regina said. "But if you stop by tomorrow, I can—"

Dylan had had enough.

"Excuse us," he said and walked away.

Since his hand was clamped over Regina's on his arm, she had no choice but to go with him.

He wanted air. He wanted the sea. He wanted to get Regina away from the people who pressed around them and the circumstances that hedged them in. He wanted her. Still. Again.

Since he could not have what he wanted, he found the nearest escape, a turn off the main road that led to the island church and a cemetery dreaming on the side of a hill.

Dylan stopped among the crooked stones and rough grass, breathing in the silence and the scent of juniper.

"Well." Regina exhaled. "That was rude."

He wanted her naked. She didn't have a clue.

"Not as rude as they were. Not half as rude as I wanted to be. How do you stand it?" he demanded. "How do you stand them? All those people. All they cared about was gossip and their own convenience. Not one of them cared about you."

Her chin cocked. "Oh, and you do."

"I . . ." His mouth opened. His brows drew together. Was he like her shallow friend, her hungry customer, focused only on his own concerns and appetites?

Wasn't he?

And why should that bother him? It hadn't bothered her last night. Or the night of his brother's wedding. He snapped his mouth shut.

Regina smiled, an odd little twist of lips that knotted his insides. "Yeah, that's what I thought."

She sighed again and leaned against the low stone wall that bordered the graveyard. "Tell me about your relationship with your sister."

What was she after now? "Lucy? I barely know her."

"So you keep saying." Regina tilted her head. "You just haven't told me why."

"I . . ." He kicked at the grass. "She was a year old when I left."

"Yeah, well, she grew up. You should, too. Just because you were taken from your family at the age of thirteen is no excuse for spending the rest of your life in a state of arrested emotional development."

Arrested emotional . . . He ground his teeth together. But the wry understanding in Regina's eyes eroded his anger and his defenses.

"I hardly see the point of forming a relationship now," he said stiffly.

"Because you don't need her."

He did not allow himself to need anyone. "Yes."

Regina met his gaze, her dark, expressive eyes surprisingly compassionate. "Did you ever think maybe *she* needs you?"

His head throbbed. "She has Caleb. And our father."

"And that's enough," Regina prodded him.

It was more than he had. But he could not, would not, let himself say so. He was selkie, he thought, half desperately. He had made his choice more than twenty years ago.

"She doesn't appear to be suffering," he said.

"How would you know? You didn't even look at her in the kitchen."

Dylan frowned. He hadn't. All his attention had been on Margred. When he looked at his sister, when he even tried to look at her, his gaze slipped away. She was like an ice sculpture, colorless, opaque.

"She is not interesting to me."

"Don't you think that's kind of strange?"

"Only by human standards." Yet he could look at his brother. "When I see her—sometimes when I even think about her—I get a headache," he confessed. He felt it now, again, an odd pressure building like a headache in his skull, tempting him to avert his gaze, his focus, to something, anything else. "It's almost like a glamour."

"A what?"

"A spell, you would call it." His mouth felt dry. "To make you look away. But this—this is different."

Regina's brow pleated. "Could your sister be selkie?"

His stomach revolted. His temples pounded. Everything in him rejected the very idea.

"No," he said positively.

"Why not?"

He reared his head like a harpooned animal. "I would know. My people would know."

"But you said yourself you don't know her very well," Regina said reasonably. "Maybe while you're here you could spend some time—"

"No."

"Why not?" she asked again. Stubborn. Irresistible. Hopeful. *Human.* The sight of her caused a fissure in

Dylan's chest as deep and painful as the dissonance in his head.

"Because we won't be here long enough." He faced her, his mouth a tight, grim line. "I am taking you to Sanctuary."

13

~~~~~

REGINA REGARDED THE BROODING EYES AND set mouth of the man she was falling in love with and felt a surge of exasperation. Never mind the choices his mother had made when he was thirteen.

"Running away is not a solution," she told him.

"I am not running away." His voice was flat. His eyes were stormy. "I am taking you where you will be safe."

"To Sanctuary," she said.

He nodded once, as if he didn't trust himself to speak or her to hear. Regina's stomach gave a warning flip. He wasn't going to give her anything she didn't ask for. Not information or anything else. Even last night, she'd practically had to beg him to make love to her.

Well, that had to change. Maybe he didn't love her, but he wanted her. And she had some pride, after all.

But right now she had more important things to worry about than her pride.

She set her jaw. "Where's that?"

"It is an island off the Hebrides. The coast of Scotland," he explained. "You will be safe there. You and the child."

"His name is Nick."

She was fascinated to see a flush spread across his hard cheekbones. "I meant the child you carry."

Right. Potential Super Selkie Baby. Regina suppressed a sudden pang. She couldn't let her own growing feelings for Dylan blind her to his true priorities.

"I can't just leave," she protested. "I have . . ." A jumble of images and concerns pressed on her: Nick, her mother, the restaurant. "A life."

"I'd like you to keep it."

Fear feathered her nerves; shortened her breath. She shook it from her head. "I have responsibilities."

"Your first responsibility is to the child."

Her heart beat faster. "I have two children," she reminded him.

"You would not have to leave Nick."

At least he remembered to use her son's name this time.

"Damn straight," she said.

"He can come with you," Dylan said.

"You." Not *"us."*

"To Scotland," Regina said.

"To Sanctuary."

"No. No way. I can't just uproot him. His home is here, his friends, his school . . . Everything he's ever known."

"He is young. He will adjust."

"Like you did?"

He hesitated. "Yes."

She didn't buy it. "You were thirteen. And selkie, as

you're so fond of pointing out. Are there other humans on this Sanctuary of yours? Other children?"

Dylan shifted his shoulders, staring out at the tilting headstones and blowing grass. "Not many."

Uh-huh. "Any?" she pressed.

His eyes were black with suppressed emotion. "He would be safe there," he said, which was no answer at all.

"There's no reason to believe he won't be safe here, is there?"

Dylan was silent.

Her heartbeat drummed. "Is there?"

His face set. "It's my responsibility to protect you. You and your child. Children," he amended before she could correct him.

Regret welled in her heart like blood. His acknowledgment of Nick was not enough. He'd said "protect," not love. He did not love her. She could not expect him to. If he did . . .

It wouldn't make any difference. She had her priorities, too.

At least he was stepping up. It was more than Alain ever offered to do.

Regina stuck out her chin. "Then figure out how to protect us here. Because we're staying."

*   *   *

The woman was impossible.

What she asked was . . . impossible.

Dylan glared at her stumping up the hill, her usual grace hobbled by her gauze-wrapped toes. The collar of bruises showed plainly above the scooped neck of her tank top. Her eyes were shadowed and strained. But nothing seemed to slow her down for long.

Brave girl. She had more courage than most men, as much appetite for life as any selkie, more strength of mind and stubborn spirit than . . . well, than anyone he'd ever known.

But she was still only human. She could die.

Fear and admiration coalesced in a hot, tight ball in Dylan's gut. "You have a touching—if misplaced—faith in my ability to save you."

She turned to look at him. The sun gleamed in her cap of dark hair and warmed her ivory skin to gold. "You rescued me before."

"I did not face a demon for you before."

"Scared?" Her tone was teasing, her eyes deadly serious.

He was terrified. Terrified of failing her, terrified of losing her. His hands clenched into fists at his sides.

"I am not . . . trained for this," he said with difficulty. "You need someone . . ." *Better. Stronger.* "Someone else."

"I don't think so." They walked on, past gardens edged with day lilies and yards full of rusting cars and lobster traps. "At least you have a stake in this thing."

A *stake*? He stared at her in disbelief. That's what she called this sickening weight of responsibility, this agonized awareness of being found wanting, insufficient, at fault . . .

"There must be somebody you could ask for advice," she continued, apparently oblivious to the storm raging inside him.

He forced himself to fasten on her words, to quell the nausea of his stomach. "There is," he replied. "The prince."

"You have a *prince*? Of course you do," she answered

her own question. "Because this situation wasn't unreal enough before."

He wished he knew some way to reassure her.

"Conn ap Llyr, lord of Sanctuary, prince of the merfolk. He took me under his patronage after my mother died."

"Like a . . . father figure?"

Dylan pictured the aloof, inscrutable selkie ruler isolated in his tower at Caer Subai. "I was never tempted to call him 'Daddy,' " he said with perfect truth.

Regina studied him a moment. Something flickered in her eyes, a perception that made him squirm, a sympathy that tore old wounds and half-healed scars. He stiffened in rejection. He was no longer that fourteen-year-old boy crying for his mother. He was selkie. He did not need her *pity*.

But all she said was, "Can't argue with you there. Mine split when I was three years old." He thought he heard her sigh. "Must be a family tradition."

As if he would leave her.

He'd intended to leave her. But . . .

"Must it?" he heard himself ask and held his breath for her answer.

She smiled crookedly. "I guess we'll find out."

Perversely, he was irritated. He did not need her sympathy. But he would not mind if she admitted to needing him.

She paused at the curb of the clinic. "You want to contact this prince of yours while I'm in my doctor's appointment?"

He shook his head. "It's not like I can call him on his cell phone. I have to go down to the beach."

"So go."

He opened the clinic's outer door for her. "I'm coming with you."

"No, you're not. I don't want you in the room while I'm flat on my back in a paper drape getting a pelvic exam."

The image made him clench uncomfortably. But he said, "I've seen you in less."

"Forget it."

He narrowed his eyes. Was she actually blushing? "Then I will wait for you."

"Suit yourself. But . . ." She broke off.

A thin, bearded man in a stained hooded sweatshirt was walking toward them across the waiting room. Dylan recognized him from the group around the fire in the homeless encampment.

Regina trembled.

Dylan put his arm around her without thinking. The man passed them, his gaze lowered. Dylan scanned the room. There was something there, something in the air that wasn't right. But when he breathed in, all he smelled was Regina's shampoo like apricots.

"It's not Jericho," he told her quietly.

"I know. Caleb said he brought another patient in yesterday." Her throat moved as she swallowed. "The day before yesterday."

She had lost almost a day in the caves.

Dylan tightened his arm around her.

A woman in a printed smock looked up from behind the counter and smiled. "Hi, Regina. The doctor is ready for you now."

And he had to let her go.

*   *   *

Regina sat up, hitching her paper sheet around her waist and over her thighs. Thank God that was over.

Donna Tomah scrubbed her hands at the tiny sink. "Everything seems to be normal. I'd say you're about five weeks along."

Stars wheeling, rocks shifting, Dylan plunging thick and hot inside her . . .

"Four," Regina corrected.

Donna glanced over her shoulder. "Your due date is calculated from the beginning of your last cycle. We can't really pinpoint the date of conception."

She could. Heat crept into her face.

"Do you want to talk?" Donna asked gently.

"What about?"

"Your options. If you're not comfortable talking with me, there's a family planning clinic in Rockland . . ."

"Oh." And then, as the implications sank in, *"Oh."*

Just for a moment, she let herself be tempted, felt the possibility expand her lungs like air. Her old life beckoned. To have *options . . .*

"No." She met the doctor's eyes. "It's not like I haven't done this before."

"Hm." The doctor shut off the water with her elbow. "If you're sure . . ."

Regina rubbed the bare skin below her collarbone. "Sure."

Donna dried her hands on a paper towel. "All right, then. Nancy will get your blood and a urine specimen. You should pick up some prenatal vitamins. Why don't you get dressed, and I'll give you a sample to get you started."

"Thanks."

Regina hopped off the table as the doctor left the

room, hissing at the pain of her swollen toes. Before she finished dressing, the door reopened. She clutched her pants, oddly uncomfortable at being caught in her underwear by the doctor who had just seen her naked. *Stupid.*

Donna appeared flustered, too. Her face flushed as she set a little paper cup of medicine beside the exam table. "Here you go."

Regina reached for the vitamins. They were small. Like yellow aspirin. "Three?"

"One for now, two for later," the doctor said smoothly, avoiding Regina's eyes. She filled a cup at the sink. "In case you don't want to face the gossip at the drugstore right away. Water?"

Regina accepted the cup, aware of the doctor's eyes on her as she forced the tablet down her throat.

"Good," Donna said, whisking the water away. She sealed the remaining pills in a tiny plastic bag. "Don't forget to take these now. And tell Nancy to set up another appointment in a couple of days."

"So soon?" Regina asked, surprised. When she was pregnant with Nick, she'd only seen a doctor every six weeks or so. But then she'd been on her own in Boston, trying desperately to make ends meet and grabbing appointments at the free clinic.

"With all you've been through lately . . . Better safe than sorry."

Anxiety snagged her breathing. "You said everything looked normal."

"Everything looks fine," Donna assured her. "Any questions? Concerns?"

Regina swallowed a hiccup of completely inappropriate laughter. No way could she share her real concerns. "Is there any way to tell the baby's sex yet?"

"I can schedule an ultrasound in the middle of the second trimester. Let's say, at eighteen weeks." Donna scrawled the prescription and handed it to Regina. "Do you want another boy? Or are you hoping for a girl this time?"

Just for a moment, Regina felt the draw of the baby at her breast and the warm weight of it in her arms, saw the cap of soft, dark hair and the fan of lashes against a smooth, flushed cheek.

A boy or a girl? *"A daughter of the house of Atargatis, who will change the balance of power between Heaven and Hell"*?

Or a black-eyed boy who would run away to sea and break her heart?

Some choice.

She moistened her lips. "You know what they say. As long as the baby's healthy . . ."

And safe.

Her heart clenched like a fist. Please, God, keep her baby safe.

*   *   *

Caleb shifted the paper on his desk a half-inch to the left and tapped the top sheet.

Regina's heart drummed in time with his fingers.

"If I take this to the DA, he's going to assume you're lying or crazy or both," Caleb said.

Regina's stomach dropped. Her chin jutted. "Dylan said you would believe me. Because of Margred."

"I do believe you." Caleb's voice was firm, his eyes

kind. "Which is why I'm suggesting you reconsider your statement before you sign."

Regina trusted Caleb. She always had. But under the circumstances . . .

"I want to talk to Dylan," she said.

Caleb frowned before rising stiffly from his desk and opening his door. "Edith, would you—"

Before he could finish his instruction to the clerk, Dylan strode into the room, his mouth a tight line, his gaze locking instantly on Regina's.

She released a breath she hadn't been aware of holding.

"That took long enough," he drawled. "Should I be jealous?"

"Your brother thinks the DA won't like my story," she said.

Caleb closed the door on Edith Paine, hovering in the outer office. "Parts of it. Sit down," he said to Dylan.

Dylan raised an eyebrow and draped himself in the chair next to Regina's. In the small, cramped office she could feel the heat under his cool. "So don't tell the DA. Drop the charges or whatever you call them."

"I can't do that." Caleb positioned himself behind his desk. "Criminal charges are filed by the state, not the victim. And with three unrelated attacks in two months making headlines across the state, you can bet the DA is bringing charges against somebody."

Regina sat forward. "But Jericho isn't really guilty, is he? I mean, if he is possessed—"

"Was possessed," Dylan corrected. "The demon left him."

"That's the part the DA is going to have problems with," Regina said.

Caleb sighed. "Actually, the DA will assume—correctly—that the defense will use demonic possession as an insanity plea. The court will take into account that this is Jones's first offense. They'll consider his military service, probably do an alcohol and drug assessment. Even so, he's facing charges of aggravated assault and kidnapping."

Dylan shrugged. "You said yourself the charges have nothing to do with us."

"Unless you're called to the stand. Kidnapping is a Class A crime. The defense will try to reduce it to a lesser charge by arguing that Jones voluntarily released the victim in a safe place."

Dylan lifted an eyebrow. "Since when is dumping a woman in a flooding cave considered 'release in a safe place'?"

"It's not," Caleb said. "I'm telling you what the defense will argue. You'll both be called to testify. Do you really want to explain under oath where and how you found her?"

"Your oaths do not constrain me," Dylan said.

"No? How about being locked up for contempt of court?"

"You guys want to settle this over a game of hoops?" Regina asked. "Or pistols at dawn?"

They turned to her with almost identical expressions of annoyance.

"What if I refuse to testify?" she asked.

Caleb rubbed his jaw. "That would definitely weaken the prosecution's case. The DA might be willing to settle in Sessions Court in return for a guilty plea to a lesser charge—say, misdemeanor assault. The case wouldn't actually go to trial."

She reached for the cross around her neck. It was in her pocket. She flushed and tucked her hands into her armpits. "And Jericho would go free?"

"He'd serve some time. Long enough, maybe, for me to get him into the new veterans' housing program downstate."

"Whether Jones is in jail or not is irrelevant," Dylan said.

"Not irrelevant to him," Regina muttered.

Dylan's black eyes glinted. "His fate is not my care or responsibility. Yours is."

"What about the rest of the island? Other threats? Other demons?" Caleb asked.

Dylan shrugged. "There has been . . . activity on and around World's End before this. But they want Regina now."

"And are willing to possess anybody else to get at her," Caleb said grimly.

"Not anybody. There are limits to their power."

Caleb's eyes narrowed. "The cross."

"And my tattoo," Regina said.

Dylan nodded. "They could not kill you. And they did not anticipate me. They cannot afford to attract Heaven's attention with a series of botched attempts. They will choose the next time and their next target very carefully."

"Are you trying to make me feel better?"

Dylan's expression did not change. "I'm trying to scare you."

"So that I'll run away with you to Sanctuary."

Caleb cleared his throat.

Dylan ignored him. "Yes."

"For how long?" Regina demanded.

"Until we know you and the child are safe."

"And how long will that take?" She pressed her hand to her stomach. "Nine months?"

He was silent.

"Thirteen *years*?"

He glared, his dark eyes stormy. "Sanctuary is the best solution."

She squeezed her hands together in her lap at the tumult in those eyes. "The safest, maybe. Not the best. Not for me or my children. In thirteen years, my mother could be dead. If the heartbreak doesn't kill her sooner."

"Regina . . ."

Her heart shook at his tone. She could not afford to give in to him. She would not give in. She had crawled and fought and worked damn hard for the life she had made with her son. She would not give it up. "No."

He flung himself from his chair; stalked to the window. "I could leave you here."

"But you won't," she said softly.

He glanced over his shoulder. A corner of his mouth rose. "No."

Her heart beat faster. "Because of the child."

He inclined his head. "If you like."

She could not read him. She did not know him. How could she be falling in love with him?

Caleb cleared his throat again. "You'll need a place to stay."

"For how long?" Regina asked.

"Nine months?" Dylan smiled in wicked echo. "Thirteen years?"

And then what? He'd leave her like his mother left his father? Like her father left her mother?

"You can't just move in with us," Regina said. "It's not fair to Nick."

"Nick is not the one with the problem," Dylan shot back.

"I have to protect him," she said stubbornly.

Even if it was too late to protect her own heart.

Caleb rubbed the back of his neck. "I don't see how we're going to protect either one of them."

Regina glanced at Dylan, startled by the easy way Caleb allied himself with his brother over her defense. Dylan hardly seemed to notice. *Men.*

"I'll have to ward her building," Dylan said.

Caleb raised his eyebrows. "You can do that?"

His jaw set. "I must."

"And if she has to leave the apartment? Or the restaurant?"

A long look passed between the brothers.

"Then I will be with her," Dylan said. "Attached to her like a lamprey. Or a lover."

"Not in the apartment," Regina said.

"You'll need a place to stay," Caleb said again at the same time. "Somewhere close."

"Is that an invitation, little brother?"

"If you need one," Caleb said steadily.

"I don't need anything from you," Dylan said. But the darkness in his eyes made the words a lie.

"You should go home. To your parents' house," Regina said.

Dylan sneered. "The way you did?"

He would not let her pity him. Fine. She wouldn't permit him to goad her.

"There's no shame in going home when you need to."

She could say that now. She could even believe it. The realization lightened her heart.

"This was never my home. I'd rather pay to stay at the Inn."

"Full up this time of year," Regina said. "Your father has room."

"Our old room," Caleb said. "Nothing's changed."

Dylan's face was blank and hard as the sea cliffs. "That's what I'm afraid of."

14

DYLAN KNELT IN THE WEEDS AND GRAVEL BE-
hind the restaurant, running his long-fingered hands over
the brick of the building the way Regina imagined another man might stroke a horse or the hood of a car. He
looked sweaty, preoccupied, and very male.

She dropped the black plastic trash bags at her feet to
watch.

At the sound, he turned his head. "Come to see me on
my knees?"

She tilted her chin at a challenging angle. "I've seen
you on your knees before."

"Ah. Remember that, do you?" he said in a satisfied
tone.

Remember his dark head moving between her legs,
the whirling stars, the whispering sea, and the heat rising
in her blood, created by his mouth and hands and breath?

"Um. Maybe. Vaguely."

His rare grin cracked like lightning across his face;

sizzled along her nerves. "Perhaps I should refresh your memory."

She swallowed hard. "I thought you had to go commune with your prince or whatever."

"I do. But I must set a ward first. I will not leave you unprotected."

He went back to his bricks. She picked up the black garbage bags and pitched them into the Dumpster, ignoring the gulls that squawked and settled on the roofs around.

Dylan was tapping and pressing on the mortared wall like a safecracker. She set her hands on her hips to watch.

"Go back inside."

She glanced nervously, compulsively, around the alley. "Am I in danger?"

"No." He looked at her and sighed. "You are distracting."

"Oh." A warm feeling melted her belly. "Okay."

She took a step toward the door and stopped, observing his careful hands and frowning, slightly frustrated expression. The warm feeling spread. He was an immortal creature of the sea whose natural home was a magic island. Yet here he was on his knees in the dirt of the alley because she would not go away with him. He was putting his own life on hold for her sake. Her sake and her son's. Under the brooding and the bluster, Dylan Hunter was a good man. Not only hot and exciting, but principled and even . . . tender.

A tender, principled guy who was also hot. Which made him about as rare in her life as a selkie.

She walked back. His dark brows twitched together in annoyance. Smiling, she brushed a kiss on the top of his head. Dylan went as still as the broken concrete underfoot, his hair warm against her lips.

She straightened. "Thanks," she said and went back to her kitchen.

*   *   *

Regina's kiss—her warm lips, her sweet smell, her simple words of gratitude—fell like rain on Dylan's parched heart and churned up a storm in his soul.

Or where his soul would be if he had one.

Alone in the alley, he closed his eyes, pressing his forehead to the rough brick. Her affection would not endure, he reminded himself. Nothing human endured. Families were torn apart. Children grew up. Parents died.

Better to live in the moment as the sea folk did than pin your heart and hopes on . . .

Love.

And yet the moment when she kissed him, not from lust or need, had been almost unbearably sweet, ripe with trust, pregnant with affection.

Pregnant. The sharp stones of the alley pricked his knees. The birds on the roof watched with bright, merciless eyes. Regina was pregnant with his child, and she would not go with him to Sanctuary.

He was responsible for her. And if he failed to protect her, he would be responsible for the deaths of the only two women who had ever mattered in his life.

He splayed his fingers on the wall.

He was not a warden. The foundation between his hands was man-made bricks and mortar, not stone and sand. He did not know if what he attempted could even be done.

The selkie flowed as the sea flowed. Their gift was like water, powerful, changeable, and fluid. Like the wind or a woman's lust, it was fickle. Ephemeral. But to protect Regina, this ward must stand against time and the power of Hell.

He was on his knees with his hands raised. As if he prayed. Perhaps he did. Perhaps he should.

He opened his mind, sent it spiraling down and down, feeling his gift like water trapped in a sponge, saturating each cell and fiber, lubricating each joint and sinew. Conn said the magic of the merfolk had declined as their numbers declined. But Dylan could feel the power in his blood like a silent sea waiting for the pull of the moon.

He tried a cautious internal pressure, making a space—between heart and lungs, between liver and spleen—for the power to fill as water fills a footprint in the sand. Slowly it seeped in, a trace, a glimmer, a pool, growing in the gaps of his ribs, in the hollow of his gut. The power rose, and hope rose, too, swirling, eddying inside him, but not enough, not quite enough, like water blocked by a twig, a trickle when he needed a torrent.

Sweat slicked his palms; beaded his forehead. He tried to force power, to wring it from his bones, to squeeze it from his heart, but like water, the magic eluded his grasp, reabsorbed into his tissues.

"You need someone else," he had told her.

And her voice replied, firm in its faith. *"I don't think so."*

He groaned. He wanted, needed . . .

More.

MORE.

Power burst through him like a wave through a flume,

sluiced his senses, roared down his veins, erupted from his mouth, shot from his eyes, exploded from his fingertips. Everything, heart and brain and loins, was swept up and carried away like burning branches borne by a flood.

He let the power take him where and how it would; until he was left, tumbled and empty, on the stones of the alley.

The magic retreated, leaving him beached and gasping. He sprawled on his stomach, with rough green weeds poking between his fingers and broken glass glittering before his dazed eyes like stars.

He heard a scrape, an indrawn breath, and turned his head.

His sister, Lucy, stood in the shadow of the door well, her usually soft, overcast eyes blazing like the sea at noon.

The ground tilted beneath his cheek.

She blinked, and it was as if a shutter dropped over her face, transforming her brightness, making her once again a tall, rather ordinary young woman in a green Clippers T-shirt and a white kitchen apron.

"Are you all right?" she asked anxiously.

His hands were scraped raw. His lip was split. A headache drove spikes through his skull. But buoyed by the power that had surged through him—*the wonder of it, the rightness of it*—he barely noticed.

"Did you see . . . Did you *feel* that?" he demanded.

She took a step back as he lunged to his feet, retreating farther into the shadows, into herself. Her lashes swept down like a curtain closing behind shutters.

"I'm glad you're all right," she said.

Like the world hadn't tilted on its axis. Like nothing had happened at all.

Like nothing happened. Fear raked him, more painful than the gravel embedded in his hands.

He turned his head sharply and inspected the building.

There. Relief shook him. *The warden's mark,* etched deep in brick and mortar. The sign of power was scoured into the eastern corner of the foundation, where it would draw strength from the sea, the earth, and the rising sun.

Even though he had placed it there himself, carved the connecting spirals with his need and his gift, the sight robbed him of breath.

He looked back at his sister.

She smiled uncertainly and turned to go.

Driven by an urgency he did not understand, he called after her. "Lucy."

She wavered in the doorway, looking quiet and inoffensive and as if she would rather be anywhere but here.

Regina's words beat in his brain.

"Do you . . ." He hesitated.

Need me? What a lame-ass question. He had robbed her of their mother. What possible use could he be to her now?

"Could I come stay with you awhile?"

She blinked again, slowly. "Stay?"

"In the house," he said, feeling like a fool.

"It's not my house. Or my decision."

"If you want me to ask . . . him, I'll ask him. But would you mind?"

"I wouldn't mind. But I didn't mean that. The decision's up to you." She smiled, an oddly aware, bitter little smile that lifted her face from ordinary to arresting. "It's always been up to you."

*   *   *

Regina frowned and applied antibiotic ointment from the kitchen first aid kit to Dylan's scrapes. He sat on a stool at the dining room counter, out of the way of the prep continuing in the kitchen. She had to stand between his thighs to dot ointment on his cheek. He flinched as she brushed an abrasion near his eye.

She winced in sympathy. "I don't know how you did this," she grumbled.

He grinned at her foolishly, making her heart lurch. "Neither do I."

"You sound disgustingly pleased with yourself."

"I am." He waited until his words caught her attention, until his gaze caught hers. "I warded the building."

"You . . ." Comprehension, relief, gratitude, all rushed in on her. "Wow. That's . . . wonderful."

"I didn't think I could," he confessed.

Her heart tightened at the aching uncertainty in his voice. She touched him lightly, unable to keep her fingers from lingering on the tender skin beside his eye, below his jaw. "Well, you did. Congratulations."

He caught her hand and pressed it to his cheek. The stubble of his beard rasped her palm. "You don't have to do this."

She swallowed and tugged her hand away to feather ointment on his broken lip, struggling to keep her tone light. "Yeah, I do. You took care of me, seems I should take care of you."

He touched his thumb to the side of her mouth, to her own cracked and throbbing lip. His mouth was so close to hers, and his eyes were close and dark and full of heat. "Now we match," he whispered, and his words and his look stopped her breath. Caught her heart.

She smiled crookedly. "I guess we do."

But she knew better than to believe it.

She wiped her fingers on a napkin and reached for the top to the ointment. However tempting she found this strange, addictive new mood of his, it would pass. Sooner or later, Dylan would remember that he was selkie and she was only the human incubator of a child who might one day be useful to his people.

And then he would break her heart.

She dropped the ointment back in the box. "So, are you still going down to the beach this afternoon?"

"I must." Dylan hesitated. "The prince will expect a report."

"Sure. No problem."

Not his problem anyway. She'd made it clear her family was her priority. Dylan had been equally up front about having other priorities. Other allegiances. Now that he'd delivered on his promise to protect her, she wasn't looking at him to hold her hand or change her life. She didn't need him hanging around, getting underfoot, in her way, in her hair, in her heart . . .

"Regina." Dylan's voice shivered through her, shaking her resolve. "What is it?"

"Nothing." She snapped the first aid kit shut and stepped from between his thighs. "I'm fine. I don't want to bother you."

"Woman." His low growl vibrated in her ear. "You have badgered, pestered, distracted, and annoyed me since I met you. Why stop now?"

A reluctant smile tugged at her lips. She stole a look at him and saw an answering smile lurking in his eyes.

Sighing, she relaxed against his restraining arm. "Well, since you put it so nicely . . ."

He laughed, attracting Antonia's glance through the kitchen pass.

Regina lowered her voice. "If you're going through town, could you stop at Wiley's? I need vitamins."

"Pills?" Concern leaped into his black eyes. "Are you sick?"

"No, I'm pregnant. I need prenatal vitamins."

"But you're all right," he pressed.

"Fine." She was almost embarrassed now to have brought it up. Since when did she need a guy to run her errands? "Well, I've had a little cramping, but—"

"Have you called the doctor?"

She blinked, confused by his urgency. And more touched than she could say. Although, of course, he had Selkie Baby to consider. "I gave her a call while you were outside. She said a little cramping and nausea were perfectly normal and to keep taking my vitamins. So—"

"What if I buy the wrong kind?"

She sighed. "Listen, never mind. I can—"

"No, I'll do it. You need vitamins, I'll buy vitamins. Prenatal ones." His tone was grim, his gaze almost panicked.

Regina couldn't decide which was more adorable, his masculine discomfort with his errand or his obvious determination to do the right thing. Good thing she wasn't sending him out for tampons. To tease him, to test him, she whispered wickedly, "Or you could stay here and explain to my mother why I need them."

His face paled beneath his golden tan. "Better your mother," he muttered, "than those squawking gulls in town."

"At least you can charm the gulls."

He raised one eyebrow. "I can charm your mother."

He probably could, Regina thought, contemplating that dark, handsome face. He could charm anyone. He'd certainly charmed the pants off her.

"Not after she learns you knocked me up."

He leaned closer, making her heart race. "You still find me charming."

Her breath went. "Ha."

"You can't help yourself." His breath skated over her lips. His lips skimmed her jaw. Desire drizzled like honey under her skin. "My power over women is irresistible."

She heard the laughter throbbing in his voice and under the laughter something else, something deeper, something almost like . . . yearning.

She felt herself leaning, melting into him, and closed her eyes. "Your ego is unbelievable."

"Let me prove it to you," he murmured, his hands circling her ribs, his voice warm and seductive at her ear. "Let me charm you, Regina. Let me love you."

Oh. Her heart contracted sharply.

"Oh." Lucy's voice, high and mortified. "Antonia sent us to . . . I didn't mean to interrupt."

Regina disentangled herself from Dylan. Lucy stood in the kitchen door, with Margred behind her.

"You're not interrupting," Regina lied, heat creeping up her face. "I was just giving Dylan an errand to do for me in town."

Margred arched her brows. "Is that what you were giving him?"

"I don't pay you to stand and talk," Antonia bawled from the line. "Let's clean those tables. We open in an hour."

Margred strolled forward, as elegant carrying a rag and a bottle of sanitizer as a sommelier with a folded napkin around a bottle of Grand-Cru.

"Is that wise?" Margred murmured to Dylan. "To leave her . . . now?"

"It's safe." Dylan looked over her head to Regina, directing his assurance to her. There was a new confidence in his voice, she realized, an energy she hadn't heard before.

"I warded the building," he said.

Margred inhaled. "I'm impressed. That was you?"

"Not only me. I thought . . . I felt . . . You?"

She shook her head, eyes wide.

Regina watched their byplay, lost.

Dylan frowned. "Then . . ."

Nick barged through the kitchen door, his sneakers squeaking on the old wood floors, and fixed Dylan with wide, hopeful eyes. "Nonna said you were going to the store. Can I come?"

Dylan glanced down. "Not this time."

Regina winced. *Ouch.*

Nick hunched a shoulder in a boy's gesture. "Okay. Whatever."

Regina read his body language as easily as his heart: *I didn't want to anyway.* Better to pretend that you didn't want something, than to hope and have it denied . . .

This was what she was afraid of, she realized. That her son would fall in love as quickly as she had done.

"Maybe you could hold on to something for me until I get back," Dylan suggested.

Nick's chin came up. He was interested, but wary. No fool, her boy. "Like what?"

Dylan reached into his pocket and withdrew a silver

coin. A Morgan Liberty Head silver dollar. Regina had looked it up online. The thing was worth a couple hundred dollars, easy. She sucked in her breath.

Dylan's gaze clashed with hers.

She exhaled slowly, without speaking.

Nick examined the coin in his grubby palm and then looked up at Dylan. "What's this, like, a bribe?"

"If it was a bribe, I would have to give it to you," Dylan explained. "Which I can't, because your mother would skin us both."

Nick snickered.

"It's a marker. Like a promise," Dylan said. "You keep it safe until I ask for it, and then I take you out in my boat."

Nick's gaze flickered to his mom. "Is that okay?"

She hugged her arms across her chest to hold in her expanding heart. "It's your deal, kiddo."

"Okay. Cool." His fingers closed on the coin. A smile cracked his thin face as he stuck out his other hand. "Deal."

Dylan nodded once, his large, dark hand encompassing Nick's small, dirty one.

This was her son, Regina thought, almost dizzy with emotion. Her family, her life. She had never had a man in her life, never felt the need for one.

But now, watching Dylan shake hands with her son, she realized how easily he could make a place with them.

And how much it would hurt when he was gone.

15

❧

THE TEENAGER BEHIND THE REGISTER AT THE grocery store blinked purple-lined eyes at the coins on the counter. "You can't pay with those."

Impatience whipped through Dylan like wind through a sail. He quivered, desperate to be gone. Browsing the pharmacy aisles had been a nightmare. Too many labels. Too many choices. What if he guessed wrong? He glared at the girl standing between him and freedom and snarled, "Take the damn money."

Her painted eyes widened. Her jaw dropped. "Dad!" she hollered.

Dylan ground his teeth together. So much for his ability to charm.

A man with a build like a barrel and a receding hairline rolled over from the meat counter. "Problem here?"

"*He*—" The girl thrust her lip ring in Dylan's direction. "Wants to pay with *that*." She sneered at the fortune in silver plunked on the counter.

"They're dollars," Dylan said tightly.

American dollars. It wasn't like he'd offered her Caesars or doubloons.

Usually when he needed cash to buy propane or supplies, he sold a few coins to a dealer in Rockland. But the past few weeks on World's End had depleted his currency.

"So I . . ." The creases deepened at the corners of the man's eyes. "Dylan? I heard you were back."

Dylan regarded him blankly.

"George," the man said.

Dylan had gone to school with a boy named George. They'd shared a classroom from kindergarten through eighth grade, shared gum and homework answers and copies of *Penthouse* that George had smuggled from behind the counter of his father's store. Wiley's Grocery. George Wiley. *George.*

Dylan managed to unglue his tongue from the roof of his mouth. "Good to see you again."

"Yeah, you, too. Boy, you look just the same." George shook his head. "*Just* the same."

Because he'd aged only half the time, Dylan thought, with an odd lurch in his stomach.

George beamed at the girl with the purple eye shadow. "That's my daughter, Stephanie, who won't take your money."

She rolled her eyes. "Dad-deee."

His friend George was a father, Dylan thought dazedly. An overweight store owner with an adolescent daughter. *Nothing human endured . . .*

"So, you want us to run a tab for you?" George asked.

Dylan scowled. "What?"

His old friend nodded at the pile of coins on the

counter. "What you got there is probably worth half my inventory. I don't know exactly how much, and I sure as hell can't make change. So we'll open you an account, and you settle up when you can."

Maybe some things endured, Dylan realized. Like a boy's casually offered friendship, long after the boy had grown.

He swallowed past a constriction in his throat. "That would be . . . good. Thanks."

"What are friends for?" George made an entry in a ledger; glanced at the prenatal vitamins as he bagged them. "How's Regina?"

"Fine."

Pregnant.

"Good." George's grin widened. "Women and the island, they get to us all, buddy. You give her my best."

Dylan walked out, purchase in hand and George's good wishes in his ears.

This, then, was what Regina wanted for Nick. The net Dylan felt closing so tightly around him could also be a web of support. Maybe the gossip and aggravation, the friction and demands, were a tolerable trade-off for this sense of community. Of acceptance. Of belonging.

Or they would be, Dylan thought, if he were human.

* * *

When you lived for millennia in the sea, a few days to send a message was nothing. But this once, the human technology that had fouled the waves and roiled the ocean bottom would have come in handy.

Dylan tread water a mile offshore, his long, pale legs dangling like so much shark bait, his balls pulled tight with cold. His human form was another inconvenience that had to be endured. Details tended to dissipate over distance in the water. Dylan needed his human brain to frame and sharpen the images he sent to Conn.

Especially since the messengers he called would filter whatever information he gave them the same way they strained the ocean for food, keeping only what they could digest.

They came, their long, sleek backs and uneven dorsals occasionally breaking the water's bright surface: huge, slow acrobats of the sea with mild, deep eyes and flukes as individual as snowflakes. Two males, a female, and a calf, drawn by Dylan's call. Not near, not too near. Their weight could swamp him, their draft could drown him, the barnacles on their sides could scrape him raw. Even the baby weighed a ton.

One of the males struck the water in greeting, and the wash broke over Dylan's head, sending a roll of amusement through them all.

He surfaced, sputtering.

They did not question why or in what form Dylan was among them. Among the *whayleyn*, presence—being—was enough. Their vast acceptance surrounded him. Their collective concern enveloped him. They circled, letting their song absorb his story, weaving his message into the harmonies that knit together the Atlantic in the great deep blue, in the clear cold dark.

Dylan had no idea how the words and images of his report would be relayed to Conn, how "homeless" or "crucifix" transposed to notes in the whales' harmonies. But they understood the importance of the child-to-be. MOTHER LOVE FATHER CARE FAMILY JOY surged over him in waves. Their song filled his ears like the surf; flooded his heart with peace; floated with him to shore.

He stood in the shallows, heart full, mind emptied, muscles loose and relaxed. Tossing back his wet hair, he scanned the beach.

And saw his father sitting guard over his pile of clothes.

Shit.

Dylan's joy drained away like the waves frothing around his ankles. They were locked in a lonely amphitheater of rock and sand, with no one to witness their meeting but the spruce standing sentinel on shore and a few wisps of cloud.

Bart Hunter sat with his elbow on one raised knee, staring out to sea.

Dylan waded from the surf. He could not avoid the old man. The best he could do was ignore him. He bent for his jeans.

"She used to come here," Bart said. "Your mother."

Dylan didn't want to talk about his mother, didn't want to share her memory. Particularly not with his father.

He jammed his damp foot into his pant leg.

"Not just with you kids," Bart continued. "Before you were born."

Okay, Dylan really didn't want to hear this. He hitched his jeans over his other foot.

"She'd come ashore there . . ."

Against his will, Dylan glanced over his shoulder, following his father's gaze to his own route from the water.

Bart shook his head. "The most beautiful thing I'd

ever seen in my life, and she tells me she loves me." He laughed in wonder and disbelief, a sound harsh as a sob. "Me, who knew nothing but lobster and the tides. I weren't much older than our Lucy then. Left school in the seventh grade. Never left the island at all. But she . . ." His voice trailed, lost in memory. He did not use her name. He did not need to. There was only ever one "she" for him, then or now.

"You stole her sealskin," Dylan said, hard and cold. "You robbed her of her life."

"I gave her a new life and three children. It should have been enough."

"You robbed her of her self."

"And didn't she do the same to me? I never had a moment's peace after I saw her. She told me she loved me." Bart's voice cracked like ice in April. "But how could I believe her? She being what she was, and me being what I was."

Dylan opened his mouth to argue, outrage hot in his blood. His father was wrong. Had always been wrong.

And yet . . .

The words stopped his mouth, bitter and unspoken.

Didn't Dylan believe the same? A selkie could not love a human.

Bart held his gaze, a sad recognition in his faded eyes. And then he stared back out to sea. "Your brother says you need a place to stay. You can have your old room if you want it."

*   *   *

Dylan came downstairs with his bag packed while Regina was sweeping the floor. The grill was shut down, the front door was locked, the day's receipts were totaled . . . and another man was preparing to walk out the door.

Regina looked from Dylan's zippered duffel to his closed expression and felt her heart clutch.

Get over it, she told herself. She should be used to men leaving her by now.

Anyway, it was only for the night. This time. He'd be back in the morning. He said.

Dylan looked around the empty restaurant. His brows snapped together. "Should you be doing this yourself?"

His tone put her back up. Good. A fight would take her mind off her fear of closing alone, would distract her from the low, achy pain in her gut, would ease the loneliness that waited to swallow her when the door shut behind him.

"You see anybody else to do it?" she asked.

Now he looked annoyed. "Your mother . . ."

"Was here half the night last night and all day yesterday. Anyway, I'm almost done."

Dylan set down his bag. "Give it to me, then."

"I don't think so."

"Regina." He gripped the handle just above her hand, humor in his voice and temper in his eyes, hot and real and so close she could have kissed him. "You really want to get into a tug of war with me over a broom?"

She thought about it. "No."

"All right, then."

With a sigh, she released the broom. He swept the floor. She erased the day's specials from the board.

"Thanks for taking Nick out on your boat," she offered. "It was all he could talk about all night."

"We had a good time." Dylan emptied the dustpan into the trash. "I'll take you out tomorrow."

Regina wiped her chalky fingers on her apron. "Can't. I have work."

"You can't work all the time."

He followed her back to the kitchen and hung the broom in the mop closet. That closet . . . Regina suppressed a shiver.

Dylan frowned. "You look done in."

"I'm fine. Tired." She dragged up a smile. "Morning sickness seems to be hitting hard and early this time around."

"You are sick?"

His instant concern should have been gratifying. But she didn't want him hanging around because he felt *sorry* for her. "I'm fine," she repeated.

"Is it the baby?"

"Yes. No. I don't know." Worry sharpened her nerves and her voice. "I have cramps, okay?" Guys hated cramps. "I've had them all day."

"Tell me what to do," he said.

If she had to tell him, what good was that?

"Nothing. I've seen the doctor. I don't need you to play nurse."

He looked at her steadily. Silent. Willing. And completely clueless.

Emotionally arrested at thirteen, she thought. No one to teach him. To touch him. Ever.

She sighed. "I could use a hug."

He put his arms around her, awkward as a boy at a sixth-grade dance.

She let her head drop on a man's strong chest for the first time since she was three years old. She wasn't used to leaning on people. On men.

She closed her eyes. He smelled like the sea.

They stood in the center of the kitchen, lightly linked, until by degrees their breathing meshed and matched, until he'd warmed her with his body. She'd observed before that his temperature was hotter than hers.

Gradually, her fears and worries, her annoyance and loneliness, slipped away. Her heartbeat quickened. His chest expanded. She could feel his erection growing long and hard against her stomach. Her hands fisted in his shirt at his back.

"I have something for you," he said.

She smiled without opening her eyes. "I noticed."

His amusement stirred her hair. "Not that. Not only that."

He eased her away from him, patting his pockets like another man searching for his keys or a lighter. Eventually, he found what he was looking for and pulled it out: a fine gold chain with a single pearl suspended in a glowing twist of metal.

A single, really beautiful, very large pearl.

Regina sucked in her breath. She put her hands behind her back so she wouldn't snatch it from him. She'd warned Nick repeatedly about the dangers of accepting gifts from strangers. Not that Dylan was a stranger any longer. But . . .

"Take it," he said. "You need a chain to replace the one that was broken."

"A chain, fine. This is . . ."

Too beautiful. Too much. Too painfully reminiscent of the kind of gift a man gave a woman he loved.

"It was my mother's," Dylan said. "It may have power to protect you, as your cross protects you."

"Oh." Her hands itched for it. "That's very . . . practical."

His eyes gleamed. "I hoped you would think so."

She dug her crucifix from her pocket and threaded it on the chain with trembling fingers. The rounded pearl and the glowing cross slid together with a faint *ching*.

"Thank you," Regina said. "It's beautiful."

She looked at the two charms lying together in her palm and then up at Dylan. Two bright spots of emotion burned on his cheekbones.

"I need your help to put it on."

"I can do that. Turn around."

She did, lifting her short hair out of the way. She felt the fumbling brush of his fingertips and then a warm, brief touch that might have been his mouth. Her heart moved into her throat.

"Well." She swallowed. "I guess you should go now."

Stay, her heart whispered.

"I could stay," he echoed quietly behind her.

She wanted him to.

"No, you can't. I told Nicky he could have a sleepover tonight."

"Then you can have one, too," Dylan said so promptly she laughed.

"Wrong."

Even if Nick would buy that argument, even if Regina were willing to ignore her own long-standing rule, there was no way she would expose them all to the comments of freckle-faced ten-year-old Danny Trujillo, whose instincts were honed by his mother's love of gossip and whose conversation, like the video games he played, carried a M-rating for blood and gore, sexual content, and strong language.

Still, Regina half expected—hoped—Dylan would argue with her. Instead he walked her through the kitchen and up the stairs, waiting on the landing outside her apartment as she unlocked her door like a nice boy seeing a girl home after a pleasant evening out.

At least, Regina imagined it was like that. She'd never dated nice boys.

"I'll see you in the morning," he said politely and kissed her good night.

He didn't kiss the way she imagined a nice boy would kiss. He backed her up against the door, plunged right in, and took her along for the dive. He used his tongue, his teeth, and the friction of his body, pulsing his hips against her, making her shake and ache and want. When they surfaced, her blood was pounding, her head was spinning, and he had a wicked glint in his eye.

"Sleep well," he said.

*   *   *

"Dude," Danny complained. "We're dying here."

The two boys lay on their stomachs in front of the TV, a bowl of fried pizza dough covered in cinnamon sugar between them. Their faces were sticky. So were their game controllers.

Nick hit Pause, and the legions of terror surrounding their embattled warriors froze. "Sorry. I thought I heard my mom."

"Yeah. So?"

Nick chewed his lip. "So, why doesn't she come in?"

Danny cocked his head, listening to the noises from the landing outside. " 'Cause somebody's with her. That Dylan guy."

"Oh." Nick relaxed. That was okay. Dylan was cool.

"He's probably kissing her good night." Danny made a giant sucking sound and then gagged.

Nick laughed, but his heart wasn't in it, because the idea of Dylan kissing his mom made his stomach feel tight. Or maybe that was the fried dough, but he didn't think so.

"He's just here to take care of her," Nick said, because that was what Dylan had told him last night. It had sounded good then, but now, in front of Danny, Nick wondered if maybe it sounded stupid.

Danny rolled his eyes, confirming Nick's suspicions. "Right. That's why he gave you that coin."

Nick squinted. "What are you talking about?"

"The coin, numb nuts. He gave you something, and now he's hanging around your mom. Dude, if a grownup does that, he wants to have sex with her."

The tight feeling in Nick's stomach got worse. He clenched his fists. "He does not. Take it back."

"Okay. Whatever." Danny regarded him a moment, his hazel eyes concerned. He smiled. "Hey, if he really wanted to do it with her, he'd give *her* presents. Not you. Right?"

Nick smiled gratefully back. "Yeah."

Then his mom came in, and she looked the same as always if you didn't look too hard at the bruises around her neck. Nick was getting good at not looking.

But the next morning when he stumbled down to the restaurant kitchen hoping maybe his mom would make more of the fried pizza dough for breakfast, he snuck another peek at her neck and felt a weight like a gorilla sitting on his chest.

"What's that?"

His mom rubbed two fingers over her necklace—not like always, there was something hanging there besides the cross, a pearl or something—and her face got kind of red. "Oh, it's a present. From Dylan. Because my chain broke."

Danny's words came back to Nick. *"Hey, if he really wanted to do it with her, he'd give* her *presents. Right?"*

Nick wasn't hungry anymore.

But even that wasn't as bad as after lunch, when Dylan came by to invite Nick's mother out on the boat. Not Nick, just his mom.

"I can't leave now," his mother said, looking flushed and excited and not like his mother at all. "I can't leave Nick."

Which made him feel like a baby. He stiffened and said, "I'm fine. I'm going to Danny's this afternoon anyway."

"No, you are not," his mother said, and she still sounded like herself, that flat voice she got when she was serious about something. "You are not leaving the restaurant."

Which was so unfair, because she wasn't stuck here all day.

"I can keep an eye on him," Margred said.

Like Nonna wasn't enough. Like Nick needed *two* babysitters, for crying out loud. And that made him so mad that even when Dylan asked if he wanted to come, Nick said no.

He was sorry about it afterward, though.

Boy, was he sorry.

16

～❦～

DYLAN HAD INVITED HER OUT ON HIS BOAT
to have sex.

Regina knew it, accepted it, had planned for it. This
time, she resolved, she would not be at a disadvantage.
This time she wasn't drunk or hurt, cold or in need of
comfort.

She stepped onto the cutter's deck armed with a picnic lunch and her best red underwear, ready to take the
battle to her lover's home turf.

Dylan raised his eyebrows at the picnic basket, but
he didn't say anything until she had wobbled to a seat on
the cockpit bench.

"This was supposed to be a break for you," he said as
he eased his craft away from the dock.

"It is," she assured him.

"Then why the basket?"

Regina rested her arms along the warm trim of the

bow and tilted back her head to watch him work the lines. He'd stripped off his shirt; his body was long and lean and golden. Watching the sleek play of muscles under his skin, the competence of those long-fingered hands, she felt something inside her flutter and rise with the sails.

"I wanted to feed you," she said. "I haven't yet."

The sails flapped and snapped like sheets on a backyard line.

Dylan adjusted them, pulling them taut, before he folded himself onto the seat beside her and gripped the rudder. "You feed me all the time."

"You eat at the restaurant all the time. It's not the same. I wanted to cook for you. It's what I do."

"Feed people."

She shrugged. "Pretty much."

"Take care of them."

She met his gaze. The wind ruffled his dark hair, obscuring his face, making his expression harder than ever to read. *Steady, Regina.* "Yes."

"I don't need someone to take care of me," he said.

Maybe not. But if they were going to have any kind of equal relationship, any relationship at all, he needed to see her as something more than a poor human female who got herself knocked up and kidnapped. Someone more than a victim.

She cocked her chin. "You only say that because you haven't experienced the full range of my amazing powers in the kitchen," she told him. "You have no idea what I'm capable of."

He glanced from the open hatch where he'd stowed the basket to her red-painted toes. His gaze trailed up her skinny jeans to her eyes. Her mouth. "I take it I'm about to find out?"

The air between them hummed with sexual challenge.

Warmth uncurled in the pit of her stomach. "Yep."

"I can hardly wait," Dylan murmured.

Regina had planned a leisurely seduction, a slow siege on his senses, an assault on his heart. She hadn't counted on the building anticipation that was itself seduction, that made foreplay unnecessary. Heat poured over the deck like sunlight, like honey, heavy and golden, thick and sweet. She breathed it in and felt desire rise in her like sap, flowing through her veins. By the time Dylan dropped the sails and anchor, she was melting inside.

She surveyed the empty rocks, the short, deserted dock, the shielding trees along the shore. Private. Perfect.

Dylan turned his head, a glint in his eyes. "Ready to eat?"

She flashed him a grin. "Yes."

His gaze narrowed, but he turned obediently enough to retrieve the picnic basket from the hatch.

She was on him in an instant, her arms sliding around his waist, their bodies bumping, her busy fingers yanking at his belt. She pressed her breasts against his back—*lovely warm skin, long, smooth muscle*—and felt him harden in surprise as he caught her hands.

She nipped his ear.

"Regina." Her name was an explosion of laughter and lust. His breath hissed as her fingers found him. He turned in her arms. "You'll flip the boat."

"Mm," she said and licked his chest. He tasted like salt, like sex, like man. Her starved palate craved him like a drug. She wanted to eat him up. So she did, trailing her tongue over the quivering muscles of his abdomen to where his jeans gaped and his body strained to meet her.

She sank to her knees on the sunlit deck, enjoying his choked exhalation. She could do this for him. For them both. He was so beautiful to her, smooth and then rough, dark and then pale, hard and silky. Inhaling his musk, she laid claim to him with her mouth. His hands fisted in her hair as she fed.

The boat rocked, pulsed, pitched. Dylan trembled and groaned. He sank beside her, his hands cradling her head, dragging her mouth to meet his. Her touch streaked over him.

He reached for the hem of her shirt. "I want to see you."

She raised her arms. He ripped the shirt over her head. The sun was warm and heavy on her eyelids, on her naked breasts.

"Beautiful," he said hoarsely.

She felt beautiful, powerful, and free. She unsnapped her jeans and worked them over her hips and down her legs. She kicked them across the deck and reached for him, blinded by the sun, dizzy with the heat, drunk with love and lust. His hands shaped and caressed her. He tucked her into his long, strong body, turned her so she kneeled with her forearms flat along the bench and her buttocks in full, warm contact with his groin. He covered her, his breath hot in her ear, his body hot at her back, thick and tempting.

But she twisted again, pushing at his chest, shoving him back against the bench seat.

"I want to see *you*." His face, his wonderful body. Let him see her. Let him see who was loving him.

She rose on her knees to straddle him, strong and broad and hers, watching her with dark, dazed eyes as she came over him. She took him, lowering herself by inches, balancing herself with her hands on his shoulders, biting her lip with pleasure.

"I need you." He gripped her hips. "Now."

A fresh thrill assaulted her system. "Yes."

She let him pull her down, felt him surge up high inside her, deep inside her, closer than she'd ever felt to anyone in her life. His eyes were hot and dark on hers as he rocked inside her, hard at her center. She was pinned by his hands, impaled by his cock, while everything around her, sea and sky, was flowing, molten, golden.

She stooped to lick his parted lips, his breath so hot it seared her.

"Mine," she said, her voice thick with satisfaction, her nails curling into his shoulders, and he shuddered and came, inside her, hers, and that was enough to make her come, too, over and over in a blinding white rush that emptied them both beneath the blue sky.

*   *   *

Regina draped over Dylan like seaweed on a rock, limp, boneless, fused to him by sweat and sex. Her hair was in his mouth. His body was lodged in her body. She was soft and slick surrounding him, and he wanted her again.

As soon as he got his breath back. His strength back. His mind.

The boat had steadied, but he was reeling still.

She lifted her head, dislodging his face from the slim curve of her throat. She smiled at him with her kiss-swollen mouth, flushed and warm and desirable, her heart right there in her glowing eyes, so beautiful it hurt his chest to look at her.

"I love you," she said.

Which hit him like a two-by-four upside the head.

Panic seized him. He didn't, couldn't, speak. What could he say? *"Thank you"?* He wasn't grateful.

"I am . . . honored," he managed.

That sounded good. Reasonable. Appreciative, even.

Her clear brown eyes clouded with annoyance. "No, you're not. You're scared."

She scrambled off his lap, her slim pale legs flashing in the sunlight, and stooped for her underwear. The curve of her butt made him dizzy. Regret weighted his tongue.

"Regina . . ."

"Don't sweat it." She scooted the thong—red—up her thighs and wiggled it into place. "You want lunch?"

Dylan watched the movement of her hips and didn't know what he wanted. He was uneasily aware of something missing, something lost: a mood, a moment, an opportunity.

"I am not scared." His jaw set. He was terrified. "You surprised me, that's all."

She shot him a glance over her shoulder before she tugged her shirt over her head. "Uh-huh. Get the basket. We don't want all that food going to waste."

"Of course I care about you," he offered stiffly.

Regina looked at him like he was the restaurant cat

and he'd just deposited a dead mouse at her feet. "Don't throw me a bone," she said. "I told you I love you. You don't love me back, that's my loss and your problem."

"My father claimed to love my mother."

She set her hands on her hips just above the line of red elastic. "So? I'm not your father. If you leave me, I'm not going off on a drunken twenty-year bender. I had a life before you came. I'll have a life when you're gone. But I'm not going to hide or lie about how I feel because you might be threatened by it."

She was blazing. Furious.

"Are you done?" he asked.

"I guess."

"Good." He picked her up in his arms and jumped with her over the side.

Water rushed over their heads, cutting off her shriek.

She surfaced sputtering and clutching at him. "You son of a *bitch*! Are you out of your mind?"

He buoyed her up, felt her shiver with shock and cold. "Scared?" he demanded.

She glared, her hair dripping in her eyes. "I'm *wet*."

"Out of your element."

"Yes!"

"Over your head?"

She squinted, adjusting her grip on his neck. "I . . . so?"

"Me, too," he confessed.

She gaped at him. He kissed her open mouth until her lips warmed and her body was soft and fluid, until her fingers tangled in his hair and they almost bobbed back under the water.

If he was going down, he was damn well taking her with him.

*   *   *

The grill hissed; the fryer belched steam. The smell of the hot grease turned Regina's stomach.

She pressed her lips together and drizzled olive oil over a piece of swordfish. *Baked potato, butter, broccoli, done.*

"Order up," she called.

Heat rolled from the pizza oven as Antonia slid out one medium pepperoni-mushroom and slid in a large with clams.

Regina reached for another ticket. *Two chowders, two pastas.* She ladled the soup into cups and added crackers.

Lucy grabbed the swordfish from the line, looking hot and harried. "The dining room's packed. Is dinner always like this?"

"Nope. Guess closing for a day was good for business."

Antonia snorted and zipped the cutter over the pizza. "You getting kidnapped was good for business. Every fool in town's been in to have a look at you."

Regina shrugged. "They're going to talk. They've got to eat. We might as well make money."

"They're talking all right," Antonia said a bit grimly. She set the pizza on the pass and began shaping another crust.

Another cramp hit. Regina pressed the back of her hand to her mouth, praying she wouldn't be sick.

"Sit down before you fall down," her mother snapped.

Regina swallowed and stirred the pasta bubbling on the cook top. "I'm fine. Tired, that's all."

"Tired, or pregnant?" Antonia asked.

Regina's gaze jerked to hers.

Antonia nodded. "When were you going to tell me?"

Regina felt a pressure in the center of her chest like heartburn. Or shame. She added shrimp to the chili peppers and tomatoes simmering on the stove, stirring to coat them in the sauce. "I . . . Soon. I didn't want you to think . . . I feel so stupid."

"Hm. When are you going to tell him?" Antonia pursed her lips toward the dining room, where Dylan watched the door.

At least her mother didn't have to ask who the father was.

"He already knows," Regina said, covering the pan.

Antonia crossed her arms over her tomato-stained apron. "And?"

"And . . ." Regina sighed. "He's still around."

For now. She watched as Hercules wound through the dining room, moving with unusual purpose for a feline, and butted his flat, broad head against Dylan's knee. Hungry for some sign of affection.

You and me both, cat.

"That's something," Antonia said.

Regina smiled weakly. It was, indeed, something. Dylan might be out of his element and over his head, but he had not abandoned them. He reached down absently and scratched Hercules under the jaw.

"He wanted us to go with him, you know," Antonia said abruptly.

Regina stopped watching Dylan with the cat. "Excuse me?"

"Your father. He wanted me to sell out, pack up, and move with him to the mainland, Baltimore or some damn place."

Regina blinked and drained the pasta. "You never told me that."

She'd always thought her father hadn't wanted them. Hadn't wanted her. Did it make a difference, after all these years, to learn otherwise?

"Maybe I didn't want to admit it, that this place meant more to me than he did. The security meant more to me than he did." Antonia spread sauce with the back of a spoon, her eyes on her work. "I don't regret the choices I've made in my life. Be a waste of time anyway. But I've wondered sometimes what kind of example I set for you."

Regina regarded her mother's floured hands and strong, lined face. Hands that had fed and disciplined her, nursed her and provided her with a home and a living. "You're a good mom," she said. "You're a great example."

"Ha," Antonia said, but there was a pleased gleam in her eyes. "Maybe. Doesn't mean you have to follow it."

Regina finished her plates and set them on the pass.

Dylan stalked through the crowded tables with the same elegance and purpose as the cat, lean and dark and so good-looking Regina's heart did a foolish little dance in her chest.

"Take that pie," Antonia said. "Table six."

He looked at her blankly.

"Corner booth."

"I've got it." Lucy balanced the pizza, cutter, and cheese and headed for the family of four in the booth by the door.

Dylan looked at Regina. "Have you seen Nick?"

His voice was low, his eyes serious.

She struggled for breath. "I . . . He's in his room. Up-stairs. I saw him when I got home."

"No, he's not."

Antonia set a floured hand on her hip. "And how would you know? Cat told you?"

Dylan's gaze clashed with Regina's. "Go check."

Without a word, she turned and ran for the stairs.

17

NICK SCUFFED HIS SNEAKERS ON THE ROAD, shooting spurts of dust. He wasn't going far. He didn't want to scare his mom. Not too much.

A little scare would serve her right. She'd scared him a lot.

Habit took him to the turn to Danny's house. Nick ducked his head and kept on walking. He didn't even want to see Danny since he'd said that thing about Nick's mom.

Anyway, the Trujillos' was the first place his mom would call looking for him, and Nick wasn't ready to be found yet. He wasn't ready to go back. There was nothing to do at home—when he turned on the TV, it was all cooking shows and grown-ups yakking. Boring. Nick had watched the cooking for a while, because it was his dad, but he wasn't really any more interested in his dad than his dad was in him. And downstairs was just more cooking and more yakking and his mom with those awful bruises around her neck.

Thinking about his mom's bruises made Nick's chest feel hot and tight. He walked faster, not going anywhere, just . . . away.

His mom kept saying that everything was fine, kept pretending that everything was normal. Which was bullshit, Nick thought, because if things were really okay, if she was safe now, why did Chief Hunter keep nosing around? And Dylan.

"I'm keeping an eye on your mother," Dylan had said, his voice and eyes serious, like a promise.

Hearing him say that had made Nick feel better, at least for a while.

Going out on the boat had made him feel better, too, in a different way. It was quiet on the water, no grown-ups talking, no motor even, just the rush of the wind and the waves white alongside the boat. For one moment, when the boat turned and rocked and the sails filled and leaned, Nick thought they were going to tip right into the water. He got goose bumps—the good kind—just thinking about it. And later, when they were coming in, Dylan let him haul on the ropes and told him he'd done a good job. That was cool.

Nick hunched his shoulders. Only maybe that was bullshit, too, because Danny said . . .

Nick kicked at a rock, watching it bounce two, three times, before skittering into a ditch.

Dylan was only being nice to him because he liked Nick's mom.

Except that wasn't true either, Nick thought, tucking his hands in his pockets. Not all the way true. He felt the hard shape of the silver dollar under his fingers. Dylan hadn't asked for it, and Nick didn't want to give it back.

Ever since his mom disappeared, everything had been all mixed up. He heard a car coming behind him and shifted to the side of the road.

He'd been so scared. Mad at her, too. Not that it was her fault, really.

He shuffled along. The car behind him was poking along like the driver was afraid to pass. Which was stupid, because there were no cars and nobody coming the other way. Nick stepped onto the grass and gravel anyway because if he actually got hit by a car, he would really be in trouble.

The engine rumbled loud and close. Too close. Maybe the driver was lost. Maybe he wanted to ask for directions. Maybe he was a jerk who liked to scare kids with his car.

Nick started to turn—to offer help? to flip him the finger?—and the world exploded in a blast of red light.

And then nothing.

*   *   *

Regina was terrified. "You have to find him," she said fiercely. *Her boy. Her baby.* "You find him *now*."

Her voice rose on the last word, practically a shriek, and the customers still in the dining room strained their necks, eavesdropping on the action in the kitchen, looking at her like she was crazy. She didn't care about any of them. She didn't care about anything but Nick, gone. Nick, kidnapped. Nick, lost and needing his mommy.

"We're going to do everything we can," Caleb said, competent and calm, and despair stabbed her, a sharp, deep pain in her belly.

Dylan wasn't calm. His black eyes were hot and dangerous. He looked ready to murder somebody.

Thank God for Dylan.

She grasped his arm. "You have to find him. You have to get him. Before the tide comes in."

Caleb rubbed his jaw. "Regina, we don't know he's in those caves."

"Where else would they take him?"

"Who would take him?" Antonia demanded. "Boy took off, that's all."

"Possibly." Caleb looked at Dylan. "Did you get anything upstairs?"

Dylan shook his head. "No sign."

"When did you last see him?" Caleb asked Regina.

"An hour ago. An hour and a half?" She twisted her hands together in her apron. Why didn't he do something? Why didn't they go find him? "Before dinner anyway."

"After the ferry left, then," Caleb said.

"I guess. Does it matter?"

"It increases the chance he's still on the island."

"Of course he's on the island," Antonia said.

"Did he say anything to you about going out?" Caleb asked Regina. "To a friend's house maybe."

"He's not at the Trujillos'. I called first thing. He's not *anywhere*."

"He's sulking," Antonia said. "He'll come back when he feels like it."

"Why 'sulking'?" Caleb asked.

Guilt swamped Regina. Nick was upset because of her. Because she'd left him. First she'd gotten herself kidnapped and then she'd gone off on the boat to have sex, leaving her traumatized eight-year-old behind. She was a terrible, terrible mother.

"He . . . I . . ."

"His mood doesn't matter," Dylan said.

"Unless he ran away," Caleb pointed out. "Without proof of an abduction—"

"He does not need to have been abducted to be in danger," Dylan said flatly. "Once outside the ward's protection, he is vulnerable."

Oh, God, Regina thought. She curled her hands protectively over her stomach.

"Vulnerable to what?" Antonia demanded. "This is World's End, not New York City."

Fear clawed Regina's throat. Her son hadn't been taken by sexual predators. He'd been kidnapped by demons.

She swallowed hard. "Why? You said he wasn't in danger."

Dylan's face was bleak. "He should not have been. He has no value to them."

That made it worse. If he had no value, they could kill him.

"Can't you put out a . . . What do they call it? An Amber Alert?" Regina asked Caleb.

"As soon as we have any indication he was abducted, I'll call the Knox County sheriff," he promised. "Get him in the database. But we need to search the apartment first, talk to the neighbors. Sometimes kids hide. Can you describe what he was wearing?"

"Jeans. A T-shirt. Blue? Oh, we're wasting *time*," she said in an agony of worry. "The tide . . . He's so little."

"I'll go now," Dylan said.

Regina's stomach was burning. Raw. She reached for her apron strings. "I'll come with you."

"Not a good idea," Caleb said. "I'll do a quick patrol, visit the encampment. Somebody may have seen him. You need to stay here in case Nick shows up. Or calls."

"He can't call if he's been kidnapped," she snapped. *If he was drowning.* "I'm going."

Dylan shook his head. "I will be faster without you."

She had never felt so helpless, so scared. Her heart was heavy, her arms ached with the weight of her missing child. "But—"

"Trust me," Dylan said.

She met his intense, black gaze. Did she? Could she? She'd never wanted to rely on anyone, on any man. Then again, she'd never known another man like Dylan.

She had trusted him with her life. And her heart. But could she trust him with her child?

She stretched out her hands. "Please. Bring him back to me."

* * *

Dylan stood on the cliffs, clutching a ragged stuffed bear with a draggled red bow. *Nick's.* Before he left, Regina had given him the toy, fear in her voice and her heart in her eyes. *"Bring him back to me."*

The sun bled over the bruised sea, staining the clouds like dirty bandages. In half an hour, they would lose the light. While Dylan could see well enough in the dark, the human searchers Caleb had mustered could not.

Somewhere, Nick would be in the dark, alone.

At least, Dylan hoped the boy was alone.

In his mind, he saw the selkie Gwyneth. Not as he'd known her in life, a small, voracious blonde with slum-

berous eyes and a sharp white smile. But as he'd last
seen her in death after the demon Tan was done with her,
her flesh torn and purpled. The image chilled Dylan's
blood. The thought of Nick—a human child, Regina's
son—in demon hands, in similar circumstances, made
him break into a cold sweat.

His hand closed hard on the bear as if he could
squeeze Nick's whereabouts from plush and stuffing.
Memories clung to the matted fur like the scent of laun-
dry soap and baby shampoo. Traces of Regina, her
laughter, her love, a quick and careless hug. Traces of
Nick, sick and sleepy, snuggled and secure. But none of
those warm and hazy impressions yielded a clue to the
boy's location. The bear had a connection to Nick; Dylan
did not. He could not use the toy as he had used Regina's
cross, to fix on its owner.

Spreading his arms, he shut his eyes and tried to call
up Nick's thin face against the dark.

He emptied himself, pouring out his power like water
on the ground, straining for a hint, a trace, a sign. He
could feel Nick's absence throbbing in his head like a
missing tooth or the pain of an amputated limb. His
senses sharpened and expanded. He could hear the wind
in the trees and the water on the rocks, the yammer of
a gull, the putt of an engine. He could smell the scents
of juniper and bayberry, the tang of rockweed and salt-
water.

But he could not sense Regina's son. Nothing shouted
"Nick" at him, nothing smelled like "boy." Only the rush
of the waves, the scent of the water . . .

Dylan's breath hissed. *The rush of the waves.*

The tide was rising.

Cold settled in his bones. He had to find Nick. Now.

*　*　*

Regina scoured pots and prayed as if she could save her son through sheer application. Scrubbing kept her hands busy and her mind occupied, distracted her from the pain in her back and the ache at her heart.

Hail, Mary, full of grace . . .

Regina took a deep breath and attacked a crud-encrusted pan, struggling to ignore the silent phone, the crawling clock, the anger and panic simmering in her chest.

It wasn't fair. This wasn't supposed to happen.

From the moment the delivery nurse had laid Nick's downy dark head on Regina's breast, she'd negotiated a bargain with God. She would take the five miserable months of morning sickness, the twenty-six long and lonely hours of labor, nights of no sleep, years with no sex, in exchange for this miracle. Her boy.

Regina would do anything, endure anything, sacrifice anything, in return for her son. Anything to keep him. Anything to keep him safe.

Regina plunged another pot into the sink. Except she'd screwed up. Literally. She'd had sex. More than once. She'd left her child to go off with Dylan, and now Nick was gone.

She hadn't protected him. She couldn't even join the search. All she could do was wait by the phone and trust Dylan to find him.

And try to make another deal with God.

She scrubbed until her fingers were pale and pruny, until the ache in her back was paired by a low, persistent pain in her gut. Sweat filmed her face and stung her eyes. Or maybe those were tears.

She blinked and bit her lip as another spasm stabbed her. Not good. She hadn't . . . With Nick, she'd never . . .

Oh. She doubled over in pain, clutching the rim of the sink.

Breathe. In through her nose, out through her . . . *Ow. Oh.*

"Regina?" Her mother's voice, dim and concerned.

Regina inhaled. Straightened, still gripping the edge of the sink. "I'm all right." She had to be all right.

Antonia was not convinced. Her dark, hard eyes examined her daughter's face. "Your cheeks are all red. Go to the bathroom, wash your face."

Regina nodded. Her head felt wobbly. "You have to . . . listen for the phone."

"Hell, girl, I know that. Take your break."

Yes. Okay. Regina took little steps to the restroom, cautious as an old woman with a walker.

It's just nerves, she told herself. Stress. As soon as she rinsed her face, sat down a minute, she'd be fine.

She pushed open the door to the women's room; splashed cold water on her face and hands before she entered a stall.

Legs shaking, she sank down on the toilet.

They were still shaking minutes later as she teetered back into the kitchen, one hand on the wall for support.

Antonia took one look at her face and scowled. "Regina? Baby? What is it?"

"Mama . . ." Her voice broke. "I'm bleeding."

*   *   *

Nick was not in the caves.

Driven by desperation and the rising tide, Dylan had searched the hole where the demon had dumped Regina and then the tunnels beyond. Nick wasn't there. Or had wiggled out of range of his voice.

Or . . . Dylan stared out at the darkening sea and purple sky, forcing himself to consider the possibilities. Maybe Nick couldn't answer. Maybe the boy was bound, gagged, dead.

Or would be dead soon.

The tide rattled over the stones, black and silver, like a chain. Dylan inhaled through clenched teeth, the weight of failure on his chest like the pressure of a deep dive. He was not a warden or a cop. He did not have Conn's power or Caleb's position. But he was here. Regina was counting on him. Nick needed him. He had to find a link to Nick.

Or the kid could die.

Dylan ground his jaw. What did he know about links and connections? He'd spent the past twenty years avoiding human contact, cutting all human ties. He was out of his element, he'd confessed to Regina. In over his head. But he'd be damned before he'd leave her to sink or swim alone.

The sea reached long, pale fingers over the rocks, plucking at his feet. Through the clouds, the moon shimmered like a silver coin at the bottom of a bucket.

Dylan's breath caught. *Like a coin* . . .

*   *   *

"Bleeding, yes," Antonia said into the phone. Regina watched dully from the kitchen stool. "I don't know, I'll ask her. Did you throw up?" she asked her daughter.

Regina swallowed hard and shook her head. She hadn't wanted this baby. It was a mistake. An inconvenience. A disaster. But it was hers now, hers and Dylan's.

She crossed her arms over her stomach as if she could hold it inside.

"No vomiting," Antonia told the doctor, her fingers almost blue, wrapped tight around the phone cord. "No, I haven't taken her temperature. All right. Yes, we will. I'll tell her."

Antonia hung up. "Donna wants to see you at the clinic. She'll be out front in ten minutes to pick you up."

Regina bit her lip. "Can't she examine me here? The phone . . ."

Antonia scowled. "I'll take care of the phone. You take care of yourself."

Herself and the baby. Regina's hand crept to the cross around her neck; fingered the pearl. Her son was out there somewhere, lost. She couldn't lose this baby, too. Heaven couldn't be so cruel.

"Ten minutes?"

"That's what she said." Antonia's mouth set in a hard, grim line. Her eyes were dark and concerned. She fumbled in her apron pocket for her cigarettes; put them back again. "You need anything from upstairs?"

Regina forced a smile for her mother's sake. "Thanks, Ma. I'm good."

Antonia's work-roughened hand smoothed her daughter's hair. "The best," she said.

Another cramp ripped her like a knife. Regina closed her eyes and leaned into her mother's hand.

* * *

Dylan called the wind to his sails until they swelled full-bellied as the moon. Another sign? he wondered. Or an illusion?

The silver dollar he had given Nick beamed a steady

signal like the lighthouse at the island's edge or a dot on Conn's map of the world. The water rippled white under his prow, following the coin's pull like a compass needle drawn true north. The boat moved by magic between the dark and the deep, between the vastness brimming with life below and a greater vastness sprinkled with stars. This was Dylan's element. His lips peeled back from his teeth. The demons had invaded his territory.

But there were a thousand islands off the coast of Maine, mostly uninhabited fortresses of spruce and stone, incursions of molten magma through the earth's crust. Nick could be hidden anywhere. Or lying at the bottom of the sea. The fire spawn could have tossed him overboard as a warning or out of spite.

From another shore, the sea birds keened over something dead.

"He has no value to them."

"Please, bring him back to me."

Dylan clenched the rudder and thought about the coin. Focused on the coin. As long as he felt that small, bright tug, he allowed himself to hope.

* * *

"You can't blame yourself." Donna Tomah's voice was gentle and compassionate. Her eyes were bright and cold. Regina pressed her thighs together, shivering under the stupid paper sheet. "There's no evidence that either sexual activity or stress can cause an abortion."

"Not her fault" was good. But . . .

"Miscarriage," Regina corrected.

The doctor raised her eyebrows. "I was speaking medically."

Regina felt her face turn red. "Right. So, can you stop it?"

Donna hesitated. "Often an abortion—or miscarriage, if you prefer—can't be prevented. And shouldn't be. It's usually an indication that the pregnancy isn't normal."

Regina supposed having a selkie father and a human mother qualified as unusual. But Dylan had said the baby was normal. Human. For now. "Is something wrong with my baby?"

"It's possible."

Just this once, Regina wished she had a hand to hold when somebody delivered bad news. She bunched her fists at her waist, wrinkling the paper sheet. "How can you tell?"

"We can't, unfortunately."

"Then why the hell am I here? What are you going to do?"

"We need to confirm that your pregnancy is in fact terminating," Donna said steadily. "We'll do a pelvic exam, possibly an ultrasound. If the uterus is clear, then there's nothing else we need to do."

So clinical. So cold. Regina's heart tightened in her chest. "And if it's not?"

Donna Tomah smiled. "Let's just see, shall we? Lie down."

A chill slithered down her spine. She didn't *want* to lie down. She felt exposed and vulnerable enough already. She didn't want to put her feet in the metal stirrups and open herself up to more disappointment.

Regina moistened her lips. "What if the uterus isn't . . . You know. Clear."

"We would take steps to prevent infection."

Steps. Misgiving contracted her stomach, sharp as a cramp. *Uh-oh.* "Antibiotics?"

"Let's get the pelvic over with before we decide on a plan of treatment," the doctor said.

Which made sense. It did. Regina opened her mouth to agree. Heard herself say, "I think I'll come back in the morning."

Donna's pleasant smile set. Well, she probably wasn't happy at being dragged from her dinner and whatever was on TV tonight just so Regina could refuse medical attention. "We could be busy."

"I have an appointment," Regina reminded her. "Ten o'clock. I'll come then."

Donna stiffened. "That's not a good idea."

Antonia used to complain that the surest way to get Regina to do something was to tell her not to do it. *"Attitude,"* her teachers said. *"Bitch,"* Alain called her. Resistance tended to make her stubborn.

She was uncertain and sick and afraid, but she wasn't giving up her baby. Dylan's baby. Whether their child was the fulfillment of some selkie prophecy or not, he was precious to her. She was not giving up.

"I'll take my temperature. I'll call if I run a fever. In the morning, if I'm still having . . ." She swallowed against the constriction of her bruised throat. "Problems, I'll come back."

So reasonable, her voice. Nothing in her words betrayed the small animal panic stirring inside her like a mouse spooked by the shadow of an owl.

For a moment, she thought the doctor was going to argue with her, and the panic grew claws that raked her gut.

Donna sighed. Shrugged. "I can't keep you here. Let me just make a few notes, and then I'll drop you at home." She pursed her lips. "Unless there's someone you want to call to pick you up?"

Half the island had turned out to help in the search for Nick. And her mother was waiting at home by the phone.

Regina gave a quick shake of her head, feeling oddly let down and relieved. "A ride home would be great. Thanks."

While Donna scrawled on her chart, Regina eased off the end of the exam room table, reaching for her pants.

"I'll be just a minute," Donna said and disappeared through the door.

Regina released her breath. Her hands were shaking, she noticed in surprise. Well, it had been a long day. Stressful. And it wasn't over yet.

The doctor's words came back to her. *"There's no evidence that stress can cause an abortion."*

Regina straightened slowly, one hand at her back.

"All set." Donna bustled back into the room carrying a big quilted bag and a paper medicine cup. "These are for you."

Regina looked down at the white pills, six-sided like little stop signs. Her stomach rolled. "What are they?"

"Antibiotics." The doctor's smile did not waver. "In case of infection."

No, Regina thought instinctively. And then, *Why not?* She half extended her hand to take the cup.

The spiral tattoo on her wrist glowed with a faint blue light.

Donna hissed and recoiled.

Regina's heart lurched to her throat. Her pulse hammered. Carefully she turned her hand to hide the glowing mark. If she could just pretend . . . If she could get away . . .

She crumpled the paper cup between her thumb and forefinger. "Thanks," she said again. Her voice rasped. "I'll take them as soon as I get home."

If she got home. She sidled along the edge of the table.

Oh, God, get me out of here.

Donna stepped between her and the door, her eyes glinting weirdly. "You really should take them now."

"I . . ." Shit. "I just want to go home."

"Take them."

"Later."

"Now."

"No."

Their gazes locked. Regina's stomach pitched. She was warded, she reminded herself. Protected. The thing looking out of Donna's eyes couldn't force her to take them. Couldn't stop her from leaving.

Donna—or whatever alien being possessed Donna—recovered itself enough to smile slowly. "Your choice. But I think you'll stay and take your medicine. Or you'll never see your son again."

18

⚬

THE FOG ROSE FROM THE WATER, SWALLOW-
ing the sea and Dylan's sails, drowning the hummocks of
land. Dylan gave himself up to the dripping twilight, letting it film his skin and bead on his eyelashes, wrapping
himself and his boat in mists and shadows to follow the
pull of his personal star.

He was very near to Nick. He could feel it. As if
they played a game from his childhood: *cool, warm,
warmer* . . .

His senses heightened—an animal's on the hunt. An
island loomed out of the sea like a kraken, smooth and
dripping, covered with knobs and weeds, dotted with
eyes. His heartbeat quickened. His muscles tightened.

Warmer . . . HOT.

Nick was here. Alone? Alive?

The rounded shape resolved into a long, curved wall.
The eyes became a row of windows, square and blank. *A*

fort. The coast was dotted with them, abandoned bunkers of brick and stone built to protect harbors and towns from the Spanish, the English, the Nazis.

Dylan snarled silently as the scent of ash blew to him on the wind. Or maybe not abandoned after all.

*   *   *

Regina's mouth dried. The edges of her vision grayed until all she could see were those bright, knowing eyes and that horrible, taunting smile.

"Nick," she whispered.

Holy Mary, Mother of God, not—

"Nick," the thing with Donna's face confirmed with a nod. "Sucks for you, doesn't it? You have to decide which child you want to save. The baby blob or . . . your little boy."

Regina's chest hurt. Her mind spun. She couldn't breathe. Where was Dylan? Where was Caleb? Oh, God, where was Nick?

"Don't hurt him." Was that her voice, that begging, breathless whisper? "Don't kill him. Please."

"Kill him?" The doctor cocked her head as if considering the possibility. "Oh, I don't think we'll do that."

"I don't think"?

A trickle of rage dripped through the icy ball of fear in Regina's gut. But the fear was greater.

"You don't want him," she said, her voice shaking. "He's not . . ."

"He has no value to them," Dylan had said.

"He doesn't have anything to do with this," Regina finished.

"No, he doesn't, does he?" Donna agreed pleasantly.

"What a shame, for the child to have to suffer for the sins of the mother."

Suffer. Oh, Nick . . .

Regina's hands clenched helplessly, convulsively.

The thing smiled slyly, watching her, enjoying her reaction. "But you're wrong to think we don't want him. Some of us have been forced to take human form for some time, living in camps, sleeping in the rough. A little distraction, a fresh . . . sensation, would be welcome. And Nick is such a pretty boy. So . . . clean."

Anger rose like bile in Regina's throat, sick and bitter.

"Take the pills, Regina." The thing's voice hardened. "And maybe we'll let him go."

Maybe?

Blind, white rage geysered inside Regina. She wanted to kill the devil woman in front of her with her bare hands. Wanted to gouge and bite, scratch and kick, with outraged maternal instinct.

But her rage, her instincts, wouldn't save Nick. This devil had no intention of letting him go. They would use him to control her and then abuse him because they could.

Unless she stopped them. Unless, for once in her life, she was careful and smart.

She met Donna's bright, malicious eyes and saw Evil peering out at her. She clenched her hands. Raised her chin. "How do I know you'll do what you say?"

The thing's mouth stretched in a grotesque imitation of a smile. "You'll just have to trust me."

"Trust me," Dylan said.

Yes. The choice had never been so clear or so hard. She couldn't do this alone.

She must, she did, trust Dylan to deliver Nick, to save her child any way he could.

Just as she would fight for their baby with everything she had. Fight to buy him time.

She loosened her clutch on the crumpled cup to reveal the pills inside. Cleared her throat. "You gave me something else before."

"Methotrexate." The demon watched her closely. "Did you take them all?"

"I . . ." Regina's mind blanked. Should she lie? *Keep her talking. Keep an eye on the door.*

The demon shrugged. "It doesn't matter. These will finish the job. Take your medicine now, like a good girl."

Regina stiffened her spine. "Not unless you tell me what they are."

The demon made a dismissive sound. "Why bother? It's not like you're a doctor."

"Neither are you," Regina shot back.

Donna Tomah seemed to grow before her eyes. "I know more than you ever will, you ignorant little slut." Her voice was guttural and deep. "I am ageless. I am immortal. One of the First Creation who saw the stars when your kind were wriggling in the muck."

"Then why are you so afraid?"

"I am not afraid!" the demon shouted.

Regina shrugged to disguise the fact that she couldn't breathe. Her heart thundered in her ears. "Whatever."

"You're just human. And not even a particularly successful human. A miserable little cook who got knocked up so you wouldn't have to take responsibility for your own failures."

Regina winced as the demon's words slid through her ribs to touch a tender spot. *Ouch.*

"You should be grateful I'm delivering you from repeating your mistakes."

"Grateful," Regina repeated. Anger elbowed for space in her chest.

The devil's eyes danced with delight. "Well, it's not as if you had a future with Aqua Man, is it? You know how those selkies are. Four or five quick ones, and they're back to sea with the boys."

Regina could barely speak around the burning lump in her throat. "I didn't know."

"And now you do. Take the pills," the demon urged almost gently. "Save your son. Save yourself."

Regina could barely think anymore. Loss of blood, lack of sleep, and worry over Nick had drained her. Her head was full of white noise like the TV when the cable went out.

"I need . . ." *Time.* "Water," she choked out.

"Of course." Donna filled a cup at the tap, held it out solicitously. "This will make everything easier," she said. "You'll see."

*   *   *

The fortress waited above him in the dark like a sleeping dragon. Baleful. Breathing.

Dylan twisted water from his shorts before he put them on. Anticipating ambush, he had slipped ashore in seal form, his black dive knife in his teeth. He retrieved the blade—salvaged years before from the wreck of a Navy boat—and hung it from the waistband of his shorts. Firearms were not reliable weapons against the children of fire.

Besides, Dylan couldn't swim with a gun in his mouth.

He bundled his sealskin under a rock at the water's edge, trusting night and the fog to hide it. He straightened from the surf, wrapping a glamour around him like a cloak to shield himself from demon eyes. A breeze whistled over the rocks, a sharp and sneaky little wind that tugged at his disguise and raised the hair on the back of his neck.

He froze, expecting something to spring at him out of the dark. A guard. A jailer. A demon.

But there was only the breeze, carrying the cold notes of mold and wet ash, drowned fires and small, dead things.

Releasing his breath, Dylan climbed the rocks.

And walked into a wall of fire.

Pain. Heat.

It seared the tissues of his mouth and throat, sucked the moisture from his eyeballs and the oxygen from his lungs.

But he was selkie. The power of the sea coursed through his blood, and a human purpose deep and wide as the ocean drove him. He would not fail Regina. He would not fail. His own power rose to the flood. The making of the warden's mark on the restaurant wall had changed him, as if his gift had burst its banks and found new channels, new rivers within him.

The fire was not real fire, he realized dimly. It was a flash of power, a wall of illusion, intended to repel. Squaring his shoulders, he walked through the flames without burning, and they died in his wake.

He drew a shaky breath. Only the faintest demon taint stained the air. Maybe they were . . . gone? In hiding. Or maybe their magic fire had fried his sinuses.

He studied the fortress squatting less than fifty yards above the waterline, its roof topped with grass like a hill. It stank of death and disuse.

And something else.

His heart pounded.

Nick.

He felt the boy trapped within those rough dark walls like a grain of sand in an oyster. So close.

Dylan pulled his knife. Crouching, he crept over the rocks, trying not to crash through bushes like a bear, awkward as a seal out of water. He should have worn shoes. When he reached the fortress, he stopped and sniffed the air again. Nothing.

It shouldn't be this easy.

It must be a trap.

He drew a deep breath and eased along the wall, searching for an entrance.

He found one tucked under the shadow of the hill and a white swirl of graffiti, the sign of human vandals, not of demons. He waited, listened, and slipped inside.

The windows piercing the thick walls had been designed for cannon, not for light. The feeble moon lay in faint, square puddles on the broken floor. The damp walls gleamed.

Dylan did not need the moonlight. His eyes were made for darkness. But the need for caution hampered him like a blindfold. Small sounds echoed in the enclosed space. The rasp of his breath. The scuff of his feet.

No other footsteps.

Where was Nick?

He heard a scrape from the lower level and a stifled whimper.

He looked down through the rotted floor that must once have covered a store room and saw Nick, his face as pale as a rag and his eyes closed, huddled and bound at the bottom of the staircase like a goat tethered to trap a tiger.

Dylan's heart squeezed. *Ah, shit. Be alive,* he thought. *Please be alive.*

"Don't move," he called down the stairs. "I'm coming to get you."

And then he realized maybe those weren't the most reassuring words to hear from a man with a knife at the top of the stairs if you were a little boy tied up in the dark.

Assuming Nick could hear.

"It's Dylan," he added.

Like that would make him happy.

The railing had rotted along with the floor. The steps were solid brick. That didn't mean they were safe. The demons might have rigged things so that somebody got hurt. Nick could get hurt. Dylan still had that back-of-the-neck, deep-in-his-bones instinct that something was wrong. But he couldn't see anything, and he couldn't smell anything, and he for damn sure couldn't leave the kid lying alone at the bottom of the stairs for the next hundred years or so while he figured it out.

He inched down the steps. Easy, easy . . .

He frowned, again with that moth-wing brush on his neck. Maybe too easy?

But then he got close enough to see the shudder of Nick's breath and the faint pulse beating beneath his jaw. Dylan dropped to his knees, shoving his thoughts about demons aside to concentrate on the child.

He used his knife to cut Nick's bonds, sliding the point carefully under the latex ties. *Latex.* Bastards.

He scowled. Who uses latex?

The boy's hands were cold. Dylan sat on the bottom step and pulled Nick onto his lap to chafe his swollen hands.

The boy's head rolled on his shoulder. "Dylan?" he asked sleepily.

"Yeah. You all right?"

Nick began to tremble, still in Dylan's arms. "What are you doing here?"

Dylan had to clear his throat before he could answer. "I came to see if you still had my marker."

Nick's hand crept into his pocket. He pulled out the silver dollar, glowing faintly with a blue light. His hand shook. His lower lip trembled. "Do I have to give it back?"

"No," Dylan said hoarsely. "Why don't you hold on to it for me for a while?"

Nick nodded. And then he threw his arms around Dylan's neck and hung on as if he'd never let go.

Well, Dylan thought, wonder and relief blooming in his chest, that was easy. He held the boy tight.

Nick was safe. Dylan had done it. He'd fulfilled his promise to Regina.

And it was all so . . . easy.

As if the demons had determined they'd made a mistake and decided to let the boy go. Or as if they'd never really wanted him in the first place.

Dylan frowned. In that case, why go to the trouble of taking him?

He patted the boy's bony back, his mind racing. Unless his kidnapping was just a diversion. Unless Nick wasn't their true target at all.

Unless . . . Dylan's blood ran cold. Unless they'd wanted to remove him from the scene so they could go after Regina.

And the baby.

19

❦

"IF YOU DO NOT TAKE THE PILLS," THE DEMON said in Donna Tomah's patient, instructive voice, "I'll give you an injection."

Regina tightened her hand on the paper cup, dread curdling her stomach. "I thought you couldn't hurt me."

The demon's smile showed all its teeth, its resemblance to the doctor fading. "Your wards protect you from possession. And from death. A shot in the arm or the ass will not kill you."

Just her baby.

Tension knotted Regina's gut. She met the devil woman's gaze. She was running out of time. How long had Dylan been gone? Two hours? Three? How long since Nick went missing? Four?

"I've always hated needles," she said, trying to buy time.

"Then take the pills." Impatience licked the edge of the devil's voice like a flame on paper.

She needed a distraction, Regina realized. She needed to get out of here. She took a deep breath. Clenching the cup of water, she threw it full in the demon's face.

Donna Tomah did not, as Regina half hoped, melt away like the Wicked Witch of the West. She didn't flinch. She did not wipe her face. The lack of that simple human gesture stuck like a knife in Regina's chest. Her pulse pounded in her ears.

They stared at one another as the water streamed down Donna's cheeks and dripped from her nose onto her white lab coat. Beneath the spreading blotch, she wore a pretty patterned shirt of blue flowers.

The devil blinked once, a lizardlike flicker of eyelids. "I'll prepare the injection."

The instant her back was turned, Regina bolted for the door.

Locked.

Regina fumbled with the doorknob. Kicked the door. There was no bolt. No visible lock. But the knob slid uselessly under her hand. The door didn't budge.

She glanced over her shoulder as the devil woman turned, syringe in hand.

Oh, shit, Regina thought as the doctor lunged at her with the needle.

* * *

Dylan held Nick's hand as they walked up the hill to the restaurant. He needed the touch as much as the boy did.

The sense of wrongness had been building since they left the island bunker. It throbbed like a headache at the base of his skull, tightened his gut, drove at his heels.

Beside him, Nick stumbled.

Dylan gritted his teeth, resisting the urge to scoop him up and run with him like a football. The kid had been jounced around enough for one night. "You all right?" he asked for what must have been the fifth or fiftieth time in an hour.

Nick stuck out his chin in a gesture that reminded Dylan poignantly of Regina. "Sure. I'm tough," he boasted.

That was what Dylan had told him on the boat. "Pretty tough kid," he'd said, and the boy had grinned and relaxed against him.

Now Dylan ruffled his hair, adjusting his stride to the boy's much shorter steps. "A regular hero."

Nick scuffled his feet along the road. "I didn't see anything, though," he said to his shoes in the dark. "I didn't do anything to stop them."

Dylan had saved the crime scene questions for his brother, the police chief. But he'd heard enough to guess that Nick's abductor had laid some kind of sleep on the boy from the moment of his capture. It was a mercy for the boy, Dylan considered. And a damned inconvenience for the rest of them. If somebody out there was still possessed, was still a threat, he had to be dealt with.

"Nothing you could do," he said, nudging the kid forward. Not much farther now. "Hard to put up much of a fight when you're unconscious."

Nick slid him a sideways glance. "Was it Jericho?"

Dylan heard the fear in the boy's voice and tried to reassure him. "No. Jericho's in jail."

"Will whoever did it . . ." Nick's voice trembled. "Will he come back?"

Dylan tightened his hold on the boy's small hand. "No," he said, flat and sure.

Not if he had to ward every building, rock, and tree on the island. He could be stuck here for months. Years.

The prospect didn't bother him as much as it should have.

They reached the center street of town, parked cars, silent storefronts, and flower boxes spilling fragrance in the dark. Dylan could see the red awning of the restaurant and Regina's apartment windows glowing like the promise of home. He lengthened his stride again.

"It was my fault," Nick mumbled from beside him, interrupting Dylan's pleasant fantasy of Regina demonstrating exactly how grateful she was for the return of her son. "Getting kidnapped."

Dylan frowned down at the top of his head. Okay, they really didn't have time for this. "No, it wasn't. The kidnappers were bigger than you and stronger than you." Immortal. Inhuman. "There wasn't a damn thing you could do about it."

"I shouldn't have gone outside without telling." Nick's voice was miserable as he tugged his hand away. He stopped and turned to meet Dylan's gaze, his eyes brave and determined. "I was mad at Mom." He swallowed and admitted jerkily, "And you."

The way Dylan had once been mad at his own father.

Dylan closed his eyes a moment, the pounding in his head threatening to split his skull. He should have seen this coming. He really wished this moment could have waited until he got the kid home to his mother.

But when he opened his eyes, the boy was still staring at him, waiting for his response, searching for judgment or absolution.

He had to say something. Do something.

Please, God, don't let me fuck this up. "Sometimes," he said carefully, "when you're growing up, you do stupid stuff. Stuff you regret. But you can't keep beating yourself up over it. You've got to learn from your mistakes and move on."

Nick cocked his head curiously. "Did you ever run away?"

Dylan nodded. "When I was a little older than you are. But I'm not going to anymore."

Nick snickered. "You can't run away anymore. You're a grown-up."

"Yeah." Dylan cleared his throat. "That's my point."

They started up the road again, side by side. Almost there, Dylan thought.

"But you ever scare your mom like that again, I'll whip your ass," he said.

Nick looked at him, wide-eyed.

"If I can catch you," Dylan added thoughtfully. "You're a quick little bastard."

Nick grinned and tucked his hand into Dylan's, increasing his pace to an almost trot. They walked like that, hand in hand, the rest of the way up the hill.

* * *

Regina struck the demon's arm, knocking aside the gleaming needle, and dodged out of range behind the exam table.

Her heart thundered. Dylan was coming. She had to believe that. She just had to buy him time. Time to rescue Nick. Time to find her. Time to save their baby.

The demon darted forward. Regina lashed with her foot at her attacker's knee. The devil blocked the blow with her thigh. Regina drove her heel down on the soft instep of the doctor's sensible shoe and Donna yelped. She struck out with the loaded syringe, and Regina jumped back to avoid the plunging needle.

They circled like boxers searching for an opening, the table in between.

"You're being very difficult," the devil woman panted.

"The most difficult woman I've ever known," Dylan had called her.

Regina grinned savagely. "You bet your ass."

* * *

"Gone," Dylan repeated blankly. He stood between the restaurant booths, staring at Antonia over Nick's head. "Gone where?"

His heart drummed in his chest, thundered in his ears. Outside the restaurant, was all he could think.

Beyond the protection of the ward.

All his earlier fears and misgivings grabbed him by the neck and shook him like a terrier shakes a rat.

Antonia looked up from cuddling her grandson, her face deeply wrinkled and tired. "There were . . . problems," she said, not quite meeting Dylan's eyes. "She went to see Donna Tomah at the clinic."

Dylan scowled. "The doctor?"

And remembered, with a clarity that left him cold, the thin, bearded man in the hooded sweatshirt passing them at the clinic door. *Christ.*

The clinic. Ten minutes on foot. Two minutes by car.

"I need to borrow your car," he said.

Antonia pursed her lips. "Van's out back. Can you drive it?"

Dylan's jaw set. He hadn't been behind the wheel since he'd steered his father's truck up and down their driveway twenty-five years ago.

Ten minutes on foot. Two minutes by car.

"I guess we'll find out," he said grimly and caught the keys on the run.

*   *   *

Regina's cheek burned from the devil woman's nails, her back hurt, and her belly was on fire. She faced the demon, her breath escaping in shallow sobs, dismally aware of the heavy flow between her thighs.

Donna Tomah's nostrils flared. "You're bleeding again," the demon observed. "Why don't you give it up?"

The doctor's neat braid was frayed and torn, her jaw was swollen, and her left wrist hung at an awkward angle. But her voice was calmly conversational. "It's still not too late to save Nick."

Regina hated, hated, the doctor's voice. But conversation gave her a chance to get her breath back. To get her strength back. She was thirty years younger than Donna, but the doctor was impervious to pain and fought with the strength and quickness of the possessed.

"Nick will be fine," Regina said shortly. Please, let him be fine. "I'm saving this baby."

"Too late." The devil smiled compassionately. "You've already lost your little whelp."

Rage and sorrow swamped Regina, flooded her brain red as blood. "Not my baby, you bitch," she said and launched herself at the demon.

Her charge carried them both to the floor with a bone-jarring thud. Regina grabbed the demon's wrist with both hands, uncaring of the teeth that snapped at her face, that gnawed at her arm. Gasping, sobbing, she crawled over the demon's body to grind her tattooed wrist against the hand that gripped the syringe.

The demon shrieked. The stench of burning flesh rose from her smoking wrist. Her hand released, and the needle skittered under the sink.

They rolled over the floor, kicking and biting, scratching and gouging. The devil woman drove a knee into Regina's groin. She doubled up, seeing red. Seeing stars. Seeing death.

The demon heaved and scrabbled over the floor toward the needle. Regina jumped on her back and grabbed her hair with both hands.

"*Not my baby,*" she screamed and slammed the devil bitch's head into the fixed leg of the exam table. Over and over and over again, until her arms had no strength, until the body under hers jerked and was still.

With a sob, Regina collapsed, slumping over Donna's back, her hands sticky with Donna's blood. So much blood. Trembling violently, she dragged herself off the doctor's body and curled into a ball a few feet away, her arms crossed protectively over her cramping stomach.

"Regina?"

Dylan's voice, she thought dreamily. Dylan's quick, sure footsteps coming down the hall. He'd come. She knew he would.

She managed to unglue her eyelids in time to see the door open and his feet enter the room. "My God, Regina!"

She tried to raise herself off the floor and on to one elbow. Struggled to summon a smile.

But when he dropped to his knees beside her, cradling her body in his arms as if she were something infinitely fragile and precious, she could only turn her face into his chest and cry.

20

❧

"I HATE HOSPITALS," CALEB SAID.

Sitting in the waiting room at Special Care, Dylan lifted his head from his hands, roused by his brother's voice. He'd never felt so scared in his life. So anguished. Helpless. Human. So aware that a life could end and snuff out the light of his world.

When he'd walked into that clinic and seen Regina, small and still, bleeding on the floor . . .

Caleb eased into the chair beside him and stretched out his injured leg with a grunt. "How's she doing?"

Dylan scrubbed his face with his hand, dredging words from the blackness inside him, bits of information he held like talismans against the dark. "Stable. Her blood pressure's good."

"Have you seen her yet?"

"No."

The memory of her ashen face, her pale lips, burned in his brain like a ghost. A brave and beautiful ghost.

Regina had been rushed from the helo pad to the Emergency Room, whisked from the Emergency Room to Special Care. The last time he'd seen her, she'd been strapped into a stretcher, hooked to two different IVs. Just before she was loaded onto the LifeFlight with Donna Tomah, her gaze had found Dylan standing outside the ring of professionals laboring over her. She'd tried to smile, raising two fingers in an islander's wave.

And shattered his heart.

He rubbed the heel of his palm over his chest. "Her mother and Nick are with her now."

"They let the boy in?"

"He needed to see her. And she needed to see him. Anyway, it's just for five minutes."

Regina was allowed visitors for five minutes, once an hour. Dylan could see her in an hour.

Hold her for five minutes.

Tell her . . . What could he possibly say to her that would make up for all she had been through? He would have done anything to help her, suffered anything to save her. But he'd come too late.

"The baby?" Caleb asked quietly.

Dylan took a deep breath. "We don't know. Antonia said they were going to do an ultrasound, take some blood."

More blood. He closed his eyes, but he could not shut out the memory of her bone-white face, the blood-streaked floor.

"I'm sorry," Caleb said. "I know the prophecy—"

Dylan opened his eyes to glare at his brother. "I don't give a fuck about the prophecy. She shouldn't have to lose this baby."

Not after she'd fought so hard, so valiantly to keep it. While he did nothing. Could do nothing.

Caleb watched him carefully. "Does she know yet that you love her?"

The question struck like a harpoon. Straight through the chest. Dylan's mouth dropped open. He managed to shut it. Opened it to snarl, "You think I should have said something while she was bleeding on the floor? Or maybe in front of the paramedics while they were shoving tubes in her veins?"

Caleb rubbed his jaw. "Seems to me you had opportunities before tonight."

He did. Of course he did.

Dylan thought of Regina braced on the deck of his boat, her chin lifted bravely and her heart in her eyes. *"I'm not going to hide or lie about how I feel because you might be threatened by it."*

What the hell had he been scared of? Why the hell hadn't he said something then?

"What good would telling her have done? It wouldn't have kept her safe. I didn't keep her safe," Dylan amended bitterly.

"You rescued her son."

"But I didn't protect her. She's not safe. None of us are."

Caleb frowned thoughtfully. "Because of Donna Tomah?"

"There was no taint of demon in her." Or Dylan would not have let the doctor live, let alone get on the same helicopter that transported Regina.

Caleb sighed. "Just as well. I'm having enough trouble explaining how two more women got the crap beat out of them on my island. Thank God nobody died."

Dylan shot him a hard look. "You cannot blame Regina for defending herself."

"I don't. I'm just telling you how the DA is going to see it."

"And how will the DA see it?"

Caleb gave his brother a level look. "I'm investigating the possibility that an unknown intruder got into the clinic."

An intruder. Dylan nodded. It was as good a description of demonic possession as any.

"Of course, that story will only work if Donna doesn't tell them what really happened," Caleb continued.

"She will not remember."

"You think her head injuries—"

"The demon did not leave her willingly or gently. Its presence may have damaged her mind. Or at least her memory."

"You sure it left?" Caleb asked.

Dylan shrugged. "Once her body lost function, it was of no further use to the demon. Anyway, I did not sense any trace of fire spawn."

"So it could be anywhere."

"Yes."

"Shit," Caleb said wearily. "I'm still looking for a witness to identify the bastards who snatched Nick."

"Whoever it was had a boat," Dylan offered.

"Which means it may not have been someone from World's End at all. Hell."

"I will do all I can to ward the island," Dylan said.

"Then I guess you're planning on sticking around."

"Yes. No." Dylan caught the gleam in his brother's

eyes and scowled. "I will not make Regina promises that I can't keep."

That she would not believe. Not after the way he'd failed her.

Caleb scratched his jaw. "Has she asked for promises?"

Another sore point.

"No," Dylan admitted.

"Then what's the problem?"

The problem, Dylan realized, was that he wanted those promises. Wanted to make a life with her. Wanted to make children with her. And now was a piss poor moment to tell her so.

"The timing sucks," he said. "There are too many factors . . . Too many dangers . . ."

"That's not necessarily reason to wait. When you know what you have to lose may be the best time to be honest about what you feel. About what you want. Any Army chaplain will tell you he performs more marriages in war time."

"And these marriages . . . do they last?" Dylan challenged.

"If you're asking me for guarantees, I don't have any," Caleb said evenly. "But if you're asking me if love is worth the risk, any risk, I'd have to say yes."

Dylan raised one eyebrow. "Is that what you tell Margred?"

"That's what we tell each other. You can get through anything if you have love. If you have trust."

"If you have hope," Dylan said.

Caleb exhaled slowly, looking at his hands. "She wants a baby," he confessed.

Dylan regarded his brother with understanding. Caleb—careful, upright Caleb—would not want to put his wife or a child at risk. "You have my sympathy. Margred is used to getting what she wants."

"She—"

The door swung open. Antonia marched out, holding Nick's hand.

Dylan lurched to his feet, his heart banging against his ribs. "Regina?"

Antonia's straight gaze met his. Her hard mouth relaxed into a smile. "They're moving her to the maternity wing."

"Then . . ." Dylan swallowed, hardly daring to hope.

"The doctors want to keep her overnight. For observation." Antonia ran a hand through her uncompromisingly black hair. "God, I need a smoke."

*   *   *

"We're all set." Antonia leaned over the metal railing to press her lips to Regina's forehead. Regina closed her eyes, comforted by the familiar tang of tobacco in the midst of all the hospital smells, fear, sweat, and antiseptic.

"Caleb is taking us back on the boat tonight," Antonia continued. "I'll talk to you in the morning after you've seen the doctor."

Nick stirred in the rocking chair, his bottom lip jutting dangerously. "I don't want to go. I want to stay with you."

Regina's heart cracked. She was tired. So tired and close to tears. Her head felt empty and her heart too full. She made an effort to summon words, to sound reassuring, but before she could tell Nick that he could stay all night if he wanted, Dylan spoke up from the foot of her bed.

"Your mom needs her rest." His voice was firm, his jaw roughened by stubble. Underneath his golden tan, his face was pale with fatigue. "And so do you. Now kiss her good night and get out of here."

Regina opened her mouth to tell him it was all right. The child was obviously traumatized. He needed coddling. He needed his mother.

But to her surprise, Nick uncurled from the chair. "Okay, okay." He slouched over, leaning his slight weight against the mattress. "Night, mom."

He puckered up and delivered a smacking kiss on her cheek.

Regina sniffed so she wouldn't start bawling. "Night, kiddo. I'll call you in the morning."

She was very aware of Dylan watching her, his hands in his pockets, as her mother collected her purse, her magazines, and Nick.

They left.

Dylan stayed at the foot of her bed, his hooded gaze on her face.

"You're good with him," Regina said.

He looked so handsome standing there, masculine and lean and as out of place in a hospital room as the rocking chair or the cheerful curtains. The deliberately homey touches of the maternity wing did not hide the bank of beeping, glowing machines by her bed. Just as Dylan's obvious determination to do the right thing couldn't disguise his discomfort.

Her heart swelled a little with love and regret.

"He'll miss you," she said softly.

Dylan shrugged. "I'll see him tomorrow."

"I meant . . . when you leave."

He wandered as far as the window, staring through the blinds at the bay and the night as if he longed to be gone. His shoulders were rigid, his profile shadowed. "I'm not leaving. I'm never leaving you again."

Her heart gave a wild leap. For one weak moment, she allowed herself to hope. Let herself yearn.

She took a careful breath. *Steady, Regina.* Dylan had already given her more than any other man in her life. He had saved her son. He had come for her when she was hurt and bleeding, held her when she desperately needed his embrace.

Now she could give him something in return. Something he wanted. Needed.

His freedom.

"That's not necessary," she said gently.

His shoulders stiffened. He turned around, his eyes black. "What are you talking about?"

She raised her chin. "I don't want you to feel you have to stay with me because I might be pregnant. That pill I took two days ago can take several weeks to work. For you to hang around waiting . . . It's not fair to you. Or . . . or to me, either."

His gaze narrowed. "I'm not staying because you're pregnant."

Her heart thudded. But she knew him. She knew herself. She knew, at last, what she wanted and what she was worth. "Dylan, I love you, but I don't need you to do me any favors. I don't want you be with me out of obligation or guilt or—"

"Responsibility?"

She hurried on as if he hadn't spoken, afraid if she stopped she'd lose her courage. "It's not going to be with us like it was with your parents, me trying to keep you here against your will and you resenting me."

"I don't resent you." He stepped away from the window, took her hands. "I couldn't resent you. Regina, I love you."

"*Oh.*" Tears stung the back of her eyes, burned the back of her throat. The temptation to take him at his word, to take advantage of his love, was an arrow in her heart. She swallowed. "I love you, too. I love you for who and what you are. I don't want you to be anything different. I don't want you to be anything less."

He shook his head impatiently. "You don't get it. I didn't understand it myself until tonight. With you I can be more. If I leave you, I leave the best part of myself." He kissed her fingers, held between his hands. He pressed his lips to her hair and made her tremble. "Every bit of courage and commitment, everything I know of love or loving, my heart, my life, my soul, I owe to you."

He kissed her forehead, her eyebrow, her cheek. "Don't make me leave you," he murmured. "Don't make me leave. You'll rip my heart out."

She squeezed her eyes shut, bowing her head over their joined hands. Heard his heart beat, wild and strong.

And let herself believe.

Epilogue

THE NIGHT OF FRANK IVEY'S SIXTY-FIFTH birthday party, Regina accepted a bottle of sparkling cider from a grateful Jane Ivey and poured herself a glass.

Champagne would have been even better, but she was nine weeks pregnant and she wasn't drinking anything that wasn't good for the baby.

The cider bubbled up and over her fingers. Laughing, she snatched back her hand.

"Careful," warned a deep masculine voice behind her.

Her heart beat faster. She turned, her lips already curving in a smile.

Dylan, tall, dark, and hot, lounged in the shadows of the picnic shelter, an answering smile in his eyes. "Let me." He caught her wrist and kissed her wet fingers, making her shiver with desire.

She chuckled and leaned against him. "What are you doing here?"

"You need help loading the van."

"I have help. Your sister's here."

At the other end of the shelter, Lucy scooped chocolate ice cream for the youngest Ivey grandchild. Competent and unobtrusive, she had everything under control.

Regina surveyed the kids and grandkids running around the blue-checkered tablecloths, the pitchers jammed with daisies, the laughing, relaxed adults, and sighed with satisfaction. "Nice party."

"Beautiful," Dylan agreed.

She glanced over her shoulder. He wasn't looking at the picnic. Her heart soared and sailed into the sky like an escaping birthday balloon.

He held out his hand. "Walk with me."

"Where?"

"The beach."

Her toes curled inside her practical flat shoes. She knew what he was offering. They hadn't had a lot of time alone these past few weeks. But tonight her work was done and Nick was settled safely at her mother's. Regina had a clean bill of health from the new clinic doctor, and Dylan was looking at her as if she were the sun and the moon and his entire world wrapped up in one.

She slipped her hand into his. "Isn't it a little cold out for a . . . walk?"

Dylan lifted an eyebrow. "I'll see what I can do to keep you warm."

Hands linked, they wandered down the grassy slope and over the shale. The sound of the children's shouts and laughter blended with the surf. The land shimmered and shifted like the sea, glowing red and gold, as if a giant box of watercolors had spilled over the sky and dripped over the landscape. The kind of golden evening when the promise of fall charged the air and even a cynic could believe in happy endings.

A burst of foam ran up and faded at their feet.

"You know I love you," Dylan said abruptly.

She did know. But hearing it still had the power to make her heart dance. "Yes."

He stopped and cupped her face in his hands. His eyes were dark and direct. "It's not enough."

She frowned. "I don't understand."

"You told me once that you had a life before I came, and you'd have one when I'd gone. A life that includes Nick and your mother and the restaurant. You don't need me, Regina."

The blood rushed in her ears, louder than the surf. "Now, wait a minute . . ."

"You don't need me," he repeated, a glint in his eyes. "But I need you. You, Nick, all of it. I need you now."

He kissed her. Almost dizzy with love and lust and relief, she kissed him back, her hands flexing on his arms.

"Um . . ." Oh, God, that felt good. "Here?"

His gaze, hot and intent, narrowed on her face. "Yes. This will do." He dropped to his knees.

Regina caught her breath, reminded of their first meeting on the beach. She stared down at his dark head. Before she could point out to him that they were practically within sight of Frank and Jane Ivey—and their daughters and all the little Iveys—Dylan reached into his pocket. Something gleamed in the golden light of the sinking sun. A coin.

No, not a coin, a . . .

Regina trembled. *A ring.*

"This ring was lost at sea, and now it's found. The way I was lost, without ever knowing it, for years." Dy-

Ian took a deep breath. "But now I've found the life I want. The love I need. With you. Because of you." His dark eyes shone. "Marry me, Regina."

Joy sluiced through her. She tugged him to his feet and threw her arms around his neck. "*Yes!* Oh, yes."

He caught her close, sliding one strong hand beneath her hair.

And there at the water's edge, he kissed her.

CONN AP LLYR HAD NOT HAD SEX WITH A mortal woman in three hundred years.

And the girl grubbing in the dirt, surrounded by pumpkins and broken stalks of corn, was hardly a reward for his years of discipline and sacrifice.

Even kneeling, she was as tall as many men, long boned and rangy. Although maybe that was an illusion created by her clothes, jeans and a lumpy gray jacket. Conn thought there might be curves under the jacket. Big breasts, little breasts . . . He hardly cared. Her hair fell thick and pale as straw around her downturned face. Her long, pale fingers patted and pressed the earth. She had a streak of dirt beside her nose.

Not a beauty.

Conn had known her mother, the sea witch, Atargatis. This human girl had clearly not inherited her mother's allure or her gifts. Living proof—if Conn had required any—that the children of the sea should not breed with humankind.

But a starving dog could not sneer at a bone.

In recent weeks, Conn's visions had shown him the girl again and again. He might not want her, but his magic insisted he needed her. His visions were rare enough, his magic as fickle as a woman confident of her power. If he ignored it, it could leave him. He could not risk that.

He watched the girl drag her hand along the swollen side of a pumpkin. Brushing off dirt? Testing it for ripeness? He had only the vaguest idea what she might be doing here among the tiny plots of staked vines and fading flowers. The children of the sea did not work the earth for their sustenance.

But she was alone. Unguarded. That was good.

Conn did not expect resistance. He could make her willing, make her want him. It was, he thought bitterly, the remaining power of his kind, when other gifts had trickled away like water through cupped hands.

She would not resist. But she had family who might interfere. Brothers. Conn had no doubt the human, Caleb, would do what he could to shield his sister from either sex or magic.

Dylan, on the other hand, was selkie, like their mother. He had lived among the children of the sea since he was thirteen years old. Conn had always counted on Dylan's loyalty. He did not think Dylan would have much interest in or control over his sister's sex life. But Dylan was involved with a human woman now. Who knew where his loyalties lay?

No, it was better, wiser, more expedient, for Conn to approach the girl alone.

Conn believed in expediency. The fate of his people rested on his ability to keep the treacherous balance between the children of the sea and the other elementals, to wrest a fragile peace from Hell's war on humankind. The survival of his kind depended on him.

And if, as his visions insisted, it involved this human girl as well . . .

He regarded her head, bent like one of her heavy gold sunflowers over the dirt of the garden, and felt a twinge of regret.

That was unfortunate for both of them.

* * *

Lucy affectionately patted the pumpkin, like a dog, and climbed to her feet. Her second graders' garden plots would be ready for harvest soon. Plants and students were rewarding like that. Put in a little time, a little effort, and you could actually see results.

Too bad the rest of her life didn't work that way.

Not that she was complaining, she told herself firmly. She had a job she enjoyed and people who needed her. If at times she felt so frustrated and restless she could scream, well, that was her own fault for moving back home after college. Back to the cold, cramped house she grew up in, to the empty rooms haunted by her father's shell and her mother's ghost. Back to the island, where everybody assumed they knew everything about her.

Back to the sea she dreaded and could not live without.

She had tried to leave once, when she was fifteen and had finally figured out her adored brother Cal wasn't ever coming back to rescue her. She'd run away as fast and as far as she could go.

Which, it turned out, wasn't very far at all.

Lucy looked over the dried stalks and hillocks of the garden, remembering. She had hitchhiked to Richmond, twenty miles from the coast, before collapsing on the stinking floor of a gas station restroom. Caleb had found her, shivering and defeated, and brought her back to the echoing house and the sound of the sea whispering under her window.

She had recovered before the ferry left the dock.

Lucy wiped her hands on her jeans. Anyway, things were better now.

She could handle her father. She could deal with the house. Both her brothers lived on the island now, and she had a new sister-in-law. Soon, when Dylan married Regina, she'd have two. Then there would be nieces and nephews coming along.

And if her brothers' happiness sometimes made her chafe and fidget . . .

Lucy took a deep breath, still staring at the garden, and forced herself to think about plants until the feeling went away.

Garlic, she told herself. Next week her class could plant garlic. The bulbs could winter in the soil, and next season her seven-year-old students could sell their crop to Regina's restaurant. Her future sister-in-law was always complaining she wanted fresh herbs.

Steadied by the thought, Lucy turned from the untidy rows.

Someone was watching from the edge of the field. A man.

Her heart thumped. A stranger, here on World's End, where she knew everybody outside of tourist season. And the last of those had left on Labor Day . . .

She rubbed sweaty palms on the thighs of her jeans. He must have come on the ferry, she reasoned. Or by boat. She was uncomfortably aware how quiet the school was now that all the children had gone home.

When he saw her notice him, he stepped from the shadow of the trees. She had to press her knees together so she wouldn't run away.

Yeah, because freezing like a frightened rabbit was a much better option.

He was big, taller than Dylan, broader than Caleb, and a little younger. Or older. She squinted. It was hard to tell. Despite his impressive stillness and well-cut black hair, there was a wildness to him that charged the air like a storm. Strong, wide forehead; long, thin nose; firm, unsmiling mouth, *oh, my*. His eyes were the color of rain.

Something stirred in Lucy, something that had been closed off and quiet for years. Something that should *stay* quiet. Her throat tightened. The blood drummed in her ears like the sea.

Maybe she should have run after all.